John Geyser—A dreamy boy with the hand of an artist and the eye of a visionary. When he left home to practice his art, his brothers called it treason.

Luke Geyser—A hot-blooded hell-raiser. Not even the threat of death could curb his appetite for adventure or a pretty woman.

Emma Geyser—She married a rich man whom war promised to make richer. Wars were good for business— it was families they destroyed.

Malachy Hale—He had always wanted to be a soldier, yet never dreamed it would mean killing the people he loved.

Jonas Steele—Abe Lincoln's personal agent, he married Malachy's sister. Haunted by visions of his own death, he was totally unprepared for the shape that nightmare would take.

Major Welles—A hell-fire soldier and preacher, he called Jehovah's vengeance down on all Yankees and runaway slaves. When God proved uncooperative, he took matters into his own hands.

THE BLUE
AND
THE GRAY

THE BLUE
AND
THE GRAY

A Larry White and Lou Reda Production in association with Columbia Pictures Television

This novel by John Leekley is based on a story by John Leekley and Bruce Catton and the teleplay by Ian McLellan Hunter

Historical consultant, Bruce Catton

John Leekley

The Blue
and
The Gray

Historical consultant, Bruce Catton

CORGI BOOKS
A DIVISION OF TRANSWORLD PUBLISHERS LTD

THE BLUE AND THE GRAY

A CORGI BOOK 0 552 12136 3

First publication in Great Britain

PRINTING HISTORY
Corgi edition published 1982

This book is set in 10 on 12 point Times

Corgi Books are published by
Transworld Publishers Ltd,
Century House, 61–63 Uxbridge Road,
Ealing, London W5 5SA

Printed and bound in Great Britain by
Cox and Wyman Ltd, Reading

For my father,
Richard Leekley.

PROLOGUE

Virginia—Spring 1856

The old woman was dying. She knew that. She didn't mind; her time had been long and good. A week ago she just lay down knowing that she would never get up. In spite of the warm day she was lying under a heavy patchwork quilt, covered to her chin. Her blood was tired and thin, and she felt cold. She looked tiny in the large bed, and shrunken. She had held her family together with strength and iron will for forty years. And it was for the family that she worried now.

The house, usually filled with her people, was strangely quiet. She could hear the clock ticking in the silence of the room. She could hear the flies buzzing and the voices of men working in the field. The voices of men . . . she closed her eyes and dreamed, listening to the voices of all the strong men she had ever loved. And she prepared to die.

Across the fields in front of the house, down by the creek, they were pulling stumps from the ground with an ox. In the shadows along the tree line you could tell them apart by the way they moved. Matthew was taller, raw boned, slow moving with an easy grace. Mark was the quick one, smaller and darker.

They were doing what the Geysers had done every spring for the last fifty years. They were turning the woods into fields for grazing and crops. Like all farmers, they knew that clearing was best done in the spring when the ground was loose and wet. The earth lets go a little from its hold and a man can pull a stump out clean. But still it's a thankless job.

From the low ground only their heads could be seen moving above the tall grass along the woods. The sun was hot, the air lazy and still. The dust rose around them as they worked, sticking to them, to their sweat, which ran in streaks on their bunching arms and down the smalls of their backs. Blue jays scolded them from the trees as they worked together against the big chestnut stump.

Mark slapped the ox on the rump. "Come on. Lean into it. Come on, big boy." The huge white ox lurched forward.

On one side of the stump the heavy roots groaned and ripped out. They cut them with axes, loosening the earth's hold. Again the two men strained against the stump, and for one long moment ox and men were poised in their awesome effort, the tree's roots holding fast to the ground. With one final heave there came a sharp snapping sound, like a gunshot, and men and beast tore the stump from the earth. The men leaned against it, panting.

Mark walked over to the big ox, stroking him on his massive neck. Taking some oats from his pocket, he fed him a handful, softly cursing him. "Jesus, you're like a bone and gristle freight train."

Matt sat down on the chestnut roots. "I always feel bad when we have to pull one of these out. Been there a long time." He looked down at the hole in the ground and then across to the woods. "I don't like to see it all change." He shook the dirt out of his bushy mustache and long curly blond hair. He always had a kind of rumpled look, as though he had just woke up.

"Get your ass off there," Mark told him as he finished wrapping the rope around the stump so it could be dragged out. He talked while he worked. "Before we started last year, this field was mostly woods. Now it's done," he said as he slapped the ox on the rump. The stump began to move.

John Geyser, their younger brother, watched trance-like from the high weeds. He was fifteen, with long sandy hair—a tall, strong boy, but with a sensitive face and a distant demeanor. His brothers' violent struggle both attracted and repelled him. He seemed to view it with his heart.

John often came down to the creek to draw the blue cranes that waded there or sometimes just to lie in the weeds and watch the clouds float by, mesmerized by their changing shapes.

The sound of the snapping stump woke John from his revery. It also roused the cranes that came loping and swooping out of the dark shadows. He looked up as they flew by, beautiful in the sunlight, gliding slowly over him. Their passage threw a shadow over his eyes and John felt suddenly weak, frozen to the ground. He knew it for certain then. She would die. Till then no one had said it; in some strange way they seemed not to have known it. He jumped up and ran wildly through the tall grass toward the house.

As John plunged through the tall weeds, a horse and

rider suddenly crashed by him, knocking him down. John knew as he fell who it was. Only Luke could ride like that, flat out, fluid. Luke yelled out as he raced toward his two older brothers. Mark and Matthew shaded their eyes to see him. He leaped the fences that bordered the lower field, pulling up in a cloud of dust.

"It's Grandma. She's turned for the worse. Pa wants us all up to the house, and I reckon he means now."

Matthew and Mark turned and ran to their horses, tied to the willows in the shade, and mounted bareback. The three rode abreast across the fields and along the creek up to the house. In Virginia riding came naturally to young men, and they rode fast and easy. Luke led, with Mark right behind. Matt rode easier, his long hair streaming behind him.

By the time John ran up from the fields, he was out of breath. His father was sawing pine boards by the toolshed. John stood for a moment, watching his father's hands. They were rough, calloused, and strong, but they were gentle in their power. He was skillful with them, and they moved as if they possessed a life of their own.

He looked at his father's face, seeking a sign, some indication of what he should do. Ben worked slowly and quietly, with total absorption. His mother was dying, and it showed in his eyes. He looked painfully at the coffin, speaking softly, as if to himself: "It has to be ready."

As John entered the house, the whole family moved nervously around the large central room. They were in their work clothes, having dropped whatever they were doing. Ben Geyser came in and stood at his mother's door; next to him were all his children: Matt, Mark, young Luke, John, and Emma. Their mother, Maggie, was standing in the doorway to the kitchen, wiping her hands on her apron. Everyone was quiet.

Ben stood taller than his sons. His slate gray eyes were the same color as his close-cropped beard. He had a wooden leg, and it knocked on the oak plank floor as he walked. He took Emma into his mother's room first. As she entered, the old woman asked her to sit by her on the bed. Her face had taken on a gray pallor, a sign that the time was short. Her eyes were sunk in their dark sockets, but they still had fire. Her body was failing her, but her mind remained strong with the power that had held this family together all these years.

She was silent a moment as she looked at her granddaughter. Emma, just turned a full-grown woman, was pretty, with gray eyes like her father and with her father's pride as well. Her high cheekbones and dark hair made her look like a full-blooded Cherokee.

The old woman's voice was almost a whisper. "I don't reckon I ever told you about this quilt. It's real special to me. I like to just look at it and remember about it. It's called Cross and Crown. You can see the sign of our Lord all over it. Each one of these patches reminds me of where it came from. This blue patch comes from your grandfather's work shirt."

She touched the patch lovingly. "Jack was wearing that blue shirt in the orchard when we planted the peach trees. This was before your time, of course. I was as big as a barn with your Pa in my belly. I started to labor and he didn't know what to do. You know how men think it's such a mystery. Well, he tried to hold me, but I was so big he couldn't get his arms around me. We just laughed like fools." She paused, smiling to herself at the memory.

"This yellow patch is from Ben's cavalry uniform.

When he came back that day, after so long in Mexico, I saw him coming from a ways off down the road. He hobbled along on his wood leg, but I knew it was him. My heart fell down when I saw his loss, but I blessed the Lord he came back at all. I wanted to run and help him, but I knowed Ben too well. He would want to walk it alone, all the way.

"This white piece was Matt's first real dress shirt. He tore it up to use as linen when Maggie bore your brother John. He was all twisted inside her. By the time we got him out, he was almost too weak to go on."

She continued to move her fingers across the quilt.

"This black patch is from our old preacher's coat. This piece always reminds me that piecing a quilt is like going to church—better maybe. Preachers always have a hard time explaining the gospel truths, things like destiny and free will. But you know, piecing a quilt is like living the gospel. You start out with pieces of cloth, whatever old pieces you have. That's the destiny part. It's what you got to start with, what you have given you in life. Then you take all those pieces and make the design you want to have. You give them meaning and purpose. That's the free will." She took Emma's hands. "So, when you make a quilt, remember what the pieces mean."

The younger children had edged into the room to see her. John walked slowly by the door, peering in. She smiled at John and motioned him to stand by her. Their bond had always been strong.

"Let me see what you drawed."

He showed her the drawing he had made by the creek.

"Looks to be Matt and Mark. It looks real—better than real. Don't forget the blue birds. They're part of it.

John, boy, no matter what happens, don't stop your drawings. They will take you through to the other side. They will bring you out the other side of the hardship."

Her talking had scared him a little. "I won't—not ever," he promised.

The old woman looked hard at the children around her, as though she wanted to remember everything about them, as if she could take that memory with her. She whispered, "Children, I'm so proud of you." For a moment, the spark in her eyes flickered; she seemed about to fade away.

Then, with a sudden surge of energy, she raised her head. "What are all these long faces? It's damn disspiritin'. Mark, Matt, carry me out to the porch. I don't want to die in bed, on my backside."

The two big men lifted her between them, their arms clasped, and carried her out. In the shade of the porch she looked out over her land, the plowed fields and woods and the rolling hills beyond.

"With our own hands we made this farm. It was just woods when your Pa and I started. Sometimes it was like the latter end of original sin and hard times. But now we are beholden to no one."

Her heart fluttered; she gasped a little. "I don't have much juice left," she whispered. "I feel as dry as a bone. I reckon I look like one. The times are changing, boys, and I have no more change left. You will have to do it without me."

She smiled to herself. "I would like to go down to the orchard now—it's so pretty in bloom."

They walked her down through the cherry and apple trees. She seemed so tiny in their arms. A slight breeze blew over the trees showering them with blossoms as they walked, carpeting the ground with their fragile whiteness. The family stood on the porch, watching through the trees. The half-finished coffin sat on workhorses to the side of the porch. The wind picked up, blowing dust across the yard.

Matthew and Mark stood still. Their grandmother lay in their arms, as though she were asleep. The blossoms covered her hair and shoulders.

By late afternoon, just as the day began to cool and the shadows stretched across the yard, Ben finished pounding the last nail into the lid of the coffin. He worked slowly and methodically, trying not to think about his mother inside the box. He just wanted to get her safely shut away and at peace. After all, it wasn't really her in there, he thought to himself. It's just her body. Her soul had gone to heaven now. She wasn't a church-going woman, but she had been religious, almost spiritual. Yes, Ben reminded himself, her soul has gone to the Lord. This is just her body lying here.

But when they lifted the coffin up, they were careful not to jar her too much. Their faces were masks of pain and loss. They walked slowly up to the family graveyard on the hill overlooking the orchard. On the left side of the coffin were Ben and Mark and Matt; on the right side were Emma and John and Luke. Maggie walked behind them; at her side she carried the quilt. She cried silently; the tears streamed down her face.

The grave was ready, the hole deep and level on the bottom, the sides smooth and even. John and Luke had dug it earlier that afternoon. Now they stood beside it, tired and solemn and secretly proud of the work they had done. John was taller than Luke, and two years older, but they had always been close. They weren't just brothers, they were best friends.

The damp smell of cool earth surrounded the family. They lowered the coffin into the grave, pulling the ropes out when it was settled. They were silent a long time, reluctant to finish. Finally Maggie said, "Mama's favorite song was 'Rock of Ages.' She always liked hearin' it."

So she began to sing, her voice strong and steady. The whole family slowly joined in. The sound of their singing carried across the field, through the shade of the orchard and into the cool of the empty house. The doors were all open, and the song whispered down the hall and into the big rooms. The breeze swirled around the old woman's room, over her bed, past the family portraits, and the ticking clock.

It was the next day that the Geysers first heard about John Brown—how he and his sons had butchered those slavery men in Kansas and washed their bloody swords in the Pottawatomie Creek. It was after the old woman died that things inexorably began to change, one event leading to another, meshing, like gears turning toward each other.

BOOK I

CHAPTER ONE

Virginia—Fall 1859

Leaning back against his grandmother's tombstone, sitting very still, John Geyser stared at the rolling Virginia farmland. For as far as the eye could see this land belonged to his family. It seemed to be spread out like a quilt; the lush blue-green of the grassland and the rich brown of the newly plowed earth blended in a patchwork of muted colors. The smell of the earth and of the newly fallen leaves floated up the hill to him. He bent over to draw.

He was sketching the scene spread out below him, his father and three brothers in the orchard, gathering apples. John's hand moved swiftly and with a sure touch, his sepia brush bringing the pencil outline to life. His drawing was sensitive, yet startling in its detail. Beside him was his watercolor box and a tin of water. He was dressed in the same clothes his brothers wore— faded overalls, work shirt, homespun jacket, and heavy farm boots.

He held the drawing up and compared it to the scene

below. As he did, he noticed a pillar of smoke rising out of the dense woods beyond the farmhouse. Scooping up the brushes and paints, with the sketchbook under his arm, he set off across the fields.

John followed the familiar path through the woods to a clearing. In the middle stood a one-room log cabin with a stone chimney and a patched roof. In back of the cabin there was a lean-to that sheltered a potter's wheel and a brick kiln, which was belching smoke. A black man sat at the wheel, head bent over to one side as he finished a tall jug. While shaping the pot, he kept the wet clay spinning on the wheel by constantly kicking the stone flywheel for momentum. With one hand inside the pot and the other hand on the outside, applying pressure in perfect balance, he finished the whiskey jug. John stood with his hands shoved into his pockets, admiring the finished piece.

"Nice, Jonathan. Real nice work," John said.

The black man lifted the pot off the wheel and put it on the long plank table with the rest of the jugs he had made. Then he washed the wet clay off his hands and wiped them on his pants. The two men shook hands warmly. Jonathan was a big man, as tall as John but broader in the chest, with a massive proud face. He was as black a man as John had ever seen.

"You sent for me?" John asked.

"You know I wouldn't do that," Jonathan said with a sly smile. " 'Course I figgered *mebbe* you'd see the smoke of my kiln . . . and iff'n you did, then *mebbe* you'd drop by and do me some designs." Jonathan pointed at the milk pitchers he had made that morning, drying on the table. They were simple kitchen ware, but to John's eye they possessed a quiet beauty.

John picked up one of the pitchers and turned it

around, studying the shape with an artist's eye. "What do you want on it?"

"Could ya do me the blue flowers again—the one you call 'Tulips in the Wind'?"

"Nothin' to it." With his brush and a small jar of blue cobalt wash, John painted a flower bent over as if by the wind, using quick, careful strokes. At the same time, Jonathan worked on an already fired blue teapot, putting on it a maple sapling handle that arched over the lid. John glanced at him and saw the teapot. "That's new. What a blue that is!"

"I made this yere teapot special. For Hattie." Jonathan smiled shyly as he said it. "I'll ask you a favor— take it up to the house for me."

"Take it yourself," John said, continuing to paint. Jonathan looked surprised at the refusal. John looked up and said, "What I mean is, Hattie don't want to get a present from *me*! It's you she's sweet on."

The Geyser farmhouse sat peacefully on a hill, looking over the valley. It was a simple country home, two-story brick with a wide white porch around the entire front. Handmade furniture stood along the railing. The house had been added on to several times to accommodate the family as it grew. There were well-kept outbuildings surrounding it and tall oak trees shading everything. The home yard was bounded by a stone wall.

John and Jonathan approached the house, with Jonathan carrying the teapot wrapped in his jacket under his arm. He glanced at the house nervously. "Did yo daddy say anything 'bout me lately?" John shook his head. "I owe yo daddy some rent. Don't seem like I can sell my pots no more."

"There ain't no better pottery in Virginia. It'll sell," John said firmly.

Jonathan shook his head slowly. "I dunno. Folks roun' here never did like no free nigger in business fo' himself. And now it's worse. They scared to even talk with me. The storekeeper—he say it's accounta what happen at Harpers Ferry."

John stopped. "John Brown's raid? They can't blame you for that!"

"Mebbe not," Jonathan said softly. "But they was black men involved. Black men carryin' guns—that's the white folks' nightmare." John was silent.

As the two men rounded the corner of the house, they passed Mark leading his horse to the stable. "Evenin' Mark," John said, but his brother gave him a hostile look, not even breaking stride. Jonathan tried to look like he didn't see anything, assuming the practiced mask he wore around whites. John merely shrugged.

As they neared the kitchen door, the slave cook Hattie stepped outside and reached for the plaited cord on the dinner bell. She was lighter than Jonathan, with the blood of generations of white masters in her. When she saw him she said in a mock-gruff voice, "Jonathan, what you doin' here?"

Jonathan kept a straight face as he played out this courting dance. "Jes' a visitin', Miss Hattie."

"Jes' a visitin'! Jes' at suppertime! Don't lie to me, Jonathan Henry! You here for my lamb stew!" She turned to John. "He can smell my cookin' . . . clear down in that cabin of his."

Jonathan put on the misunderstood and wounded lover look. "You got no call to say that, Miss Hattie," and he took the teapot from the folds of his jacket. "I brung you sump'n."

When Hattie saw the teapot she dropped her pretense of anger. "Oh, Jonathan!" Her voice was sweet and inviting as she held the teapot up to admire. "It's the purtiest teapot ever!"

John eased up to her and in a hoarse whisper just loud enough to be heard by Jonathan said, "It's worth a plate o' stew, ain't it, Hattie?"

"And a piece a pie," she whispered back, again loud enough to be heard by Jonathan. She turned to him and in a gruff voice said, "Git on inside, Jonathan! Go on now, move it!" As Jonathan stepped into the kitchen, she turned to ring the bell, her eyes shining.

Ben and Matt, bare to the waist, were washing up when the bell rang out. Both men were strongly muscled from a life of labor. Ben, toweling off his face and neck, saw John coming around the front of the house and scowled. "Where you been boy?"

"Working," John said simply.

"You mean drawing pictures . . . in that book?"

"Yes, working," John said again.

"You must be all tuckered out," Matt said, looking straight at him. John, who was used to this tension, turned for the porch.

John laid his sketchbook on a porch chair and held the door open as Ben and Matt went into the house. Young Luke and Emma were just finishing their before-supper checker game on the porch. Luke yelled out, "She beat me!"

"She always beats you," John said as they all went in to supper.

The family sat around the long harvest table, passing the food up and down the line. Hattie brought in more bowls of steaming stew. Maggie sat at one end of the table with Ben at the other. She filled a plate with food for Mark, who hadn't come in yet, and sat it in front of his empty chair.

Ben turned to Emma. "Did you hear anything in town today, Emma—anything new about Harpers Ferry?"

"Nobody's talkin' about anything else," she replied. Everybody waited to hear the news. Emma, secure in the limelight, put a forkful of food in her mouth.

"Come, child, tell us the news," Maggie finally said.

"John Brown was wounded some, but they moved him and the rest who weren't killed to the jail in Charlestown. The governor's called out umpteen thousand militiamen to guard him."

Maggie spoke again. "Why all the soldiers? What are they afraid of?"

"All I know is what the sheriff said," Emma replied, stringing it out a little further.

When Emma started to put another forkful in her mouth, Matt reached over, restraining her arm. "What did he say?"

Emma quoted carefully. "He said that the nigger-loving abolitionists up North might stop flapping their jaws for a change and march on Charlestown to free John Brown."

There was a moment of silence in the room as the possibilities dawned on them for the first time. Hattie slipped out of the room. Matt spoke first. "Pa, Mark and I been talkin'. We're thinkin' we oughta put in some time in the militia, get some trainin'. Just in case."

"In case of what . . ." John began to ask, but was interrupted by Mark's voice as he entered the room.

"If this don't beat all," he said, holding John's sketchbook, angrily staring at the drawing of them working in the apple orchard. He handed the book to Matt, who was also angered at what he saw. The book was passed around the table until it got to Maggie.

"I think it's wonderful! I can tell who's who, even at this distance."

"It's a damn insult!" Mark yelled angrily. "Us sweatin' out the day's work, and he's up on some hill doin' nuthin', just watchin', like he was our lord and master."

"I'm with Mark," Matt said. He wasn't hot-tempered like Mark, and spoke quietly but firmly. "John ain't been pullin' his weight. There's no room on a farm for a man that don't earn his keep."

"That ain't for you to decide, Matt," Maggie said, turning to Ben. "Pa . . . ?"

"It's true, Maggie," he said. "When John works with us, he works hard, I'll give him that. But he ain't showed up much lately. He's givin' all his time to that hobby of his."

John tried to make his father understand. "It's not a hobby. The way I feel, it's my profession . . ."

Mark broke in with a laugh. "You aimin' to earn a livin' doin' *that* stuff?"

John didn't take his eyes off his father. "People do. I think I'm good. And I think I'll get better."

Mark continued to bait him. "How much money you made so far John?"

"Nuthin'. And I won't make nuthin', not around here." John paused. He had hoped for a better time to tell them. "I'm plannin' to go up North, to Gettysburg. I'm gonna ask Uncle Jacob to give me a start, on the newspaper." He turned to his father. "I'm asking for your blessing, Pa. Yours too, Ma."

There was a long silence in the room. Ben finally

shook his head. "It'd mean one pair of hands less to work the farm. It might cost us, and things are mighty lean around here."

"I thought on that a lot," John said. "I aim to pull my weight by sending money home. I want six months, Pa. A trial, like. If I don't get nowhere in six months, then I'll be back, ready to work the farm."

"Leave him go," Mark said angrily. "He ain't no use around here anyways."

"That's enough, Mark!" Ben pondered a moment and then looked down the table at his wife.

Maggie was the only one who really understood what all this really meant. It meant she was losing a son. The family had never spoken of it before, she thought to herself, but it had always been assumed that Matt or Mark would be the first to go, to start a family of their own, possibly with a piece of the Geyser land to build on. Or the beauty, Emma, would be taken away by one of the men who had tried to claim her. Or even Luke, the youngest, the wild one, might strike off on his own, but not John. Not John, the gentle one, the one that seemed to need his family the most. Or maybe it was just that he had *wanted* them the most. She had been the one to stand up for him since he was a boy, even more so since his grandmother had died. He had always been a dreamer. But now she realized that his dreams were bigger than his home, bigger than any of them. So when she finally spoke, it was with resignation.

"I always knew John was different from the rest of us. He has a gift. To me, a wondrous gift. And it didn't come from us, Ben. So I figgered, when he makes a picture like this, it must be God as guides his hand." She looked hard at her husband. "Mebbe God's guiding him now, Ben."

Ben put a hand over his eyes for a moment. Then he looked at Maggie and began to nod.

At dawn John stood saddling his horse outside the stable. He was dressed for the road in a heavy home-spun suit and a wide-brimmed hat. He heaved his bed-roll to the saddle and cinched it down as the horse-drawn wagon pulled up next to him. Aboard were his father and brothers, dressed for the day's work. Ben got down with some difficulty, his wooden leg swinging wide to clear the wagon wheel.

"Set?" Ben said. John nodded. They shook hands. It was an awkward moment; Ben was not built for senti-ment. "Well, can't stay around all day," Ben said ab-ruptly. "There's work to be done." Ben pulled himself back into the wagon.

"Work!" Mark said. "I figgered we'd jes lie around till John sends home all that money." Mark and Matt laughed as they whipped up the horses. John grinned good-naturedly and saluted a good-bye as the wagon drove off. He walked the horse over to the porch, where Maggie stood waiting for him, Emma and Luke by her side. Luke carried two sacks, connected by a rope, slung over his shoulders.

"Sling them up behind the saddle," Maggie in-structed Luke. To John she said, "One sack has got four days' vittles—enough to get you there, I reckon."

John hefted the other sack. "What's this? Ballast?" Maggie slapped the sack. "A ham. A twenty-four pound-er. Best Virginia smoked. Give that to my sister, with love from me 'n' Ben."

Emma gave him a warm hug and turned toward the house. Luke shook his hand. "Write me 'bout them fast

Northern girls." He darted off as Maggie aimed a cuff at him. John stood there with his mom.

"I noticed something this morning when I was saddling up that I never did before. Just before dawn, the darkness seemed like it gathered itself, to hold on to the night a little longer. For a few moments, it really got darker. Then I noticed a slight breeze starting to swirl around, trying to blow all the night away. And just then the first light appeared. It's funny I never noticed that before."

Maggie reached for him and they embraced. She had tears on her cheeks as she whispered into his ear. "I believe in you, John. You know that. But if things don't work out jes' right, you know the way home." John nodded. He broke away and leaped on his horse. Maggie watched him until he was out of sight.

Half a mile down the road, John reined his horse. He looked back at the house, the rising sun flooding Geyser Hill with light. Then he turned back to the road at a gallop.

CHAPTER TWO

Gettysburg, Pennsylvania

It was a chilly, raw day when John Geyser rode into Gettysburg. His broad hat was pulled low against the wind. Only a few people were in the streets, and those who were darted from one door to another trying to stay warm. He pulled up in front of a two-story clapboard building; the sign out front read THE GETTYSBURG COMPILER—JACOB HALE, EDITOR. Both John and his horse were tired and mud-spattered from the wet, rough roads. John tied his horse and pulled out his sketchbook from the rest of his gear.

John stood on the sidewalk in front of the newspaper office, nervous about entering. He felt a little awkward, bundled up in his muddy homemade suit, his face rough with a four-day beard. He looked down at the sketchbook, trying to work up the courage to go in. He mumbled to himself a few possible openings he might use on his uncle about the job he wanted. Finally he entered, trying to appear as casual as possible.

A wizened old man was working the printing presses on one side of the long room. John had to yell over the noise of the presses to ask where Jacob Hale was, and without even looking up the old man pointed with his thumb to the office in back. John went through a swinging wooden railing, past the potbellied stove that stood in the middle of the room. He stopped in front of his uncle's desk. Jacob Hale was a stocky man in his fifties, a man of intense beliefs, an abolitionist, and sometimes a little absent-minded. He was busy writing an editorial and didn't notice John.

John quietly said, "Uncle Jacob?" Hale lifted his bifocals and glanced up with a puzzled look.

"Uncle Jacob, I'm John Geyser."

Jacob leaped to his feet with a loud "John!" Jacob started to embrace his nephew, but when he got close enough to smell him, he settled for a lusty slap on the back. Dust flew all over his desk from the dried mud.

"A pleasure to see you, my boy!" Jacob wiped his hand. "Didn't recognize you under the mud. Just rode in, I gather. Damn but you need a shave. And a bath."

"And a job," John said bluntly. Jacob's smile faded. John hurriedly reminded him that the last time the Geysers had come for a visit, Hale had promised to give him a start doing illustrations for the paper. With a sheepish grin Hale sat him down and proceeded to outline for him the realities of operating a local newspaper. "I rarely run illustrations—it's just too expensive to make a litho block or an etching. Oh, occasionally if I can pick one up cheaply from New York . . ."

As Hale was giving his speech, hoping to let John down as easily as possible, John casually placed his sketchbook on the desk and opened it to the first page.

"I'm really sorry, my boy," Jacob said as the first sketch caught his eye. "I like you. And I hate to turn you down." He turned to the second sketch and studied it. "I only hope . . . that you . . . understand . . ." Hale's voice trailed off as he felt the impact of John's work. There were drawings of people working in the fields, of landscapes and barns, and of a few public speakers. Hale was stunned by the emotion of John's work, especially as expressed in the faces of the people. And because of John's technical skills, his work could be easily converted to etched illustrations without losing their feeling. Hale turned to the rest of the sketches.

"I'm just askin' to get a start, Uncle Jacob. I'd work cheap."

There was a pause. Jacob took a final look at the work and closed the portfolio. "Cheap?" he said.

John nodded.

Jacob looked up at him and said, "Three dollars a week?"

"Yessir! That's mighty generous!" John cried out.

Hale had something special in mind, something so radical for a small-town paper that he dared not let himself think it through to the end. He would act on this fortuitous event and possibly turn the fortunes of his paper around. "The John Brown trial . . . it's set to start in two days in Charlestown, Virginia. It'll be the trial of the century. If you can capture that fierce old goat John Brown in a portrait and get a few drawings of the trial, then you got the job. But you only have a day and a half to get there. It'll be a hard ride, and not a moment to lose."

John thanked him profusely, shook his hand, grabbed the five dollars in expense money his uncle held out, and ran out the door. Jacob stood staring after him, too surprised to speak. Just as suddenly John ran back in and dumped a mud-encrusted sack on Jacob's desk, then scooted for the door. "Wait! What the hell is this loathsome object?" Jacob called after him.

At the door John turned. "It's a twenty-four-pound best Virginia smoked ham."

Jacob was suddenly purring. "That's different."

John leaped on his horse and, without rest or a wash, he galloped toward Charlestown, and John Brown.

The man at the Charlestown telegraph office had never sent so many urgent messages in his life. He was the only telegrapher in town, and he was rising to the occasion. John stood in front of the line of reporters and reread his message.

> JOHN BROWN TO BE SENTENCED TODAY. WILL SEND WORD IMMEDIATELY.
>
> JOHN GEYSER.

"Where do you want me to send this?" the operator asked.

"Send it to the editor, *Gettysburg Compiler*."

"Where?"

"Gettysburg. It's in Pennsylvania."

"That'll be a dollar." John paid him. "Some doings—we've never had anything like this in our town, and you can *believe* that."

John walked out into the dusty town square and across the street to the courthouse. He carried his sketchbook under his arm. When he got to the court-room, people were crowding through the doors, trying to get a look at John Brown. Militiamen in dress uniform were posted all around the courthouse and inside along the walls. John found a seat in the jammed press section and opened his sketchbook, ready to draw. The courthouse was overflowing with people—they all knew that today would provide the climax of the trial. The air was close and filled with tension.

In the only open space in the entire room was an army cot with a pillow and a lap robe lying on it. There was a sudden stir as John Brown entered the room assisted by two guards. He stretched out on the cot and one of the guards pulled the robe over him. John studied Brown's cruel, hawklike face. His flowing white beard fell away from the cot as he stared blankly at the ceiling.

The clerk of the court rose. "Silence in the court." The buzz of conversation died down. "Those assembled will please rise." Everyone stood up. "His Honor, Judge Richard Parker."

Judge Parker emerged from his chambers, crossed to the bench, and sat down. He leaned toward the clerk, holding a whispered conversation. The clerk took the floor again. "Whereas the prisoner, John Brown, was yesterday found guilty of treason, conspiring with slaves and others to rebel, and of murder in the first degree . . . His Honor has charged me to direct a question at said prisoner."

Brown shifted to look directly at the clerk. "Is there any reason why sentence should not now be passed upon you?" A murmur of anticipation spread through the crowd.

Brown threw off the robe and struggled to his feet, standing firm and tall. John quickly began to draw, hardly taking his eyes off Brown. He drew the gaunt face and the burning eyes. He was a brutal killer, surely mad, but his attempt to arm slaves for revolt in his savage raid on the Federal Arsenal at Harpers Ferry had galvanized North and South in their differences. People were taking sides, not just in Virginia or Pennsylvania, but everywhere. Brown was like a hinge in time. He had opened the fateful door and the whole country had stepped through. Nothing would ever be the same again. Because of John Brown there was no more room for talking, no time left at all.

When John Brown spoke, it was with a deep, almost hypnotic voice. "I have, may it please the court, a few words to say.

"In the first place, I deny everything but what I have all along admitted of—a design on my part to free slaves.

"Had I interfered in the matter, which I admit, and which I admit has been fairly proved, had I so interfered in behalf of the rich, the powerful, the intelligent, or the so-called great, and suffered and sacrificed what I have in this interference, it would have been all right. Every man in this court would have deemed it an act worthy of reward rather than punishment.

"I see a book kissed which I suppose to be the Bible, or at least the New Testament, which teaches me that all things whatsoever I would that men should do unto me, I should do even so to them. It teaches me further to remember them that are in bonds as bound with them. I endeavored to act up to that instruction. I say I am yet too young to understand that God is any respecter of persons. I believe that to have interfered as I have done—as I have always freely admitted I have done—in behalf of His despised poor, I did no wrong, but right. Now, if it is deemed necessary that I should forfeit my life for the furtherance of the ends of justice and mingle my blood with the blood of my children and with the blood of millions in this slave country whose rights are disregarded by wicked, cruel, and unjust enactments, I say, let it be done."

John Geyser had stopped drawing and sat with his eyes riveted on Brown. In that brief moment before the judge spoke the final words of death, Brown stood there like some wild Old Testament prophet. He had done his work; now he could rest.

The judge spoke. "I have listened to the words of the accused, but I find in them nothing that challenges the verdict arrived at here by due process of law. Nor do I find, in my mind or my heart, any reasonable doubt that the prisoner is guilty. John Brown, I sentence you to be hanged in public on Friday, the second of December."

John Brown received the verdict with granitelike composure. One man began to clap, a strange, hollow sound that echoed across the ancient, faded courtroom. A guard stopped him. Then there was only silence—no murmur from the crowd, no cheers, no weeping. It was all over. Yet it had just begun.

The tavern of the Charlestown Inn was crowded and boisterous. The John Brown trial had attracted a great many spectators—farmers and other locals, who wished to be touched by history, and seekers of gain, such as politicians, military officers, and prostitutes. There was a feeling of jubilation in the smoke-filled tavern. Everyone there seemed to have found what they had come to find, and now they were happy.

A tall man walked in out of the cold night and stood

looking over the crowd. He wore a dark frock coat and a broad-brimmed black hat that concealed much of his face. That part that could be seen in the dim light was hard and leathery. He seemed to stand apart from the other patrons in the crowded bar, and those around him yielded him plenty of space in which to move.

His eyes finally settled on John Geyser, who was standing near the bar. John held out his empty beer mug to the bartender, who took it and filled it. While this was happening, a whore, standing behind him, smoothly lifted John's wallet and slipped it between her breasts. The tall stranger watched the theft without re-action. His eyes stayed with John as he made his way back to his table with the fresh beer.

John had proceeded with his meal when a shadow crossed his plate. Looking up, he found the stranger standing over him.

"Mind if I sit?" the man asked in a quiet voice. John gestured at the chair opposite him. "Name's Jonas. I been lookin' for you." John waited with interest. "You drew a picture of the old man, just before the judge ordered him strung up." John nodded. "Could I have a look?"

John hesitated a moment, weighing the man. He was tall and rangy, with deep black eyes and furrowed cheeks. His long hair was dark and pulled straight back. His steady look never wavered. John reached for his sketchbook, opened to the drawing, and handed it to Jonas.

Jonas looked it over carefully. "Like I thought, I'm in it. I felt your eyes on me." He handed it back to John. "You got the devil's way with a likeness." John looked at the drawing. There among the spectators sitting directly behind John Brown was Jonas.

Jonas spoke again. "I wouldn't want for that to be printed in your newspaper." John's look hardened, but Jonas quickly continued, "I'm not tellin'—I'm askin'."

John spoke for the first time. "Maybe you'd like to explain."

"Wish I could. All I can say is this—the business I'm in, it could do me a lot of harm if certain people knew I was at John Brown's trial. Now that ain't much grounds for askin', but . . ."

John took out a pencil, made a couple of pencil strokes in the sketch, then showed it to Jonas. "Your Aunt Rosie wouldn't know you now."

Jonas nodded and abruptly got up. "I'm obliged." He stuck out his hand and John shook it. As Jonas walked away, John's eyes followed him for a moment and then he resumed his dinner.

At the bar Jonas stepped behind the whore and reached out and took her arm—not roughly enough so that anyone would notice, but rather with a slight smile. She smiled back at him in a professional way. He leaned toward her and whispered something into her ear, motioning toward John. She protested and tried to pull her arm free. Jonas' grip still held, imperceptibly tightening like a vise. Again he leaned forward and whispered something in her ear. She hesitated and then nodded. Jonas took his hand away, and she moved across the room to John. Jonas watched for a moment and then walked out.

"I'm Nell. I got something for you, love. Follow me upstairs."

John looked flustered. "Upstairs . . . ?"

"You checked your wallet lately?" She turned on her heel and walked away. John felt for his wallet and immediately stood and followed.

The door to the room was open and John stopped at the entrance. Nell was sitting on the bed, lighting a lamp. "Bolt the door," she said.

John stood in the doorway, not knowing what to do, feeling foolish. He bolted the door. Nell reached down into the great crevice between her breasts and produced his wallet.

"Where'd you find it?" he asked, still not understanding.

"In your pocket."

"You stole it?" John said with a grave tone.

She leaned back on the bed and looked at him with a puzzled half-smile. She figured him to be either a simple dolt or fresh off the farm. She studied him from head to foot, taking in his well-worn homespun suit and the broad farm hat he held in his hand. John looked through his wallet.

"There's two dollars missing," Nell said. "I owed the bartender." She stood up matter-of-factly and started to take off her dress. "You can take it out in trade. For two dollars you can stay all night."

John began to back toward the door. "Thank you kindly, but I really got to go."

Nell stepped out of her dress. She had only her panties and her garter belt on. John was desperate. "Look, Nell, keep the two dollars." He looked around for an avenue of escape.

Nell's pride was hurt. "It's already paid for! Look at me! Am I ugly or somethin'?"

John was tugging on the doorknob. His mind had gone blank; he suddenly couldn't remember how to unlock a door. His fingers seemed to have a life of their own, and each of them was trying to do something different. "Oh, no!" he said. "You're real good-lookin'. It's not you! It's me!"

Nell stood with her hands on her hips, watching him. "You know what I think . . . you're green. Tell the truth, love—have you ever been with a woman?" John did not answer, and he stopped fiddling with the door. He looked embarrassed, almost ashamed. "It's true, ain't it? You're blushing! I've caught me a virgin!" She sensed his shame and did not laugh.

Nell walked over to John and gently took his hand. "Well, you're in luck, love." He stood as though paralyzed while she slowly took off his jacket and shirt. Then she sat him down on the bed and kneeled in front of him, taking off his boots and setting them carefully aside.

John looked at her in the candlelight. To him she appeared luminous in her beauty. "Really, Nell. I think I should go," he said softly, not meaning it.

"Shhh." She sat on the bed beside him. "I got enough experience for the both of us." With great delicacy and tenderness, she cupped his face in her hands and kissed him. John responded with his lips, but he didn't know what to do with his hands. Sensing this, she lay down next to him, taking his hand and holding it against her breast. She closed her eyes so that John could enjoy looking at her without being watched.

He bent over and kissed her on the mouth. She put her arms around him, slowly pulling him toward her until he was beside her on the bed.

John let her lead him. She was more aroused by this seduction than she had ever been, servicing the rough and callous men who used her.

He learned many things that night. Nell was a good and cheerful teacher.

CHAPTER THREE

Charlestown, Virginia

John Brown lay in his small cell drenched in sweat. Even in his sleep he was held captive. In feverish dreams of the raid on Harpers Ferry he saw again the torn bodies of his sons.

There was Watson Brown, the steady one, who had written to his wife and seven children waiting for him back home:

> Oh, Belle, I want to see you and the little fellow very much, but must wait. There was a slave near here whose wife was sold South. They found him hanging in Kennedy's orchard next morning. I cannot come home as long as such things are done here. I sometimes think that we shall not meet again.

When they were finally trapped, John Brown had sent Watson out with a white flag and had watched as he was ripped apart by rifle fire. And there was his son

Oliver Brown, the young, handsome one, who, shot in his stomach, took all night to die, screaming all the while to his father for the water he did not have to give him.

In his dreams John Brown saw again the doomed attack across the bridge, the slaves refusing to carry weapons, and he remembered the final charge by the Marines, the terrible carnage that followed. When they came, in that final moment, he looked up through the smoke-blackened air to the hill, and there sat the colonel on his gallant horse. It was Robert E. Lee, son of Virginia. Lee looked down at the final charge of his men. For a moment his eyes met those of John Brown. The gears of fate turned toward each other, meshed with blood.

The Marines were professionals and they did their job well. With ruthless efficiency the raiders who stood with Brown were pinned to the floors and walls with bayonets. It only took a few minutes. Lee, sitting quietly on his horse, checked the time and then closed his watch.

In his cell John Brown sat up with a jolt. He shook the dream from his mind. The guard was calling his name. He had company. The reporters had arrived.

The cell was furnished with a desk, an upright chair, a cot, and a potbelly stove. On the desk was a Bible, a pitcher of water, a glass, and a pen and paper. As the reporters came in, Brown, still damp with the sweat of his dreams, sat down at the desk. While the reporters gathered around, John Geyser sat down on the cot and began to draw a portrait.

The reporters told Brown that there was a rumor of

rescue, of guerrilla forces headed this way to liberate him. He replied, "I am worth, now, infinitely more dead than alive." They asked him if he was ready to die. "I'm entirely ready. I know that I and my fellow captives *must* die. But mark my prediction! Our deaths will be the beginning of the end for slavery."

John was drawing swiftly, capturing in his portrait all the violence and fascination of this steely fanatic. Brown's self-taught eloquence had a direct power—it plunged straight to the heart.

When asked about the possibility of a peaceful solution to the chasm between North and South, Brown dropped the calm facade. "I am now quite certain that the crimes of this guilty land will never be purged away but with blood!"

John Geyser looked at him in doubt, and then asked, "Sir! In everyday language, do you mean the North and South are gonna fight? Is there gonna be a war?"

Brown turned and looked him directly in the eye. "I mean that there will be wailing and lamentations in a million homes! And grief and sorrow will sit with every family in the land!"

John Brown's cortege approached the hanging ground. In the lead were a general and his staff, superbly uniformed and mounted. Behind them marched a squad of infantry. And then came a clumsy wagon, drawn by two big white horses. In the front of the wagon there sat a driver and two men; in the well, John Brown sat on his coffin as they took him to his gallows.

It was a bright winter morning, with a strong breeze coming off the Blue Ridge Mountains. John Brown looked with admiration at the countryside. He showed no fear; he had prepared himself. He wore an un-pressed black suit, white shirt without tie, black hat, and red felt slippers. His arms were bound at the el-bows, held together by a rope behind his back. The road was rutted and muddy and the ride was bumpy.

They turned off the dirt road and crossed the grass to a large hollow square around a raised platform and scaffold. The wagon halted at the foot of the crude steps that led up to the platform. The jailer jumped to the ground, then reached up to help John Brown. Though his arms were pinioned, the old man shook his head and jumped to the ground unaided. Near the steps a mounted colonel waited, his drawn saber held verti-cally. At the foot of the steps was Sheriff Campbell of Jefferson County, a stout man in frock coat, striped trousers, and top hat. Unaided, John Brown mounted the steps, following the sheriff.

At the edge of the hanging ground, the man named Jonas sat on his horse. He watched the proceedings with a stony composure much like John Brown's. He spotted John Geyser standing under a nearby tree and rode over to him. John looked up as Jonas halted. "Ever seen a man hang before?" Jonas asked him. John shook his head, looking somewhat queasy. Jonas dis-mounted and stood next to him.

John Brown stood on the trapdoor, the noose dan-gling overhead. The sheriff approached with a white hood. Since he couldn't raise his pinioned arms, Brown lowered his head until his hands could grasp his hat. He dropped the hat to his feet and straightened up to his full height. He looked around calmly, with a slight smile. He noticed Jonas standing by the tree but made no sign of recognition. He spoke to the sheriff for the first time. "A man couldn't have asked for prettier weather."

The sheriff put the hood over the old man's shaggy head and then placed the noose around his neck. A guard handed the sheriff an ax, its sharpened blade gleaming in the winter sun. The sheriff stood poised with the ax over the rope that when cut would release the trapdoor. The officer on horseback seemed to flinch as he raised his saber. "We are ready, Mr. Campbell."

The hooded John Brown stood motionless. Behind him sheriff Campbell brought the ax down, cleanly severing the rope. John Brown fell through the trapdoor. The rope tightened, snapping his neck. His legs kicked and jerked for several moments, and then stopped.

John Geyser turned away and fell to his hands and knees, vomiting. Jonas took a flask from his coat and, holding John's shoulders, poured a mouthful of brandy down his throat. John gasped and choked but was able to fight down the nausea.

"Thanks." John, pale and unsteady, got to his feet. "I didn't think it would be like this. I mean, this bad."

"It's always this bad," Jonas said grimly. "It's over. Let's go." He led John toward their horses. As they rode away, Jonas looked back for a moment. They were taking John Brown's body down from the scaffold.

They rode along together side by side. Jonas offered John the brandy flask again; they both took a long drink.

John turned toward him. "Which way you headed?"

"Philadelphia."

"Gettysburg is right on your way," John said, as he reached again for the brandy. "Tell you what, Jonas.

Let's ride together far as Gettysburg. That's where I work. I guarantee you a good dinner, good company, and a warm bed."

Jonas didn't say anything. He was used to riding alone.

John looked at him. "It's a long ride."

Jonas nodded, relenting. "Sounds good."

"Where do you come from—I mean originally?"

"Kansas," Jonas said.

John waited for more information, but none was forthcoming. "John Brown came from Kansas, didn't he?" he asked, probing.

"Yes," Jonas said, "I believe he did." It started to rain as they rode on in silence.

It was pouring rain as John and Jonas passed through the streets of Gettysburg. They were soaked, hunched down in their saddles, with collars drawn up and hats pulled down. Jonas was dozing, his horse following John's. It was something that a man learned to do, spending so much of his life on a horse with nowhere to lie down. But when John pulled up in front of the Hale house, Jonas was wide awake before John could turn around and rouse him.

They turned into the lane. Before them stood a tall house, three stories with an attic, white clapboard with frills on the porch and a stable to the side. They headed into the stable and unsaddled their horses, putting a dry blanket on both. The news of their arrival spread through the house before they even reached the door. The youngest boy, James, who was fourteen, saw them through the window and ran through the house, calling the news to his father, who was upstairs, and to his mother who was in the kitchen making supper. She was being helped by Annie, the youngest of the family, who ran out after James to the front door.

Evelyn Hale wiped the flour off her hands. She too was excited to be seeing John, who had always been her favorite nephew. She crossed to the mudroom, a small parlor where people could leave their muddy shoes and coats as they came in the back door. Mary, their oldest child, stood in front of the basin, washing her hair in rainwater. At first glance she seemed a plain girl, but there was a certain fullness about her, a generosity in her character and spirit. She possessed full, proud breasts and strong, wide hips and moved with an open, unapologizing sensuality. Her mother told her that John was there and that he was not alone. Groaning in frustration, she hurried with her hair.

Except for Mary, the whole family gathered around John and Jonas. Besides James and Annie, who stared in awe at the visitors, there were the older sons, Malachy and Jacob, Jr., called Jake, both in their early twenties. Because he worked in the local bank, Jake was dressed more formally than the others. John introduced Jonas to the family, and Evelyn invited him to stay for dinner and a night's rest. When she went to give John a hug she realized just how wet both men were. Herding them into the kitchen, she ordered them to take off their wet clothes.

While she got blankets for them, John and Jonas stripped off their shirts. Both were wearing long johns under their clothes.

"And the pants," Evelyn said as she came in. John slipped out of his pants and wrapped himself in a blanket.

She turned to Jonas: "Well?"

"You see, ma'am . . . I, uh . . ."

"Jonas, I *am* the mother of grown sons."

"Yes, ma'am. But I'm not one of them."

With a friendly laugh, Evelyn threw him a blanket. She put her arm around John and led him out of the kitchen. Jonas took off his pants and, putting the blanket around his shoulders, stood with his back to the wood stove. He heard the splashing of water in the mudroom as Mary finished rinsing her hair. The door to the mudroom slowly opened and Mary peered into the kitchen. Because the stove was blocked by the door, she couldn't see Jonas, and, thinking she was alone, she walked into the kitchen, vigorously toweling her hair. She was fully dressed from the waist down, but wore only a light camisole on her top. As she bent over and toweled her hair, her large breasts tumbled out of the camisole. She had taken several steps toward the stove before realizing Jonas was there. Gasping, she stood for a second too stunned to cover her breasts. Jonas, hovering under his blanket, wearing only his long underwear, could only stare at her, frozen with embarrassment. There was a shocked pause, during which he wrapped himself more securely with the blanket, and Mary quickly covered herself with the towel, leaving her hair in a damp tangle falling around her face.

"I'm Jonas, John's friend."

"I'm Mary, John's cousin."

There was another pause before Jonas spoke again. "I heard once that women don't wash their hair on rainy days 'cause it don't dry so good—on rainy days."

"That's true, but I wash mine on rainy days because fresh rainwater leaves it soft—and then I dry it in front of the stove."

Jonas, realizing he was blocking the stove, quickly stepped aside. "Sorry. I'm in your way."

Mary stepped in front of the stove and with a deft and practiced motion concealed by the towel slipped her breasts back into her camisole and resumed drying her hair, but with considerably less vigor. She glanced back at Jonas. "There's room. Come, warm whatever you were warming."

Jonas stepped to her side. He lifted the blanket slightly, enough to expose his backside to the heat. He looked over his shoulder at her. She looked back at him. They smiled at each other, and their eyes lingered.

After dinner, the whole family sat around the parlor talking of the John Brown trial and passing John's sketchbook around. The parlor was Victorian, like the rest of the house, furnished in heavy oak with red damask. John leaned against the mantel.

"Did you get the stuff I sent by train, the trial sketches?"

Jacob was studying the sketches. "I printed them two weeks ago. Talk of the town, they were. Got a whole gaggle of new subscribers. John, this portrait of John Brown is amazing—first time I felt I understood the man."

The gaslight cast a warm glow across the parlor. Evelyn led the youngest children toward bed, and there were goodnight kisses all around. Mary sat on the floor near Jonas. Jacob was in a celebrating mood. He took down the whiskey jug, and he and Jonas and the other men drank deeply. They talked of John Brown and his prophecies. As usual, Jake was the first to recognize the deeper meaning. "If there *was* a war, John's family would be on one side and us on the other. It's hard to imagine."

Malachy warmed to the subject. "If there's a war, I'll be the first to sign up. Betcha I'm a born soldier!"

"I want no more talk about the war, boys," Jacob said. "It's not going to happen. Too many wise heads in Washington."

He took down his old fiddle and while he tuned it up asked Evelyn to play something on the piano. John went to his saddlebag and got out his beat-up harmonica, which he called his "harpoon." They played some old English ballads and coaxed Mary into singing. She had a high, clear voice, which seemed distant and a little longing as she finished the song.

"Barbara Allen was buried, in the old churchyard,
Sweet William was buried beside her.
Out of Sweet William's heart, there grew a rose,
Out of Barbara Allen's, a briar.
They grew and grew, in the old churchyard,
Till they could grow no higher.
And in the end, they formed a true lovers' knot,
And the rose grew round the briar."

It was late when Evelyn finally said, "Bed." At the door she turned back. "Jonas can use the back bedroom."

"Thank you, ma'am," Jonas said as he finished the drink in his hand.

"Tired?" Mary asked him. Jonas nodded. "Come on, I'll show you the way."

Jonas stood in the middle of the small bedroom and watched Mary prepare the big brass bed. She was taking her time, making this moment with him last. She was aware of him watching her body as she moved, and she liked that. A single candle burned by the bed. They both felt the long silence, aware of the closeness of their bodies in the small room.

"You haven't told us much about yourself," Mary said as she worked.

"Not much to tell, really."

"It doesn't matter. I won't ask questions." She had turned down both sides of the bed and placed the pillows side by side. Jonas didn't miss the gesture. She turned to him. "Will you come back? To Gettysburg, I mean."

"It could happen," Jonas said. He paused a moment; that wasn't all he really felt. "I'd like to."

"Then make it happen." Mary said it plainly, looking him straight in the eye. She started out but turned at the door. "I hope you don't mind bold girls."

CHAPTER FOUR

Virginia—December 1860

John Geyser was still a mile from home when he reined
up. He wanted to take a good look at Geyser Hill.
Home—he had thought about it every day that he'd
been gone. The farm had not really changed, but it appeared different somehow. It looked smaller than he
had remembered; not that there was less land, but he
saw less of himself in it. He saw the farm for what it
was, but still it looked wonderful. He could see one of
his brothers hauling an armload of wood across the
yard to the house. The smoke spiraled out of the fireplace chimney into the fading December light. He
thought of staying there and drawing it, just as it looked
now, but it was too chilly and he had come a long way
today. He was anxious to see his family and he spurred
his horse on.

It had been fourteen months since John had left
home. He had changed. He now wore city clothes, and
he sported a closely trimmed beard. He'd traveled to
the great cities of America—Philadelphia, Boston,

Washington, and New York. He had sold his drawings of John Brown to *Harper's Weekly* in New York and, as a result of that, to newspapers in other cities. He was making his way in the world.

Inside the house, Matt and Mark were putting up the Christmas tree. Matt held the ladder steady while Mark leaned precariously to put a star on the top of the tree. They wore the uniforms of the Virginia State Militia. In the kitchen Maggie was working with Hattie on the Christmas feast: turkey, ham, candied yams, mashed potatoes, creamed peas and onions, pumpkin pie, mince meat pie, cookies, fresh cream. A delirious mixture of smells flowed from the house.

John was unsaddling his horse in the stable as his father wandered in carrying a harness. He smiled proudly at his son and looked him over carefully. "You're all dandied up son. All growed up, too—a year sure makes a difference."

"You look fine, Pa—same as always."

The two men shook hands and walked toward the house together. "Is everybody here?" John asked.

"Yep. Matt and Mark came home yesterday. They been spendin' time in the militia, learnin' to be soldiers."

John nodded. "I heard . . . Ma's letters."

"Emma's fie-ancy got here this morning, from Vicksburg. They still want their weddin' on Christmas Eve. Did ya ever hear of such a thing?"

John smiled. "Do you like him?"

"He's a businessman, but not too bad of a feller." Ben stopped in the yard. "John, we appreciate the money you sent. It helped."

"It wasn't much."

Just then his mother yelled out, "John!" He looked up to the porch, where Maggie waited for him at the top of the steps. The rest of the family was coming out of the door. He dropped his saddlebags on the bottom step and bounded up the stairs and gave his mother a hug. She squeezed him very hard, as if to prove to herself that he had really come home. When she let go, she turned her head so he wouldn't see her tears.

John next hugged Emma, and kissed her cheek. "Emma, congratulations." He reached his hand out. "And to you, Lester."

"Thanks," Lester said with a thin smile. "It's freezing out here. Shouldn't we be inside?"

"There's coffee in the kitchen," Maggie said, herding them into the house. "Cookies, too."

As everyone got settled with a cup of coffee, there was a pause in the general chatter as everyone waited to hear from John about his adventures—the places he had been and the things he had seen since he had been gone. But John had something else on his mind, something he had just heard in town as he rode through. It was on the telegraphs; everyone in the country would know within hours. The unthinkable had happened. South Carolina had voted to pull out of the United States and go their own way. A state had seceded from the nation. The rest of the deep South was bound to follow—Alabama, Georgia, Mississippi, Florida. If it continued, there could be two countries; there could even be ten.

If John thought he was bringing his family bad news, he was wrong. Matt and Mark let out a whoop and the rest joined in. Ben took down the hard cider jug, declaring, "We're going to start celebrating as of now."

Obviously his father felt the same relief, the pride, and the exhilaration most Southerners would feel. "We can live as we please now, like we always have, and the goddamn Yankee can't tell us what to do or how to live."

"Does it mean fighting?" Maggie asked him. In her heart she felt a chill; she knew the answer.

John felt the same chill. "Abe Lincoln takes office in a couple of months," he said. "I suppose it depends on him."

"There'll be fightin', all right! And I'm ready for it!" Mark said proudly.

"So 'm I," Matt said, and he put his arm around John's shoulder. "If the Yankee cowards come down here, we'll kick their ass! And chase them all the way home!" Everyone raised their mugs. John sipped his coffee and said nothing.

Lester's mind was racing. He understood business and had made a lot of money at it. He saw immediately the potential for profit that a war would bring. He traded in cotton, and an army needed cotton—lots of it. They needed uniforms, coats and clothes, tents and sails. And there was something else. *Both* armies needed these things. An arrangement could always be made with Northern businessmen. Yes, this was a time to celebrate. He looked over at Emma and smiled. He was a lucky man. A beautiful bride, a thriving business, and a war—what else could a man ask for?

Luke, dressed in his Sunday best, nearly a man now, made his way through the Christmas Eve wedding party. In the cleared dining room a dozen couples were doing the one-step, farmers in black Sunday coats and their wives in long plain dresses, businessmen from town in three-piece suits and tight collars, and girls in party dresses leading around awkward boys. A fiddler and his band were going strong, playing old country clog music. The Christmas tree was lit up with candles and hung heavily with homemade ornaments, many brought by neighbors.

Luke slipped into the kitchen. The feast had been spread out on tables; there were jugs of whiskey and hard cider to help wash down the food. Maggie and Hattie presided over the festivities, leading a line of people around the tables, helping them pile food on their plates. Luke shot through the line, snatched a turkey leg, and made for the door. The newlyweds, Emma and Lester, stood in the doorway, receiving congratulations and gifts from the guests.

As Luke eased into the hallway, munching his turkey leg, his attention was caught by Mark as he walked out of the dining room with a pretty young girl. He led his prize to the dark rear of the hallway. Luke followed them and tiptoed up the stairs to listen.

". . . and I'll be the first to go, Sarah . . . on account of I'm already in uniform. One of the first to fall, wounded in some great battle . . . and the last thing I'll remember, as I die on the battlefield, will be your kiss."

"I never kissed you, Mark Geyser!"

"I forgive you," Mark said as he leaned to kiss her, but she turned away.

"Mark . . . my reputation!"

"The secret will die with me, on the battlefield."

"Promise?"

"I promise." With a sweeping, gallant gesture, Mark took her in his arms and kissed her.

Luke moved silently away and with a sly smile started to look for a prize of his own. She appeared down the hallway in the robust form of Mandy, the daughter of a neighboring farmer. She, like Luke, was at loose ends, and she smiled at him as he approached. He motioned to her in a conspiratorial way, and she followed him out the front door to the porch.

". . . and there I'll be, lying on some battlefield, dead as your Uncle Henry, and the last thing I'll remember is your kiss."

"Did you bring me out here to kiss me?" Mandy asked simply. Luke nodded solemnly. "Why didn't you say so?" She took him in her strong arms and gave him an elaborate kiss.

Suddenly there was the sound of horses in the road, heading toward the house. Luke and Mandy rushed inside, calling for Ben. The horsemen pulled up and halted in front of the porch. There were four of them: they carried torches, and the eerie flickering light played on their faces, filling the yard with garish flame. Leading them were the paunchy local sheriff and a tall, fierce, bearded man wearing the black coat of a preacher. Ben stood waiting for them on the porch, backed by his four sons.

The sheriff and the preacher dismounted and stood at the bottom step. The lawman spoke first. "Evenin', Ben. Sorry to come when you're partyin'. You know Preacher Welles?"

"I know him." Ben nodded at the preacher, who made no sign of reply. John Geyser stared at the preacher's face, frozen into the mask of a fanatic possessed by a lifetime of retribution in the name of God. His eyes were like burning coals. With a start John realized who the preacher reminded him of: John Brown.

"Who're they?" Ben said, peering off into the torch-light.

"Them's the Gault brothers. They make a livin' chasin' runaway niggers. They been trackin' two of 'em clear from Georgia."

"What's it got to do with me?" Ben said curtly, making no effort to hide his disgust. As far as he was concerned, slave trackers were the worst kind of white trash—they trafficked in misery.

"The slaves are hiding on your land, Ben. In that cabin in the woods. Least, that's what the brothers tell me."

John stepped forward. "Jonathan's cabin?"

"That's him!" The preacher cried out. "Jonathan!"

Hattie, who had slipped out to the porch behind the family to hear, now moved quickly back into the house. She dashed through to the kitchen and ran out the back door into the night, heading straight for the cabin, running along the dirt road, stumbling on her long dress.

"I've been waiting a long time to get that nigger!" Preacher Welles moved toward his horse.

"I'll check Jonathan's cabin in the morning, sheriff," Ben offered.

Preacher Welles turned and fixed Ben with a challenging glare. "Tonight, Ben." There was a long moment, and then Ben nodded and walked to the stable, his sons following.

With the torches in the lead, all nine men rode to the cabin. Hattie heard them pounding down on her and realized she was too late. She would never reach the cabin in time. She hid in the ditch as the men rode by her, and then she cut off the road, across a field.

The group halted at the edge of the cabin clearing

and dismounted. The Gault brothers carried the torches.

Welles turned to Eli Gault. "Cover the rear of the cabin." Ben took the torch and Gault ducked into the woods.

The sheriff and Gault cocked their rifles and the men spread out, advancing on the cabin. When they reached the middle of the yard, they suddenly jumped back in surprise as Jonathan stepped out of the cabin and, closing the door behind him, walked into the torchlight.

"Evenin', sheriff. Evenin', Mr. Geyser," Jonathan said casually.

"There's talk you hidin' runaway slaves, Jonathan." The sheriff licked his rotten teeth.

"Runaway slaves?" Jonathan grinned. "No, sir. Not me."

Preacher Welles looked at Jerome Gault. "Search the cabin."

Jonathan backed up to the cabin door. "I live here legal, sheriff! I pay rent! Ask Mr. Geyser. You can't come bustin' in to a man's house! It's agin the law!"

Jerome spoke in a quiet, lethal voice. "Not for slaves, it ain't."

"I'm a free man, an' I got the paper to prove it. I . . ." Eli Gault had come quietly up behind Jonathan on his blind side and smashed the butt of his rifle against the black man's head. The big man went down. Eli Gaunt, who was about a foot shorter than Jonathan, stood over him and kicked him viciously in the side. Then both Gault brothers walked into the cabin.

John ran to Jonathan and knelt at his side, lifting his head, looking for a sign of life. With a groan, the black man rolled over. John whispered in his ear, "Tell me quick—you're not hidin' anyone, are you?" Jonathan stared helplessly up at his friend.

The Gault brothers pushed two runaways, skinny and spent, out the cabin door. The slaves, a man and a woman, held each other in fear. "Like we said! They here!" Eli Gault took out his manacles and chained the two slaves together. Preacher Welles took the torch from Eli. "You've got your prisoners. Wait for us at the horses. The rest of this is a local matter."

The Gaults shrugged and led the slaves off. The barrel-chested Eli put his arm around the woman slave as they moved away, yelling back at Welles: "You shoulda been there, Preacher. I ain't had so much fun since my sow got out. Yes, sir, chasin' these niggers through the swamps all night, we had quite a time. Why, we was pitching around like a blind dog in a meathouse. Yes, sir!" The Gault brothers laughed out loud as they disappeared into the shadows.

Preacher Welles dragged Jonathan to his feet and the sheriff handcuffed his hands behind him. Welles looked him in the eye. "Free man, are you! Those two niggers are going to live. Because they're slaves like our Lord intended them to be. And slaves are worth something. But you, free man, you're not worth spit in the wind!" He turned to the sheriff. "String him up!"

John moved instantly. One step and he had Welles's rifle. He leveled it at the Preacher and the sheriff. Ben stepped forward. John held his hand out in warning at his father. "They got no right to hang him, Pa! He's free, and he's got his rights!"

"Looks like you done raised a nigger lover, Ben," the sheriff said.

Ben came closer to John. "Put down that gun, John."

"Not while they're fixing to hang him, I won't."

Mark lunged at John from the side, and the rifle fired, missing Ben's head by only inches. Mark smashed John in the face and he crumpled. Ben was furious. He plunged into the cabin and grabbed the kerosene lamp, hurling it at the crude kitchen table. It exploded into flame.

"I had to stop you, John," Mark said as he tried to help John up. John was dizzy and off balance, but he swung at Mark as he stumbled to his feet. Mark knocked him down again. "Get ahold of yerself, John! I don't wanta hurt you! But we have to live here." John swung wildly again, missing completely as Mark stepped away. John fell to his knees.

Out of the darkness Hattie ran to help him. As she got him to his feet, they heard Jonathan cry out in rage and terror. John lurched around the corner of the cabin, grabbing the wall for support. The whole yard was lit up by the burning building. In the hideous blinding light they could see Jonathan's body hung from a tree, slowly turning. Hattie screamed and fell to her knees. John stood, his face contorted in horror, the tears streaming down his face. He tried to cry out, but he couldn't make a sound.

John was tying his bedroll behind his saddle when his father and two brothers came into the stable. He was drained of anger now, drained of everything. He felt hollow.

Ben spoke first. "We come to ask you not to go."

"We know you liked Jonathan," Mark said gently. "And maybe he got more than was comin' to him. But he done wrong, helping the runaways."

John strapped on his saddlebags. He hadn't looked at

them. Ben went on. "Anyways, it's no time for you to go up North. There's gonna be a fight—you know that as well as I. It's time to choose up sides, and you belong here."

John turned to face them, with a cold, steady look. "I don't belong here." He pointed at Matt's tunic. "And I'll never wear that uniform."

Matt finally spoke. He was always the big brother to John, the one John looked up to the most. "John, all our lives we've lived under the same roof. We ate at the same table. So many nights we couldn't sleep because our backs ached from the work. This is our land. Virginia is our home. These people are our neighbors. You can't turn your back on them."

When John spoke his voice was icy. "They murdered Jonathan last night on 'our land.' You did nothing to stop it—none of you did." John scooped up a handful of dirt and held it out. "Our land. What's wrong with this land that we reap such a bitter crop?" He held the dirt up in his clenched fist, in front of their faces. "Don't ask me to fight for this . . . this dust! It's not sacred soil. Not to me. Not anymore."

He tossed the dirt onto Matt's tunic. Turning his back on them, he climbed on his horse and rode away.

CHAPTER FIVE

Gettysburg—February 1861

In his stuffy room above the newspaper office John lay sprawled on the bed, asleep, snoring fitfully. It was past noon. He had fallen asleep while looking at *Harper's Weekly,* and it covered his face. His clothes were tangled around him. His shirt had white sweat stains under the armpits, and his pants were grimy and wrinkled from being slept in.

The room was littered with books, old newspapers, empty whiskey bottles, and half-empty plates of food, dried out and moldy. It had been months since that day he left his family in Virginia. Now he was finding out what it meant to have no family, no home.

Someone knocked on the door, once, twice, before he woke up. It hurt to keep his eyes open. He had a headache, and he felt slightly nauseated. "Who is it?" he asked, his voice weak.

"It's me, Mary."

John rolled to his feet, suddenly wide awake. No one

had been up to his room—not since he had gotten back. He had wanted to be alone, and they had stayed away. He straightened his clothes as best he could, thought hurriedly of trying to neaten the room, but instead poured himself a shot of whiskey and quickly threw it back. "Come in."

He got up as Mary entered. He was embarrassed to have her there. "Sorry about the mess. I wasn't expecting anyone."

"I wanted to find out how you were. No one around here seems to know." She looked around the room. There was all the answer she needed.

John shrugged. "I'm okay. How are you, Mary? Have you heard from Jonas?" He attempted a smile.

Her face darkened, and she shook her head. "Have *you* heard from him?" she asked hopefully. John shook his head.

Mary frowned and began to wander around the room. "Why don't you come to the house anymore, if only for a decent meal? You can't live on biscuits and cheese forever."

"I've been doing a lot of reading."

"You've been brooding, John. Ever since you broke with your family. You've gotta put that behind you. Make yourself a life *here*. You have a second family, if you'd just give us a chance."

John sat on the bed. "I don't fit in here, no more'n I did back home." He poured himself another whiskey and swallowed it. When he spoke, it was as much to himself as to Mary. "Pa was right. A war's coming, and it's a time to choose up sides."

"But you *made* your choice already," Mary said as she sat down by him.

John shook his head. "I chose not to fight for the

South. But I won't fight for the North either. How could I carry a rifle against my own people?"

"Then don't enlist, for anyone."

"I'd be the only man my age left in Gettysburg. Walkin' around in civilian clothes with a Virginia accent. They'd get out the tar and feathers." He put the glass on the table. "No, I figure I got to go. I just don't know where. I ain't *got* no place. No home. Soon I won't even have a country."

"Tomorrow we'll get out the buckboard and go for a long drive in the country." She got up to leave.

"No, Mary, I . . ."

She turned at the door, her face glowing with a wicked smile. "Well, you do as you please, but we're all going for a ride tomorrow. Mr. Lincoln's train is on its way to Washington, and it's supposed to stop near here tomorrow. Pa thought you might want to go along and draw the whole thing, but I'll tell him . . ."

"What!" John jumped to his feet. "When do we leave!"

The train station in the little town of Leaman Place was a half day's buggy ride from Gettysburg. By the time the Hale family and John got there, hundreds of people had gathered to get a glimpse of the new President. There were gigs and buckboards, saddled horses, and barebacked mules, all milling around on both sides of the tracks. They had come from miles away— farmers and businessmen, clerks and soldiers, miners and bankers, politicians, servants, and, of course, the press. They all waited for Mr. Lincoln with a strange silence. The train station had been hastily festooned with flags and bunting. For most of the people gathered there, this would count as one of the biggest moments of their lives. For as long as they lived they would tell the story of actually seeing President Lincoln.

They heard the train whistle in the distance. John hopped off the buggy and maneuvered for a spot in front, where the train would stop. Jacob and his family stayed in the buggy, which was high and well situated. The crowd began to cheer as the train pulled in. An officer was standing on the rear platform of the last car, and even before the train stopped he stepped aside and Mr. Lincoln came out. The President was bearded, which surprised everyone, because during his campaign the pictures they had seen showed him clean shaven. He wore a stovepipe hat and he had a black shawl on his shoulders.

The country had never known a President like Mr. Lincoln. He was from the plains, the first Westerner to be President. He was rough-hewn in manner, yet eloquent. He stood before them, gaunt, craggy faced, but obviously in a jovial mood.

"Ladies and gentlemen of Leaman Place, I want to express my pleasure at being here, and thank you for the friendly greeting. I appear, not to make a speech. I have not time to make them at length, and not strength to make them on every occasion—and, worse than all, I have none to make." There was a polite laughter from the crowd.

"Furthermore, it is well known that the more a man speaks, the less he is understood." This time there were a few guffaws and a few amens. John quickly began to draw.

"I come before you, then, merely to see and be seen. And, as regards to the ladies, I have the best of the bargain." The crowd laughed.

"But, as to the gentlemen, I cannot say as much."
This time the ladies laughed loudest.

"Let's have a look at Mrs. Lincoln!" a man yelled
out.

"Right! We want Mrs. Lincoln!" another called.

"We want Mrs. Lincoln!" was the chant.

Lincoln gave in good-naturedly. He turned to the
railroad car door behind him and suddenly Jonas appeared. A word and a gesture from Lincoln and he disappeared. The Hale family had seen him and were astonished. Mary leapt from the buggy, calling out,
"Jonas!" John, bent over his drawing, had not seen
him.

Jonas reappeared and ushered Mrs. Lincoln to the
President's side. Then he was gone again. Mary struggled to work her way through the crowd but found it
impossible.

Mrs. Lincoln wore a bonnet and carried a bouquet of
flowers. She stood side by side with her husband, facing
the crowd, waving in response to the cheers and applause. He was six-foot-four, thin as a rail, and wore a
stovepipe hat a foot high. She was five-foot-two, and
stocky. The contrast was pronounced. Lincoln raised
his hand for silence.

"Ladies and gentlemen, since you seemed determined to meet Mrs. Lincoln, I concluded I had better
give you . . . the long and the short of it." The crowd
burst into laughter.

While they were waving farewell to the crowd, Lincoln noticed John in front of him, drawing madly without even looking up. As he reentered his railroad car,
he turned to the officer and gave an instruction, nodding toward John.

Mr. Lincoln's railroad car was divided into several sections. The first was a receiving parlor, used for the press and local politicians. The next was his private office, where he met with his closest friends and allies. The innermost area was a place of retreat and privacy, reserved for Lincoln and his wife, whom he affectionately called "Mother." Mrs. Lincoln spent most of her time here with her entourage. Jonas met John in the parlor as he was brought in by the officer.

"Howdy, John," Jonas said. He had to grin at the stunned look on John's face.

"You're full of surprises," John said as he shook his hand warmly.

Jonas took John into Mr. Lincoln's private office and introduced him. Lincoln motioned to a chair. "Sit down, young man. Jonas warned me of your formidable skills with a pen. When I saw you outside, it was my assumption that you were sketching Mrs. Lincoln and myself." John nodded, nervous in his presence. "As it happens, Mrs. Lincoln and I have never been photographed together, nor sketched together, as far as I know. I'd be most interested to see your drawing."

"Oh . . . yes. Of course." John opened his sketchbook and took out the drawing. He was concerned about how Lincoln would react. In the sketch a grinning Lincoln loomed over his wife, who was glancing shyly up at him. John had captioned it, "I give you the long and the short of it." He handed it to the President.

For a very long moment Lincoln said nothing. John glanced at Jonas for a sign of hope. Slowly Lincoln began to chuckle. And then he laughed out loud. John breathed a sigh of relief. "It might not be prudent to show it to Mrs. Lincoln, but it tickles me."

John made a bold request. "Sir, could I make another sketch? More of a portrait? Something we could show Mrs. Lincoln?"

Lincoln smiled. John had phrased it just right, and Lincoln liked his audacity. "The conductor tells me we will be leaving in five minutes. Can you do a five-minute portrait?"

John whipped out his pencil and worked quickly, while Lincoln tried to remain reasonably still. After a moment of silence, Lincoln spoke. "That accent of yours—you're not originally from Gettysburg."

"No, sir. I'm from Virginia. My family has a farm near Charlottesville."

"And what is the sentiment in your county as to secession or no?"

"On our farm . . . well, I have three brothers who can't wait to fight for the Confederacy."

"And you?" Lincoln was studying him.

"I'll not fight for the South."

"Nor, I dare say, for the North."

John glanced up quickly. Lincoln was a good judge of men. "You're right, sir. I'm caught betwixt and between. I want to *do* something but I don't know what."

"Should it come to war, were I you, I should look to my talent for the solution." John stopped working and listened to Lincoln. "Your talent suggests the role of correspondence, artist correspondent. You would be where history is made, yet not required to carry a rifle. And your work would be a great contribution. Through it the people back home would come to know the real face of war."

Lincoln leaned forward and took John's sketchbook. He examined the portrait and then nodded. "You'll do well. You *see* more than most men."

* * *

After Mary finally worked her way through the crowd, she walked down the platform peering in train windows, trying to find Jonas. She spotted him as he came out of Lincoln's car with John, and again she called out his name. He saw her, but as she started toward him, the train lurched and began to move. Mary started to run. Jonas moved to the bottom step of the car. Mary, running along the platform, came abreast of him. For a moment, the train and Mary were moving at the same speed.

"Mary . . ."

Between breaths, Mary asked him. "Why . . . haven't you . . . written?"

"Mary. I'm sorry. I'll explain everything when I see you."

"When will . . . that be?"

"Soon!" The train had pulled ahead and Mary was unable to keep up. Jonas leaned recklessly over the platform. "Soon, Mary. I promise . . . !" The train pulled out of sight.

Torn between frustration and anger and her need for Jonas, she stood on the platform in a crowd of people and cried.

CHAPTER SIX

Charleston, South Carolina—April 12, 1861

"You are the chosen ones! The sword of God has been given you, the people of Charleston! From out there in that harbor the invading hordes will come to rape and plunder, sent by the Lincoln devil! I tell you that God in heaven is angry! He *will not* allow this to happen! He has spoken unto me . . ."

Preacher Welles stood in front of the crowd inside the revival tent and preached to them of hellfire and damnation—and of the way to salvation for the South. He was an imposing, almost terrifying figure. Dressed completely in black, with cold steel-gray eyes, he held the people in awe and made them tremble. With one hand he pointed a finger directly at the crowd, while the other held his Bible high above his head.

It was just past midnight and the tent was lit by lantern. It had been a long night of exhortation and frenzy. Welles had come to Charleston because in that city's harbor was a federal fort that had refused to surrender the Stars and Stripes to the new nation that claimed the land on which the fort was built, the Confederate States of America. Fort Sumter had become the eye of the developing storm. It was a tinderbox, and Preacher Welles, a man on fire, had come to spread the flame.

There was a commotion in the streets outside the tent, and the sound of a gathering crowd. A man ran into the tent. He took off his hat when the congregation turned toward him, but was afraid to speak until Welles motioned to him. "Preacher . . . the fort's been ordered to surrender."

Preacher Welles cried out, "Jehovah, you have heard my voice!" And then to the crowd, "The holy war has come!" He stalked out of the tent, calling out for his people to follow him, and they streamed out into the street.

Welles stood by the main gun battery as the rowboat came out of the darkness. It was four in the morning; dawn had begun to glow in the sky. The negotations inside Fort Sumter had been carried out in a very gentlemanly manner. The negotiators brought cigars and fine wine to the men in the fort, but in the end the demand for surrender had been refused. The negotiators, wearing red sashes and silver swords, returned to shore.

All the politics and posturing were reduced to a single fact: Americans were going to fire on other Americans. In crisp military style a mortar gun was fired as a signal. Arching high in the night sky, the red streak came down like a falling star and exploded directly on top of Fort Sumter. And then the cannons began. Preacher Welles and his frightened son Homer manned one of the mortars; they were the first to fire. The preacher's face was a mask of frenzy and hatred.

"Go on, boy," he shouted above the roar of cannon.
"Fire the gun, let the Lord hear us!"

It had begun.

April 15, 1861

In Gettysburg war fever was high. The whole town
was on holiday. The stores were closed, but not the
bars, which were filled. Main Street had been barri-
caded to traffic, turning the town square into a huge
carnival. On a raised platform in the middle of the
street a uniformed brass band blared out martial music.
The street was filled with people, celebrating and waving little flags. A few veterans of the Mexican War
stood around in their old uniforms; town dignitaries sat
on chairs mounted on the platform, hoping a little of
the glory might rub off on them; children and dogs ran
around in circles. The young men of the town stood in
clusters, kidding and taunting each other nervously.

A very old man, wearing a military blouse with medals from the War of 1812, stood at attention the entire
time the music played. There were tears in his eyes as
he remembered the day he had enlisted, nearly fifty
years ago. In his mind he was the same brave young
man, and today he was ready to reenlist.

There was a huge brewery truck next to the band-
stand. The side stakes had been left on and they held
large canvas signs that said ENLIST NOW! and SAVE THE
UNION! Three pretty girls stood on the wagon bed,
wearing their nicest white party dresses and colored rib-
bons in their hair. An elaborate barbecue was laid out
in the town square, where the womenfolk served roast
pork, corn bread, and lots of foamy beer. The buggies,

carriages, and buckboards were parked in a row around the barricades. The Hale buggy arrived at the edge of the square. Mary held the reins and Evelyn sat next to her, anxiously looking around. Anna and James were in the back seat.

Evelyn turned to her young son James. "Do you see Jake anywhere?"

James was staring at the veterans in their uniforms. "Nope," he replied absently.

Evelyn turned to Mary. "Help me find Jake and Malachy!"

Mary put her arm around her mother's shoulders. "Stop fretting, Mama. They're old enough. You couldn't stop 'em anyway."

Suddenly the band stopped playing and everyone turned toward the speakers' stand. Phineas Wade, a paunchy, middle-aged, small-town politician, mounted the rickety steps to the platform. It had been hurriedly constructed from raw lumber and was covered by a large draped flag and bunting. Wade wore the nondescript uniform of the state militia with a long sword that clanged on the steps as he climbed. He was greeted by applause.

"Friends, you've all known me as State Senator Phineas Wade. Now you see me in the role of warrior, sworn to destroy with naked sword . . ." He managed to draw his sword on the second try and he brandished it aloft.

"Sworn to destroy with naked sword the contemptible Southern traitors, the cowardly secessionists, who are out to bust up the noblest form of government on earth!" The crowd clapped enthusiastically. Several of the young men, including Jake and Malachy, moved closer to the platform.

"President Lincoln has just sounded the clarion call for volunteers! I need hot-blooded young men! I ask you to sign up for three months—ninety days of adventure and educational travel during which you will be paid the generous sum of eleven dollars a month!" The young men nodded approval of the generous pay.

"Enlist now to drive the Secesh back to their alligator swamps and then return to our beloved Gettysburg wearing the medals that will mark you as heroes!" Once again he brandished the sword. "Furthermore, I will lead you!" While the crowd cheered and applauded wildly, Wade struggled to return the sword to its scabbard.

"Please observe that wagon, the one with the pretty girls!" The girls waved as the crowd turned toward them. "Those of you who want to be soldiers and heroes, just hop aboard! And if the beautiful young ladies insist on kissing you, well, that's only natural, 'cause everybody loves a soldier! Young men, the rest is up to you!"

As the brass band started to play, Malachy moved toward the wagon like an iron filing to a magnet. When the first pretty girl said "Come on up, soldier!" he leaped aboard. All three girls kissed him at once as the crowd cheered the first volunteer. Jake took off after Malachy and jumped aboard the wagon, getting a kiss as he came up.

Evelyn watched from the buckboard, her hand held over her mouth. She wanted to cry out to them, but knew that it would be no use. It was done.

Mary tried to comfort her. "Be proud, Mama. Your sons were the very first."

"Yes. Well . . . of course I'm proud! We're all

proud!" She turned to Mary with tears in her eyes. "Aren't we?"

Young James also looked on with tears, but his came from frustration. He was crushed that he could not join up; he was only sixteen.

John Geyser had been busy all morning in the newspaper office, trying to keep up with the incoming telegrams, getting the updated news to the people, and helping Jacob and the old man to set the type for a special edition. But when the speeches started, he and Jacob stopped work and went outside to listen.

John stood apart, leaning against the building, hoping not to be noticed. He watched Malachy and Jake enlist; he saw Jacob beaming with pride. He saw Evelyn sitting stiff as a statue, her hands clenched in her lap. And when he heard them talk about being gone ninety days and whipping the cowardly rebels before fall, he had to smile. He thought of his brothers saying the same thing, but about these people, gathered in this square. With a shudder he thought of the terrible things the innocent will do.

He watched as other young men leaped to the wagon. He felt that he knew them, knew what they dreamed of. He had once been just like them. All he had known of America was Christopher Columbus and Valley Forge, the stuff that came from storybook histories. For most of John's life his world had always been what he could see from his attic window. In a way, John thought, this war fit in nicely with the storybook: brass bands, cheering crowds, pretty girls waving, boys' faces filled with innocent pride.

But that had all changed now, because *he* had changed, and he knew that he could never go back. The three pretty girls began to sing "I Am Bound to Be a

Soldier's Wife or Die an Old Maid." He watched as the brewery wagon, filled to overflowing with brash young men, started down Main Street amid the cheering crowd. And then he realized something else: how much he wished he were one of them.

Young James Hale stood in a long line at an enlistment center outside Washington, D.C. It was an old state armory near the training camp, but to him it seemed like a madhouse. White, black, brown, yellow, and red—the whole room was jammed with boys and men of every age and color speaking a babble of different languages, few of which James had ever heard about. Like all of the boys around him, James had never really been away from home, and he felt more than a little lost.

He had run away from home a week ago, the night after his brothers had enlisted and left for camp. He had heard what company they were in and he planned to join them. In fact, he was determined. It had been easy so far, he thought. In the middle of the night he had thrown his bag out the window of his room and climbed down the tree, being careful all the time not to wake anyone. He had gotten rides most of the way in buckboards and with traveling peddlers. He had already seen more different things in one week than he ever had in his whole life in Gettysburg, and he wasn't even a soldier yet. This must be the adventure they had all been talking about.

Some of the boys around him were carrying old rusty blunderbusses and some had huge bowie knives strapped to their belts. What they shared in common was that they were all trying to look as mean and tough as a soldier should. James finally got close to the front and he was able to see how it worked: the captain asked the man if he was eighteen or more and, if he was, he waved him through to the enlistment clerk. The man in front of him got his turn.

"You over eighteen?" the captain asked.

"Yes, sir!" he replied, and the captain waved him through.

"You over eighteen?" the captain asked James.

"Darn near. I'm sixteen, going on . . ."

"Sorry, lad," the captain told James, and pushed him aside. Feeling crushed and miserable, James turned and walked out the door.

He stood outside the armory, watching while other boys became soldiers. He knew he could be just as good a soldier as any of them. It never would have occurred to him to lie about his age to an officer; he just wasn't reared that way. But he had been taught to be inventive. In front of him he saw a hand-painted poster tacked to the window; it read OVER 18? SIGN UP HERE! Immediately he knew what to do. He fumbled in his pockets and came up with a stubby pencil. Glancing around to see if anyone was watching, he tore a corner off the poster. Licking the pencil, he wrote very carefully the number "18." Slipping off one shoe, he put the little piece of paper inside and put the shoe back on. Thus prepared, he squared his shoulders and marched back into the enlistment center.

He made sure to get into a different line this time, and after another long wait he reached the front. Just as he stepped forward to be questioned, the officer facing him was replaced by the captain he had already seen. Overcoming an initial instinct to run, he instead announced with a strong voice, "I'm your man!"

"Are you over eighteen?" the captain said.

"I sure am!" James said with the greatest of confidence.

The captain looked him over carefully. His brow knitted and his eyes narrowed. After a long pause he warned, "It's against the law to make a false statement."

James only smiled. "I stand on my statement, sir."

"All right." The captain turned to the clerk. "Sign him up."

The clerk took his name and asked him to make his mark. James surprised him by actually being able to write his name. Then he was sent to another table, where he was told to strip to the waist. The old doctor tapped his chest a few times and then counted his eyes.

"Ever have rheumatiz?" the doctor muttered.

"No, sir."

"Conniptions?"

"What's that?"

"It's when you go like this . . ." The doctor began to shake violently.

"I don't think so . . ."

The doctor scrawled his name on James's papers. "Congratulations. You're fit for service."

He was sent to the far corner of the armory where there was a series of long tables, each piled high with all the old used uniforms that the local militia could muster. No two were alike. They varied in design and even color; some were blue, others were gray. They had been roughly sorted: on one table sat a pile of hats, on another there were tunics, another held pants, and one was piled with woolen underwear. The young recruit in front of James, obviously a country boy, picked up a pair of the underwear and turned around, asking, "What the hell is this?"

James looked at him. "It's underwear."

"Well, what do I do with it? When am I supposed to wear it?"

"Wear it under your clothes when it gets cold." James smiled at his own sophistication.

"Well, I'll be danged. This is gonna be somethin'!"

Mary stood at the blackboard with her back to the class, demonstrating the difference between cursive writing and printing.

For more than two seasons she had been the schoolteacher in Gettysburg. The school, on a hill at the edge of town, was a solid-looking brick building, with one large classroom for kids of all ages. Mary was so absorbed in what she was teaching that she didn't hear Jonas enter the room. He stood quietly in the back, watching her. He knew he probably shouldn't be there, but he had wanted to see what she did every day. He wanted to know everything about her—and he didn't have much time. He wore his usual high boots and broad-brimmed hat, but in addition he had on something new: the tunic and striped pants of an army captain.

Mary turned around and gasped when she saw Jonas; the chalk dropped to the floor. The children also turned, following Mary's gaze. There was a long moment of silence. He realized this was a mistake. "I'm sorry for the intrusion," he said, and turned to go.

"Wait!" Mary said urgently—too urgently, she realized. "Mr. Steele, would you come up to the front of the room, please. Class, today Mr. Jonas Steele is our guest. He works for President Lincoln." There was a murmur of excitement among the children. Mary continued, looking directly at Jonas. "We are all very lucky, because Mr. Steele doesn't come to Gettysburg very often. In fact, almost never." Jonas understood what she meant. She was still angry.

He stood by the wall with his hat in his hand while she finished the lesson. She was a good teacher, allowing the students to discover things on their own. They were curious, bright children, mostly rough farm kids, but she was able to handle them. She called to the blackboard a child who was having a particularly hard time understanding the lesson. The boy could print but could not write. Mary turned to Jonas. "Mr. Steele, would you show Billy how we 'write' words."

Jonas felt ill at ease. He hadn't spent much time in a classroom where he grew up. "I'm not too good at schoolwork," he mumbled.

Mary was enjoying having the upper hand with him; she knew that didn't happen very often. "Why, Mr. Steele, you're just being modest." She handed him the chalk.

Jonas stood awkwardly in front of the class, holding the chalk. After a long, uncomfortable silence, he put the chalk back in its tray. "I can't write," he said softly.

As the realization dawned on Mary why Jonas had never returned her letters, her eyes pleaded forgiveness. "Class dismissed for the day," she said, without taking her eyes away from his. When the last child had left the room, she whispered, "I'm sorry, Jonas."

"I shouldn't have come," he said, turning toward the door.

She touched his arm. "Would you take me for a ride? There is a place I like to go."

He took her hand. "I'd like that."

They drove into the country in her buggy down a tree-lined road, his horse, tied behind them, following at a trot. It was late in April, and while the sun was warm, the air had a slight chill. The light green shoots were just starting to show in the fields, and the new bright leaves were startling against the stark black branches. There had been a calm silence between them the whole way. They knew how they *felt* about each other, yet they did not really know each other very well. Jonas had no idea when he came back to Gettysburg what he was going to tell Mary. He had never told anyone anything about himself. But as they rode along in silence, he decided. He would do something he had never done; he was going to trust someone. In his line of work, trust was the rarest commodity.

They were near the place Mary wanted to take him. She pointed off into a meadow sprinkled with wild flowers. Beside the meadow was a spring that ran out of the hills and formed a brook. Jonas stopped the buggy and they sat quietly, each at ease admiring the beauty, the peacefulness. He realized that this was one of the things that Mary gave him: when they were together, he was at peace with himself. The violence that lurked inside him was stilled.

He began to speak, slowly, softly. "I travel with Mr. Lincoln. I guess you could say I have been his bodyguard. That's why I was on the train that day. I've known Lincoln a long time, since I was a Pinkerton agent in Chicago. The Pinkerton Agency handled the security for the Illinois Central Railroad, and Lincoln was the railroad's lawyer. When Lincoln was nominated, I took care of security for him at the Chicago convention. And when he was elected, he asked me to come East with him." Jonas didn't mention that the night before they had left to go to Washington Lincoln's friends had taken him aside and told him that if anything should ever happen to Lincoln they would kill him. That was how strongly they all felt about Abe Lincoln. Friendship aside, they knew what he meant to the fate of the country.

"How does a simple country feller from Kansas get to be a detective in Chicago?"

Jonas knew that this was going to be the hard part. "When Pinkerton came to Kansas for the railroad, I was recommended to him by John Brown. And Pinkerton offered me the job."

"*The* John Brown?" Mary was stunned.

"I rode with John Brown." He fell silent for a long moment. He didn't know how to explain what John Brown had meant to him, what an influence the fiery man had had on his life. "Sitting here now, it seems like a hundred years ago. I once went with Brown to the top of a mountain. We found the bones of a large bird on the rocks, perfectly laid out. He took a bone from the wing and carved it while we talked. I told him about a dream I'd had in which I was landing a boat alone on a strange shore, carrying a man in black. I remember it had disturbed me. He told me not to be afraid of dreams and visions, but to believe in them. He had made a kind of whistle from the bone, and he played it. To me it sounded like the wind whistling across the open prairie at night. I think that's probably how he felt then, getting near the end—kind of empty. He and I both knew he had to die." Jonas was silent for a while. "Before I rode with John Brown, I had never fought. I found I had a taste for it. I . . ." He searched for the right words.

"You liked it," Mary said. Jonas nodded. "What he did was wrong, Jonas."

"The only thing he did wrong was to be the first to kill."

Mary thought of asking him about the raid on Harpers Ferry, if he had been there. But she had heard enough. It didn't matter. She knew that she wanted this man, had known it from the beginning. She wouldn't ask questions; she would just follow her heart. She looked around at the meadow in bloom. "Will it ever be like this again?" She turned to Jonas. "Let's walk awhile."

Jonas got down and reached up for her. She leaned out, and he carried her down to him. They held each other a long time. Finally Mary said, "The first time I took you up to that room, I asked you if you liked bold girls." Jonas nodded.

"You didn't answer," Mary said.

"The bolder the better."

"Good." Mary lifted her mouth to his. Jonas pressed her to him.

CHAPTER SEVEN

Outside Washington, D.C.

The Hale brothers, Jake, Malachy, and James, had been in camp for more than a week before the high command found anyone who knew how to march. Phineas Wade, now Colonel Wade, attempted to drill the men on marching maneuvers, but by the time he found the next set of turns in his instruction book the company usually had marched away. Everyone eventually was issued boots, but they quickly discovered that the War Department had allowed the shoe factory to save time and money by making each boot the same. There was no right or left boot; each boot was supposed to fit either foot. They didn't, of course, and it kept everyone in pain until they managed to get real boots sent to them. Since there weren't enough guns to go around yet, the men had to march around carrying sticks for rifles. The general effect on the Hale brothers was to make them feel more than just a little ridiculous.

One of the men in their company was Alvin Mooney,

also from Gettysburg. At home he had been the village idiot. He looked goofy, as if he had been put together from spare parts: big nose, bushy eyebrows, and a crop of short hair clustered atop his head. Mooney was well liked in Gettysburg—enough so that he was considered a special fixture in town, like the mayor or the post-man. He supported himself by running errands and doing odd jobs such as raking leaves or hauling trash. He was frequently seen around town pulling a little wagon, collecting bottles along the streets. No one really knew how old he was—somewhere between twenty and thirty was the usual guess—but he had the mind of a child. He had been enlisted because no one had the heart to say no. They figured that he would be with other young men from Gettysburg and that they would look out for him. And they were right. No one wanted Alvin Mooney to miss out on any of this adven-ture.

After several days of struggling to learn how to march, it was Mooney who finally fell out and offered a suggestion to Colonel Wade: "Say, Phineas, let's quit this damn foolin'." It was this suggestion that prompted Colonel Wade to make his first wise military decision. He found assistance in the form of a regular army offi-cer, a real soldier, who had been in the army since the Mexican War: Sergeant O'Toole.

O'Toole took command and began to turn raw re-cruits into soldiers. "Hep, two, three, four! Hep, two, three, four." A few of the men were still out of step, especially Mooney. "By the right flank, march!" The company made a ragged response to the command. Mooney turned the wrong way and bumped into every-one. O'Toole looked on in despair. "Halt!"

He gathered them around him in a semicircle. To

each man he passed out a real gun, a Springfield .58 muzzle-loading rifle. "Men, if you never learn nothing else, you're gonna learn how to load a rifle! Now, remove one paper cartridge from your holder." O'Toole took a cartridge from a leather case at his belt, illustrating each step, asking the men to follow suit.

"Observe . . . one round ball ammunition at this end . . . powder in this paper here . . . we bite off the paper twist . . . like so . . . put the cartridge in the barrel . . . tamp it down snug with your ramrod . . . and don't forget to remove the ramrod from the barrel." He looked around to see how everyone was doing. Malachy, Jake, and James followed the instructions easily enough, but Mooney was still examining his paper cartridge, baffled. Jake reached over, bit the cartridge, put it in the barrel of Mooney's rifle, and handed him his ramrod. Now Mooney looked at the ramrod, baffled.

"Take out one firing cap . . . cock the hammer . . . place the cap right here . . . on this nipple . . . the rifle is now ready to fire."

Mooney, trying to catch up, left the ramrod in the barrel as he took out a firing cap. Again Jake had to help. Mooney held the rifle toward him, finger on the trigger, as Jake put the firing cap in place.

"Now we're gonna step over to the range and you'll each get to fire one shot. Be careful. When you move with a loaded rifle, keep it pointed down at the . . ." At that moment a rifle went off with a roar. O'Toole ducked as a ramrod and a minié ball whistled by his ear. Mooney stood looking at his smoking rifle, very impressed with it. O'Toole walked over and stared at him with a look of concentrated loathing.

Colonel Wade was sitting in his tent smoking a cigar

and writing an inspiring letter about the rigors and discipline of army life for editor Jacob Hale to print in the
newspaper. Sergeant O'Toole entered the Colonel's tent
with Mooney in tow and suggested in very strong terms
that Mooney was too stupid to be in the army, and that
he be sent back home. Wade assured him that he would
take appropriate action and commended O'Toole for
bringing it to his attention.

Of course, Colonel Wade had no intention of sending
Alvin Mooney home. Alvin came from a very large
family of Mooneys, and Phineas Wade couldn't risk
losing their votes come next election. So Wade made
the second wise decision of his military career: he made
Mooney the cook.

Malachy, Jake, and James stood in front of their
tent, striking a proud and defiant pose for the photographer who was stooped over focusing the camera, his
head covered by a black cloth. Behind him was his
traveling wagon with a huge canvas sign that read DA-
GUERRIAN ARTIST. Malachy and James were leaning
flamboyantly on their new rifles, trying to look stern,
while Jake stood more easily, with his hand on James's
shoulder.

The photographer instructed them to hold very still,
and they stood in a frozen pose for several seconds.
James's face began to show signs of strain. When they
were told they could relax, James dashed away to the
latrine in back of the tents.

"What's wrong with him?" the startled photographer
asked. Malachy smiled and told him it was the "Tennessee Quick Step." The photographer didn't understand.

"The screamers," Jake offered. The photographer
hurried over to his wagon to develop the picture.

James came back looking a little pale and wobbly. Jake asked him what medicine he had been given by the regimental doctor. James shrugged. "Ever' time I go to see old sawbones, he gives me somethin' else to swallow."

"Well, what did he give you?"

"First, he gave me opium and turpentine. Then yesterday he gave me strychnine and chalk. Nothin' seems to help—it just gets worse."

To cheer himself up, James went for a stroll down the long line of tents that ran through the middle of the camp. It was a leisure period and the men were enjoying the long hot summer evening. In front of one tent five soldiers played poker on the head of a half barrel. Their uniforms were hanging on the branches around them, and two of them were stripped to their waists. Nearby, a group of men sat listening to a banjo player strumming, and they passed a whiskey bottle around openly. Discipline was lax in Colonel Wade's camp. Listening to the banjo, James didn't see the gang of soldiers, with Malachy at the head, chasing a rabbit. They almost knocked James down as they ran by, laughing and yelling. They continued on, running through tents, rousing soldiers who were quietly reading or writing letters. The rabbit scampered around, running in circles, eventually leading his pursuers through the infield of a baseball game, the ballplayers joining in the chase.

By the time James wandered back to his tent, it was surrounded by cheering soldiers crowded around a piece of canvas spread on the ground in the middle of the tent. Little piles of money were scattered around the edge of the canvas.

Malachy sat on his haunches next to the canvas, talking enthusiastically to a louse in a mason jar, exhorting it to take heart, have courage, and run like the wind. Crouched next to him was a bearded soldier named Sykes, who was holding his louse in his fist next to his ear, pretending to listen to it. In front of each man was a tin plate. James had walked in just as a louse race was about to start.

Sykes claimed to have the fastest race louse in camp, although since every man in camp was infested with lice his claim was frequently challenged. Nevertheless, he had not lost a race with Jeff Davis. Sykes came from West Virginia, a part of Virginia that was strongly pro-Union, and most men from there had enlisted to fight for the North. But he had a Southern accent, which made him few friends. In defiance he had named his champion louse after the man declared president of the Confederate States, Jefferson Davis. Malachy Hale had openly challenged Sykes to a louse race, and by the time Sykes called for quiet, over one hundred dollars had been laid down.

"Okay, gentlemen, you know the rules. The first grayback off the plate wins it all."

Malachy taunted him. "Sykes, you sad cracker, you are looking at the next race louse champion in this regiment. This here is Abe Lincoln, and he's a perfect curiosity."

Sykes laughed. "He ain't worth a pinch of sand, kid. You ready?"

"Let her rip!" Malachy said, opening the jar.

As soon as the two lice were dropped down into their respective plates, Jeff Davis raced for the edge. He was highly trained, and it showed. Malachy had found his louse only that morning, but it had shown real potential when Malachy had chased it for five minutes across his scalp, through the swamp of his armpit, across the plains of his chest, into the jungle of his pubic hair, finally cornering him in the sinkhole of his belly button. But in this race, at least, Abe Lincoln was no match for Jeff Davis, who quickly got to the edge of his plate first and toppled over into Sykes's hand.

Sykes, holding Jeff in one fist and hauling in the cash with the other hand, exclaimed, "Who else wants to challenge the champ!"

Too many men had lost money to Sykes, so there were no takers.

Suddenly James spoke up, "Three dollars says my louse is faster'n even Jeff Davis!"

"Whoa. Another Hale wants to give his money away. That's a bet, sonny. Where's the challenger?"

"Next door in Mooney's tent . . . trainin'." James got up. "Back in a coupla minutes." He sauntered out and then ran into Mooney's tent. Malachy and Jake just looked at each other and shrugged.

James put Mooney's tin plate on the cook stove, still hot from the last meal. He knew Mooney was out of the way washing pots. He searched frantically for a louse, finding one in the seam of his underwear. Emptying a matchbox, he put the louse inside. Suddenly a flash of pain tore through his guts. It was getting worse all the time. James forced himself to put it out of his mind; there was the Hale family honor to be reclaimed. He carefully picked up the hot plate, holding it by the edge, and strolled confidently back to his tent. The betting was heavy against him.

At the "go" signal, they both dropped their racers into the separate plates. Jeff Davis, like the thoroughbred he was, made for the edge. But the instant James's louse hit that hot plate, its tiny feet made a sizzling noise and it nearly leapt out of the plate, sprinting with astonishing speed off the plate and across the floor, never to be seen again. While the spectators yelled and stomped, James calmly gathered up the money he had won—more than enough to repay his brother's loss. Sykes knew he had been conned, but he didn't know how. He sat for a moment, bug-eyed, and then he leapt across the floor and began searching frantically for James's lost louse, under the tent and out into the camp.

As the tent cleared, Malachy and Jake slapped James on the back in pride. "How the hell did you do that?" Malachy asked him, but James only smiled.

The grin faded from his face as James sank to his knees still grasping his money. His guts felt like they were on fire. He clutched his belly, his face a mask of agony, and looked up at his brothers. "It's bad . . . real bad."

The hospital was a large walled tent. Inside, two rows of posts supported the roof and formed an aisle down the center. Kerosene lamps hung on every other post. It was the middle of the night and the light was low. On both sides of the tent there was a long row of cots, all filled with sick men, many of them soon to die. In addition to dysentery and other common camp diseases, many of the men were dying from children's illnesses, such as measles and the pox. Occasionally a man would scream out in agony, for water or simply for comfort. They filled the night air with their crying. A doctor moved here and there among them.

James was lying on a cot near the entrance. On a crate near his head was a candle. His face was thin and as white as alabaster; his eyes were closed and his breathing irregular. Jake and Malachy were sitting on one side of the bed. Jake watched young James, his own face drawn and tired. Malachy sat dozing next to him, unable to stay awake. On the other side of the bed Mooney knelt in prayer, holding his hands like a child would while saying nightly prayers.

The doctor came by making his rounds and Jake got up quietly and went over to him. "Doctor, I think he's dying!" Jake's eyes pleaded with the doctor to do something, anything. He was struggling to keep from breaking down.

The doctor looked at him, somewhat absently but not without compassion. In the two months he had been here he had seen more death than he thought possible, and the fighting hadn't even begun. "It's some kind of galloping dysentery. I've tried tartar emetic and Epson salts. That's all I've got. That's all I can do. I'm sorry. Excuse me."

Jake walked back to the cot, and as he looked down, James's eyes opened slightly. Jake bent close to him and whispered, "James, it's me . . . Jake."

James eyes moved to Jake's face, trying to focus on him. "Jake?"

"That's right, it's me."

"Tell mother . . . to come up . . ."

Jake's tears fell on his young brother's face. "Sure. Right away." Jake's voice was almost too hoarse to hear.

James looked at him. "Tell her . . . I feel . . . poorly."

Jake continued to look into his brother's eyes for a long moment. And then somewhere inside of them he saw the light go out.

Jake had to look away, because his brother's eyes had suddenly become like glass and he could only see himself reflected in them. He cried out. Malachy woke with a start and stared around him in confusion. Mooney was still on his knees, his hands in the attitude of prayer. He had tears running down his cheeks, but he made no sound at all.

BOOK II

CHAPTER EIGHT

Washington, D.C.—July 15, 1861

"Mr. Geyser, I presume." Mr. Arbuthnot proffered his manicured hand.

John smiled slightly to himself as they shook hands. So this was the ubiquitous Mr. Arbuthnot. John had been instructed by *Harper's* to come here to Willard's Bar to meet him, and while he wasn't sure what he had expected, he knew this wasn't it. He had heard a lot of odd stories about the legendary Arbuthnot from other journalists. Among his daring exploits, he was supposed to have shot and killed three men in separate duels, all over the questionable virtue of a single woman. If not an actual prositute, she was at the very least a lady who spread her charms around in a wide area. And Mr. Arbuthnot, her ardent admirer, was a jealous man, proven lethal in his icy anger. He had covered wars in every corner of the earth, from Europe overland to China, across Africa, over to the jungles of South America, back up the Amazon, and into Mexico. It was said that he had even fought in more than one of those wars, usually for the side with the highest principles and the most hopeless cause. But, according to the legends, even in the most remote places he always had the best wines and liquors, freshly starched shirts, and silk ties—yet he carried only one small battered bag. And here he stood, a small man, slight of build, with delicate features and the manners of a true gentleman. He was dressed in a stylish frock coat with a dashing red scarf.

"Pleased to meet you, Mr. Arbuthnot."

"I'm the correspondent for *Harper's Weekly* now stationed here in Washington. I understand you've joined the fold. Welcome, and may I offer you a drink?"

"Brandy," John said. The bartender nodded and moved away.

Arbuthnot produced a bulging envelope from his coat pocket. "My instructions from New York are to give you this." John took the envelope. "You'll find your credentials, instructions about where and how to send your stuff, and a nice little sheaf of expense money." He finished his drink. "That's about it. Be a good fellow and pick up the tab." He got up and walked away.

"Mr. Arbuthnot!" John called out. Arbuthnot paused. "Who's going to show me the ropes?"

"Not I," Mr. Arbuthnot said simply.

"But I don't know anything about covering a war." John looked at him in confusion.

"No doubt you'll learn." Mr. Arbuthnot gave John a reassuring nod and walked out. This one won't last three months, he thought to himself.

Taking a long pull on his brandy, John turned his attention to the officers that surrounded him at the bar. They were from all over the country and wore wildly different state militia uniforms. Local politicos mostly, like Colonel Wade from Gettysburg, they had raised a group of men from their home state and found themselves officers. The most colorful of them was a Zouave captain from New York. He wore baggy red knickers, a short blue jacket over a big red sash that was wrapped around his waist, and a red fez on his head. The Zouaves were very popular, because it wasn't every day that a country boy got to wear a costume like that. This dashing uniform combined elements of military outfits that had caught the public's fancy: Turkish, French, and even Oriental. The uniform was much less popular, however, after the men had been in a few battles and discovered what colorful targets they made.

One man, a regular army major, stood apart from the rest at the bar, trying to ignore the chatter around him.

"Look at that!" The Zouave captain pointed out the window. "Another regiment arriving. We must have fifty thousand troops in the city!"

"Seventy-five thousand!" a colonel from Pennsylvania joined in. "And all itching to fight!"

The regular army major glanced over at them and shook his head in disgust.

The Zouave captain turned to a captain from Vermont. "Have you been reading the *New York Trib?*"

"*On to Richmond!*" he yelled, repeating the headline.

"Correct," the Zouave said. "The rebel congress meets in Richmond on the twentieth. And we simply must be there to prevent it!" There was a general roar of approval from the other newly commissioned officers.

The regular army major turned to them. "Gentlemen, may I comment?"

"Of course, sir," the Zouave said.

"You're damn fools, the lot of you."

"Really, Major!" The Vermont captain was shocked.

"Boasting about how many troops you have. I'll tell you how many—a handful. The rest are ninety-day enlistees who'll be ready to go home before they learn to fire a rifle. What you have out there, gentlemen, is an army of civilians!"

The Zouave captain came toward him, fists clenched. "That's uncalled for, Major! My men are soldiers, and they're ready!"

The regular army major laughed in his face. "How would you know, pasha? You're a civilian yourself." He threw a coin on the bar and walked out. Jonas, who was coming in the door as the major was going out, stepped aside quickly to let the man through.

John opened his envelope and laid the money on the bar. "Another brandy," he said to the bartender, and then, seeing Jonas walk in, he said, "Make it two."

Jonas pointed at the money. "How long have you been rich?"

"Since I became combat artist for *Harper's*."

Jonas raised his glass to John. "Congratulations."

"What's your assignment?" John asked him.

"Army scout."

"What are you supposed to do?"

"I ride ahead until I locate the rebs, then I ask the rebs what they're up to, and after they tell me, I ride back and tell General McDowell."

John ignored the humor. "Listen, can I ride with you?"

" 'Fraid not. An army scout has to be a loner."

"Jonas, I have to cover the war! At least show me where it *is*!"

Jonas could see that John was serious. He looked around them at the crowded bar and then nodded his head for John to follow him to the back corner of the barroom. They sat down at a table, and Jonas took a map from his pocket. Turning up the wick on the kerosene lamp, he spread the map out. Jonas spoke quietly, and with care.

"The entire army is moving out tomorrow morning, toward Richmond. They are going down this road, called Warrenton Turnpike, through Fairfax Courthouse, Centreville, and on to Manassas. But to get to Manassas they have to cross this little stream—it's called Bull Run. The reb general Beauregard is waiting on the other side with around twenty-five thousand men. There's twelve thousand more rebs under General Johnson in here. Now, see this stone bridge, where the turnpike crosses Bull Run? If I was an artist lookin' for a battle, I'd start lookin' right here." He looked up at John. " 'Cause I believe we're goin' to have ourselves a fine old dustup."

"When will they get there?" John asked.

"Four or five days, I reckon."

John pointed at the stone bridge on the map. "Then that's where I'll be when they get there."

Bull Run—July 21, 1861

On this morning, Abraham Lincoln woke with a start. It was dawn. He sat up in bed and looked around at the dark, still bedroom as if to reassure himself he really was awake. He had once again dreamed his strange dream, the one he'd first had the night before Fort Sumter was bombarded. In the dream he was on a boat, moving rapidly forward on a stormy sea toward a dark and indefinite shore. He tried to see the land ahead, but he could not make it out. This dream aroused in him the deepest fears, because he knew that it meant some great event was about to take place. He dressed quickly, taking care not to waken his wife. He rushed to the telegraph office adjoining the White House to wait for the news he knew would come.

John Geyser also woke suddenly at dawn, to the sound of cannon fire. It had been a warm summer night, and he had fallen asleep waiting for the Union army to pass by. He was in a wooded knoll overlooking the stone bridge that crossed the stream they called Bull Run. He looked out through the leaves with his binoculars and saw them marching down the Turnpike, thousands upon thousands of Yankee soldiers moving ponderously, like an enormous caterpillar, a great swirling, living thing that flowed across the land. At shouted commands they turned off the road and moved along the creek. The cannons and caissons were deployed along the bank for miles, drawn by straining horses. As soon as each was readied, it boomed out as quickly as the expert artillerymen could fire. These men were regular army, and they knew their jobs. John pulled his boots on and, taking out his sketchbook, began to draw the cannon crews in action.

Jake and Malachy and the rest of Company B waded across Bull Run, the water to their knees. The morning was already hot, and the water cooled their feet. Malachy pushed his brother forward, almost at a run. Like most of the boys, Malachy was afraid the battle—and possibly the whole war—would be over before they got into it. He urged everyone on. They could hear the cannons booming in the distance, and they knew that the battle had begun. Malachy called out bravely, "Come on, boys. Let's not be late for the ball." Alvin Mooney ran along with them, grinning like a child, trying to keep up. In the confusion before battle someone had handed him a rifle. He had never been happier. He was a real soldier now, like everyone else.

The main force of the Union army splashed across the creek and spread out all across the field as they advanced up the slope. Rebel artillery began to burst among them, and they heard for the first time that peculiar whine of the minié balls. But the Union army's rapid deployment had been a surprise, and the rebel firing was not yet organized.

Suddenly a shell exploded in front of Malachy, tearing a crater in the earth, instantly killing the soldier just ahead of him. He looked down at the mangled body, torn apart by the force of the explosion. Malachy stopped running and stared about in horror, really focusing for the first time. He felt the urge to vomit, but Jake gave him a shove and he moved on, looking back over his shoulder at the dead man.

They could see now that the reb firing was coming from behind a stone wall. Yelling as loudly as they could for courage, Company B charged the wall. In front of Jake and Malachy more and more men went down, but as the brothers neared the wall, the rebel firing suddenly stopped, and Company B went over the wall. The rebels ran wildly in retreat, with the Yankee soldiers now in halfhearted pursuit. Jake grabbed Malachy's arm and pulled him down against the stone wall.

They were hot and drenched in sweat; the shade of the wall and the cool stones were welcome.

Jake turned to Malachy, panting. "I'm scared. Are you scared?"

"Me? Hell, no, I ain't scared." Malachy was shaking, almost in tears.

"You all right?" Jake asked him.

"Don't tell anyone."

"What?"

"I peed in my pants." Malachy tried to cover himself, but Jake could see his pants were wet.

"Hold still," Jake said as he poured water from his canteen all over Malachy's head and uniform, wetting him from head to foot. "You fell while we were crossing the creek."

Malachy looked at his brother with a sheepish smile. "And I thought I'd make a great soldier."

Jake helped him to his feet. "So far, so good."

Company B moved forward under fire to the foot of a ridge. At the top of the ridge was a plateau and at the edge the rebels knelt down and fired down on them. To the right of Company B, along the plateau, was the Henry farmhouse. From all of the lower-floor windows rebels fired at their flank. In the crossfire the men took cover behind anything they could find; some simply burrowed into the ground, clawing with their hands and feet. Jake and Malachy and a few more of the company huddled behind an overturned caisson and a dead horse. The horse's entrails were spilled over the ground and the stench was terrible in the heat, but no one moved from the hiding place. The exploding shells and the continuous roar of gunfire were so deafening that no one could hear commands anyway, so they stayed where they were.

* * *

A confederate officer on horseback galloped to the top of the ridge from the reb side. He had a long beard and the burning eyes of a man possessed. Preacher Welles, now Major Welles, rode among the rebel infantry, raising his sword so he could be seen above the confusion.

"Virginians!" he shouted, and they gathered around him. Matthew and Mark Geyser moved away from the ridge to his side. "Virginians! I have word from General Jackson! This stretch of ground is the key! The general counts on you to hold your sector! *I* count on you! Remember this is a holy war! Hold this ground and the Lord Jesus Christ stands with you! Run, and you run into the arms of Satan!"

Major Welles rode off across the ridge to the next unit, paying no mind to shells exploding around him. He rode within sight of the Union rifles, firing directly at him, but he rode on without a scratch, as if shielded from any harm. He rode without fear; he knew that God would not allow him to be struck down.

Matt and Mark moved back to their position overlooking the Yankees. As they fired, they heard the whine of an incoming shell and they clung to the dirt as it burst near them. "Much more of this, and it's me for the arms of Satan." Mark grinned as they both rolled on their backs and loaded their rifles, working with a quick, sure hand. They turned back together and continued to fire at their enemy.

Sergeant O'Toole darted behind the caisson and knelt down next to Jake. "You guessed it, boys. We gotta take that hill." They all looked fearfully at the ridge. Malachy was breathing rapidly, fear stamped across his face.

"We go straight up! No pauses! No turning back!" O'Toole looked around to see if the others were ready. "Let's go!" he screamed, and the men rose as one and charged up the ridge.

"Here they come!" Mark called out, and they raised their rifles and fired as rapidly as they could. The Company B flag-bearer went down and another man picked up the flag. And then he too went down. On the Yankees came, firing up at the rebs, stopping only to reload. All around them the air was black and heavy with the acrid smoke of gunpowder. Their faces were streaked with black rivulets of sweat. The carnage was terrible, but Jake and Malachy stumbled on.

On the ridge General Thomas Jackson galloped along the line. He was a cold-eyed, fearless fighter with a full black beard. "Fall back to the fence!" he ordered, and then he barked the order again, bringing discipline to the chaos. All along the line, the rebels dropped back to a split-rail fence and reloaded. Company B, roaring in apparent victory, reached the level ground. They beckoned the men behind them forward, and the entire line poured over the ridge. The rebs behind the fence held their fire, as General Jackson waited for the right moment. Malachy and Jake climbed over the ridge, cheering in triumph.

"Fire!" The rebel line behind the fence cut loose in one terrible volley. The rifles all along the fence exploded, almost as one, bringing the Yankees down like wheat before the scythe. The ridge became a slaughterhouse, the bodies and pieces of bodies, scattered violently around. Half of the Yankees who had made it to the top were cut down. The air was filled with flying bits of lead, like a rainstorm. Men were shouting and screaming, many dying. Company B was shattered. Some of the men in other companies had never even fired a rifle while in camp. Now they tried to remember what they had been told as they knelt to load and fire, fumbling frantically with the powder and the paper cartridges.

Alvin Mooney had managed to load his rifle by himself while they had been pinned down behind the caisson. He appeared amazingly cool under fire, as though his mind was on something else. He seemed to hardly notice the carnage around him. His only concern was to fire his gun. He raised it, pulled the trigger, and immediately began to load again. In the concussion of rifle fire around him, he didn't notice that his own gun had not gone off. He had forgotten only one step in the process—he had forgotten to insert the little firing cap. The second time he loaded, he made the same mistake. The third time he loaded the rifle, he remembered. But by then he had three full loads of powder and lead in his barrel. He raised the rifle, pointed it in the general direction of the rail fence, and pulled the trigger. The exploding gun blew the top half of his skull off, filling the air with a pink mist and pieces of his brain. Malachy, standing behind him, was splashed red with his blood.

The Union line wavered under the deadly fire, and then they broke and ran. Malachy's nerves were shattered. Throwing down his rifle, he turned and ran down the hillside. The further away he got, the faster he ran.

Others around him followed. The Confederates rushed from behind the fence and charged after them yelling a chilling, high-pitched scream, firing down on the retreating Yankees who ran in panic, abandoning their rifles, their packs, and even canteens. Anything that slowed them up they threw aside.

At the Henry farmhouse the battle was taking a different turn. The Union artillery, under a withering fire, had pulled the cannon up to the ridge and trained it on the farmhouse. In the second story of the farmhouse the smoke-filtered sunlight slanted in through the bedroom window onto an iron bed in the corner. On it lay an old woman, her eyes open. She was Judith Henry, eighty-four years old and a helpless invalid. There was something ghostly about her—her hair was as white as the sheets and the plaster walls. Only her blinking eyes moved in this white world. She seemed to be listening.

The rebels continued to fire from the lower windows, aiming their fire at the Union artillerymen as they moved their big guns, aiming them at the farmhouse. Only two Yankees were left to man the gun when it was finally ready to fire. The first shell burst outside the house, killing several rebels in the windows. The second shell hit the house directly below Mrs. Henry's window, penetrating the wall. It exploded with tremendous concussion inside, blowing out the wall, caving in much of the roof.

The line of Union soldiers, pinned down by rebs firing from the farmhouse, bellowed in angry relief and charged up the ridge. They drove the rebels away from the house and off the ridge, using their rifles as clubs when they got close. The rebels ran down their side of the hill, away from the battle, but a Confederate officer rode his horse in front of the disorganized mob, making them halt. "Look!" he shouted, pointing with his sword. "There's Jackson, standing like a stone wall! Rally behind the Virginians!"

The frightened soldiers looked back and saw General Jackson on his horse, standing on the ridge, leading a fresh squad of Confederate infantry as they fought back through the smoke to reinforce the ridge. The retreating rebels took heart and started back up the ridge, eventually driving the Yankees back across the plateau and to the farmhouse, where the Union line held. For a moment the two armies seemed to stand toe to toe, but the momentum had turned, and the Yankees began to retreat. As they came down from the ridge, they saw ahead the soldiers from Malachy's regiment in utter flight, and they too began to flee, running past the artillery battery that had smashed the farmhouse, stumbling over the bodies of their fellow soldiers which lay strewn all around their cannon.

The rebel riflemen knelt at the edge of the ridge and fired one more volley at the retreating Yankees, felling many more. It was now a wild rout.

John Geyser sat on his horse and looked through his binoculars at the hillside in the rear of the battle. He was stunned by what he saw. He could see dozens of horse-drawn carriages on the grassy hillside, with many other stylish rigs arriving. It was Sunday, and many senators and congressmen, along with their elegant ladies, were laying out blankets and opening their picnic baskets. Hundreds of Washington civilians had come to Bull Run to have the fun of watching a battle. Officers who had gotten lost from their units or had run away from the battle moved among the spectators and gave pompous running commentaries on the action before them, as though it were a sporting event. They pointed to the bursts of fire and the puffs of smoke in the distance, and the tiny figures of soldiers scurrying to and fro across the ridge. The dignitaries were all thrilled by the pageant of battle.

As John continued down the stream, ahead of him he saw a Union soldier splash across the water at a dead run. And then another, and another few, until the creek was clogged with thousands of soldiers running mindlessly away from battle. John saw Malachy, gasping for breath, but still running.

"Malachy . . . Malachy . . . stop!" John cried out to him. Malachy stopped and turned, looking about with eyes like a madman's and then he ran again, disappearing into the trees on the far side. John rode after him through the woods and up to the Turnpike.

Ahead of them, all along the road toward Washington, the Union army was more or less in orderly retreat, grimy soldiers slouching along, most without weapons, many wounded, some simply lost. In the procession also were ambulances filled with the mortally wounded, white-topped supply wagons, lumbering caissons, and riderless horses. They were all overtaken by the panicked Yankee soldiers, with Malachy in the lead, running through the fields on both sides of the Turnpike. Their panic infected everyone, and those who could run began to race with them. Drivers whipped their horses into a gallop. Those still armed dropped their rifles as they ran. The Turnpike became littered with guns, canteens, haversacks, even uniforms.

The VIP's from Washington saw the oncoming mob and then, as the rebel shell bursts approached them, they too began to panic. They left their picnic baskets and pushed their ladies into the carriages, setting off at a gallop across the grassy slope, joining the speeding traffic along the Turnpike toward the only bridge, called Cub Run.

The exultant rebel artillerymen, in pursuit of the fleeing Yankees, set up a cannon at the edge of the woods on their side of Bull Run. Just as the mob got to the bottleneck at Cub Run, the rebels began to fire. The shells burst all around them, causing complete chaos. One shell came down directly on top of a supply wagon crossing Cub Run, knocking it over on its side in the middle of the bridge. The vehicles behind it rammed into each other, and the wagons, carriages, and screaming horses became completely tangled. Many drivers and passengers simply deserted their vehicles and companions and ran off.

An ambulance driver pulled off the road in front of John, leaped out, cut the horse loose from the traces, mounted, and rode off. John could hear the cries of the wounded men inside and peered in. Five badly wounded soldiers were jammed into the back of the ambulance. Those that were conscious lifted their heads and appealed mutely for his help.

John led his horse to the front of the wagon and quickly hitched it up. He was terrified like everyone else, but he knew he couldn't leave these men behind. Shells burst all around him, showering the ambulance with shrapnel. A VIP carriage appeared out of the smoke, careening around the ambulance. It ran directly over a shell hole and overturned. A young woman, dressed in white, was thrown from the carriage. She raised her head and screamed for help. John started toward her but he lost her in the smoke. Then she appeared out of the smoke in front of him, wild eyed and ranting hysterically. She threw herself at John, clinging to him.

"Help me, help me! Get me away from here!" She hung on to him with surprising strength, pinning his right arm to his chest. He had seen too much hysteria in the last few minutes. He struck her in the face with the back of his hand. The blow was harder than he had intended, and it split her lip, spattering a little blood on her white dress. She was so startled that she just stared at him, dumbfounded. He grabbed her by the arm and pulled her to the back of the ambulance.

"Get in there! Help those men!" he yelled.

She looked in and recoiled from the mangled soldiers. "I couldn't!"

"If you want the ride, that's the price!"

She hesitated, and then climbed into the wagon. John drove the ambulance away from the chaos at the bridge. The soldiers on foot had found a shallow place to cross the creek, and John followed them at a gallop. He drove recklessly down the slope and into the stream. Fighting the current, he whipped the horse across and up the far bank. Crossing back to the Turnpike, he galloped for the field hospital.

In the midst of the vast traffic jam voices began to cry out, "All is lost for the Union!"

At dusk a lone horseman rode slowly along the ridge of battle. Jonas was stunned by the human wreckage around him. The entire plateau was littered with dead and dying men of both armies. For a mile around the cries and screams of the wounded pierced the stillness. Hundreds lay where they had fallen, bleeding to death. Even louder than the cries of the men was the humming made by the cloud of flies that swarmed like vultures over the battlefield. Jonas stopped by the shell of the Henry farmhouse and took a long pull on his brandy flask. The smell of death had made him nauseated.

Near him a Confederate soldier held the body of a friend in his arms, rocking back and forth. A woman from a nearby town had found her son. She lay across the corpse, quietly sobbing. Her husband stood nearby, his hat in his hand. A couple of civilians carried away a wounded Union soldier. Squads of Confederate soldiers gathered up the boots and weapons of dead Yankees. Some rebs stole what the corpses had in their pockets; many more could not bring themselves to do it.

Jonas dismounted and walked into the farmhouse through a gaping hole in the wall. The floor was littered with bodies. A Yankee soldier and a rebel lay in each other's arms, dead. Each had done his job well.

Jonas climbed the narrow staircase to the bedroom. Strangely the door to the room was still intact. He opened it and looked inside.

The body of Judith Henry had been blown into the corner, where it huddled on the collapsed bed in a half-sitting position. The roof had fallen in on the old woman, and the debris almost covered her. There was plaster on her face, making it appear pure white, like her hair, except for a startling rivulet of blood down one side. Only a few feet from her body the entire wall was missing. Through it Jonas could see the plateau outside and the bodies strewn all over it. He shook his head in wonder.

Jonas backed out of the bedroom slowly, closing the door behind him.

CHAPTER NINE

Outside Washington, D.C.

The "Rogues' March" hovered over the camp like a chilling fog. The entire regiment was drawn up on the parade ground in a hollow square with one side left open. In the center a post was imbedded in the ground. The regimental drum corps played with slow and ominous beats as a young soldier was marched slowly into the square by an armed escort of four soldiers bearing rifles with bayonets fixed. He was handsome, with pale, delicate features. He held his head high, trying to be brave, wanting everyone to see that he had as much courage as any man there. But his eyes were filled with terror.

It was dawn. A cold weak light enveloped the camp like a shroud. The men shivered in the morning chill, and here and there along the line a man would cough. They were not yet fully awake. Jake and Malachy had awakened to reveille as always and had stumbled out to the parade ground still half asleep. They had not been told that a sentence was to be carried out, but when they saw the stake in the middle of the field, they knew immediately. The soldier who was to be punished had been court-martialed a few days earlier, charged with running away at the Battle of Bull Run. A shameful silence hung over all the men as the soldier was marched before them. Malachy stared at the young man with a stricken, haunted look.

The new colonel in command of the regiment rode through the open side of the square and stopped in the middle. Unlike Colonel Wade, who had been given the opportunity to resign his commission "due to pressing political needs back home," this man was regular army, very official, all spit and polish. He sat stiffly in his saddle and addressed the gathering.

"Men, the army to which this regiment belongs is now under the command of Major General George B. McClellan. The mistakes of Bull Run are being corrected. Never again will a half-trained civilian mob be marched into battle! When next you march, you will be soldiers! When next you march, you will be part of General McClellan's new army—and you will march to victory!"

The colonel pointed toward the prisoner. "Mark you well the lesson of this morning. In this new army there will be no room for shirkers and layabouts. And certainly no room for cowards!" He turned to a first lieutenant and barked, "Take over, Lieutenant."

The lieutenant came to attention. He turned and shouted, "Ten . . . shun!" The entire regiment snapped to attention.

In a loud and clear voice he read the verdict. "By order of regimental court-martial. Private Lawrence Jones, having by his own admission fled from the Battle of Bull Run, is declared guilty of desertion under fire, and in the face of the enemy, and is hereby sentenced to be branded a coward and dismissed from the Army of the United States."

He turned to the sergeant who stood at the prisoner's side. "Sergeant, carry out the sentence!"

The sergeant had in front of him a brazier filled with red-hot coals. He removed a branding iron from the fire; at its end was the letter "C," glowing red. One of the armed guards lashed a leather belt around the prisoner's forehead, pulling his head rigid against the post. When he saw the glowing brand, the young man began to shake uncontrollably. Tears ran down his face, but his jaws were clamped shut; he did not utter a sound. He was determined not to give them that satisfaction. The men in the ranks were squirming as they stood at attention. Malachy watched with a tortured expression. The prisoner's eyes, so filled with terror, darted from face to face, searching for someone who would step forward and stop this from happening. But the other men only looked away, unable to meet his eyes.

As the sergeant pressed the burning iron into the young man's pale cheek, it made a searing sound that could be heard by everyone in the awe-filled silence. He shrieked for a long moment, recoiling from the branding iron with such force that the cords in his neck stood out like taut steel cables. And then his body slumped into unconsciousness, his head still held rigid by the leather belt. Few actually watched the branding; they turned their heads at the last second. Malachy tried to swallow the bile that filled his throat.

John Geyser did not turn away. He had made a drawing of the entire scene on the parade ground. At the last moment he had forced himself to watch. It was his job, he told himself; someone had to watch it. His job was to draw and report what really happened, so that the people back home would know the truth. But the real reason he forced himself to watch was that he was angry. He had been there at Bull Run, and he knew the truth. They all knew the truth. If they branded all the cowards at the Battle of Bull Run, only dead men would have unscarred faces. He wanted to capture all of the hateful, savage injustice in his drawing, so that everyone could see it. As the regiment was dismissed, John continued to draw, moving his pen with angry slashing strokes. He tried to capture the whole awful hypocrisy of the branding iron. His rage made the drawing as violent as the act itself.

Only much later did he come to understand why no editor ever printed this drawing. They didn't want the truth. They didn't want branding irons and hypocrisy; they wanted the swords and the roses. Later he wouldn't care either, but for now the drawing helped John to make it through the morning. Because in his heart he knew that if he had been a soldier at Bull Run he would have turned and run too.

Much had changed in the months since Bull Run. There were no more state militia uniforms with their gay colors and bursts of local pride. The checkered hats and flannels of the "Michigan Lumberjacks" had been put away. The jaunty hats with sprigs of green worn by the Irish Brigade were gone. Now every man wore the Yankee blue. They drilled endlessly, every day, and gradually they began to feel like real soldiers. McClellan was making them into one vast engine of destruction to be hurled against the South.

The camp was turned into a permanent city. The tents were replaced with winterized cabins made of logs and chinked with mud. Some still had canvas walls, but with dirt piled around the outside walls to give added warmth. Their roofs were still canvas, but now they had fireplaces with chimneys, also made of logs and mud. The cabins stood in long rows, and the backs of the cabins formed an alley of chimneys, which they called "Smoky Alley."

Jake sat outside their cabin and made the morning coffee. He took the whole coffee beans out of his pack and put them into a big iron bucket. With the butt of his rifle he pounded the beans into grounds. Everyone else all up and down the line of cabins was doing the same thing, and the banging rhythm filled the camp. An uncovered pot of water was boiling on the fire. John sat near him, wrapping up his sketchbook in oil cloth.

"Malachy has the blues, John. He's had 'em bad ever since Bull Run. He says he's the one they shoulda branded." Jake dumped the ground coffee from the bucket into the boiling water.

"Everyone feels that way," John said, lost in thought. "He'll get over it."

"I don't know, John. When we were kids, he fought our battles for us. He was our soldier. I don't know what's happened to him."

Inside the winterized tent there were four rude bunks built against the log walls. Malachy lay facedown on one of the lower bunks, covered with a blanket. He was not asleep, although he wished he were. He did not feel the constant torment when he was asleep, although he would dream then and live through it again and again, endlessly fleeing an enemy from which there was no escape.

Malachy raised his head for a moment when John came in, his face expressionless. Then he buried his face in his arms. John sat down next to him on a half barrel beside the bunk. "Coffee?" John offered, holding out a steaming cup. There was no answer. John took a sip of the coffee himself, wincing at the bitterness. He sat with Malachy for a while in the quiet of the cabin. He had no idea what to say.

"Heard a story about Bull Run. This reb general, he was riding up from the rear, toward the fighting. Saw so many rebels hightailing it away from the battle that he thought the South was licked for sure." John moved a little closer to Malachy. He wanted to reach him somehow; he knew what Malachy was feeling, shared the same pain, the same doubt. He felt like he'd run away from the whole war and deserted the South. "Thousands ran that day, Malachy. On both sides. Why act like you lost the battle single-handed?"

Still there was no answer. John reached out and touched his shoulder. "Leave me be!" Malachy said, jerking away from his hand.

"Your problem, cousin, is you thought you'd be the best damn soldier in the army. You said it once, back in Gettysburg—you said you were a born soldier. Well, you're not. Nobody is. You went into your first battle untrained. It scared the shit out of you. So what. It just proves you're a human being, like the rest of us."

Malachy rolled over onto his back, staring up into the shadows. He was listening. "You don't have to be a hero. Just do your share. You're needed," John said.

"What the hell are you talkin' about?"

"I'm talkin' about your brother. Jake's a young

banker, a desk man. It's gonna be a tough war, and Jake's not exactly the type for it, is he?"

"No, he's not." Malachy was looking at him now. John handed him the coffee and walked out.

After a while, Malachy sat up on the edge of the bed. The dead look in his eyes was gone.

President Lincoln slammed another shell into the firing chamber of the Spencer rifle, pumping the lever action. Squinting down the barrel, he aimed carefully and fired. He pumped the lever action and fired again until the gun was empty.

Christopher Spencer, a quiet little Connecticut Yankee, had the day before brought his new invention directly to President Lincoln's office. His new gun had been ignored by the War Department. Lincoln, who had fought in the Indian wars and tramped the woods of Illinois with guns countless times, had handled the repeating rifle with expert care. He asked Spencer to show him the "inwardness of the thing." He was so delighted with the gun that he had arranged to shoot it himself the next day.

President Lincoln was intensely interested in new weapons, especially rifles. He was just about the only person in Washington who was, however. The War Department and the Army Ordnance were run by traditionalists who believed that soldiers should not have rifles that fired more than one bullet at a time for fear that they would fire too fast and probably waste ammunition. Lincoln was determined to fight this inertia. He knew that if he had a reliable repeating rifle for his entire army, it would shorten the war and save thousands of lives on both sides.

They met in the open field in front of the half-finished Washington Monument. People who were wandering through the field stopped and gathered around to watch the President shoot. Jonas stood at Lincoln's side as he fired the rifle. The target was a board six inches high and three feet long, with a black spot painted at the center. It was set against a woodpile near the monument about seventy-five yards away. With the last shot Lincoln lowered the rifle. Spencer consulted his watch.

"You fired the seven rounds in twenty-eight seconds, Mr. President."

"The barrel remains cool," Mr. Lincoln murmured, running his hand along the gun. His initials, A.L., had been engraved on the stock. A clerk from the War Department ran back with the target board. There was one shot in the bull's-eye and five more clustered around it. One had missed entirely, possibly hitting the Washington Monument.

Lincoln turned to Jonas with a sly smile. "That's not too bad, is it, Jonas?"

"It's good shooting, sir."

Spencer reloaded the rifle, slipping seven 50-caliber, rim-fire, copper cartridges down the tubular magazine in the stock. He handed it to the President. Lincoln turned to the clerk. "Set the board up at a distance this time. Back by those trees."

The clerk turned around and looked off into the distance. The trees were several hundred yards away. With a worried look he ran to the edge of the woods. Lincoln tossed the rifle to Jonas, who caught it easily with his right hand. "Let's see what an expert can do."

Jonas hefted the rifle, getting the feel of its light weight and the lever action. "This will be an excellent test of your invention, Mr. Spencer," Lincoln said, obviously enjoying himself immensely. "Captain Steele is an army scout attached to General McClellan's staff and one of the best shots in the army."

Jonas stepped up to the firing line, adjusting the sight for the new distance. Then he glanced toward Spencer. The inventor had his eyes on his watch and was counting down. "Four . . . three . . . two . . . one . . . fire!"

Jonas pulled the rifle to his shoulder and fired. Then he pumped and fired six more times so quickly that it seemed like one continuous roar. His hands moved with extraordinary skill and he never took his eyes off the target.

Spencer was stunned. "Twelve seconds! Incredible! That is, if you hit anything."

Lincoln turned to Jonas with a smile. "What do you think of it, Jonas?"

Jonas was looking at the gun with real affection. "She hefts well, sir. Lever action is smooth. Capability for rapid fire is . . . well, amazing."

The clerk ran back with the target board. Two shots sat right on the edge of the black center, five more had nearly torn the bull's-eye away, all striking on top of each other. Jonas barely glanced at the target. He had known the results the moment he pulled the trigger.

Lincoln smiled when he saw the target and nodded confidently to Spencer. "There will have to be an official test, Mr. Spencer, but I'll recommend to the War Department that they evaluate your rifle right away. You'll hear from them." He shook Spencer's hand warmly, and he and Jonas walked off across the field together, Lincoln holding the rifle cradled in his arm.

They walked in silence a long while, and finally Lincoln spoke. "We've known each other a long time, Jonas. So I know what I'm about to say won't surprise you. But I need to talk to someone, and I know, of all people, you understand. Mother, bless her, is made of a delicate balance. It worries her to distraction when I talk of such things."

They stopped by the edge of the woods. They were both tall men, and as they talked their eyes were on an even level. "I've had strange dreams. Like the comets sent to earth, they foretell great events. I am convinced by them that my destiny is at one with this war. I sometimes feel that I will not live to see the end. In my dreams I am in a boat, on a dark stormy sea . . ." Lincoln saw the shocked expression on Jonas's face, and he stopped.

Jonas finished the dream. "You are rapidly approaching a strange dark shore, shrouded with mist." President Lincoln could only stare at him and nod. Jonas did not tell him that in his dream—the one he had told John Brown years ago, the one that had so deeply disturbed him—he was carrying a man in black. He knew suddenly that Lincoln was that man.

Lincoln smiled gently. "McClellan tells me you are to be married."

"Next week."

"Does she know of your visions?"

Jonas shook his head. "I haven't wanted to frighten her, or hurt her." And then with a grin he added, "Or hurt my chances of having her."

Lincoln nodded. He knew what pain and worry he had brought to *his* Mary. He put his hand to Jonas's shoulder. "My fate is tied to yours." It was said simply.

But they both knew that there was a bond between them that only death could break.

"We're like sleepwalkers, you and I. Our fate is somehow written in the stars, and we are just the instruments of the Almighty." With both hands he held the rifle out to Jonas. "I want you to have this. You will go to war for me—you will be my hands and eyes and heart. I want you to take my place. When you walk into battle, I'll be with you. And I'll know what you suffer."

President Lincoln turned and walked down the path toward the White House. Jonas, rifle in hand, stared after the lank, receding figure until he was gone.

CHAPTER TEN

Gettysburg, Pennsylvania

". . . and Mary, wilt thou have this man to be thy wedded husband. Wilt thou love him and comfort him, honor and obey him, in sickness and in health . . ."

Jonas stood in his captain's dress uniform next to Mary at the altar and watched her face as the preacher spoke the vow. She shone with a luminous beauty at this moment. He had been lucky. Fate had brought him to this place, here at her side; he hadn't searched her out. His life had been hard and mean, and he had walked it alone, never considering that any woman would want to share it with him. He hadn't even thought he would live this long. But now he couldn't imagine life without Mary. She was stronger than he was; he knew that now. She had changed him, given him new life.

He cherished her, loved her, but he was afraid that she might be hurt someday because of what he was and what he did, that in sharing his life she might share as well in its violence.

". . . and forsaking all others, keep thee only unto him so long as you both shall live?"

Mary looked at Jonas before she answered. She realized that she had never really known a man until she met him. But it wasn't until she came to know his vulnerability that she realized she loved him. She could see through his stern face, past his steely eyes to the lonely heart. And when he touched her, she felt only gentleness in his rough hands. As she stood with him in her mother's white lace wedding dress, she knew she was already his. She trembled as she reached out and touched his hand.

"I do."

"The ring, please."

John, dressed in his best city clothes, had been watching them. He saw the beauty in Mary's face, and in Jonas's he recognized the gentleness beneath the hard facade. He watched them touch, and he saw her tremble.

"The ring, please," the minister repeated.

John quickly dug into his pocket and handed the ring to Jonas, who carefully slipped it on her finger.

"For in as much as Jonas and Mary have consented together in holy wedlock, I pronounce that they are husband and wife."

Mary lifted her veil and Jonas kissed her hard on the mouth as the preacher added hastily, "Those whom God hath joined together, let no man put asunder. Amen."

It was a wartime wedding, without any frills. The Hale family and their close friends from Gettysburg grouped around the church doors as Mary and Jonas emerged from the church. Mary held up the skirt of her wedding dress as she ran with Jonas amid flying rice and the well-wishes of everyone. As Jonas helped Mary into the gig, there was a rumbling of distant thunder, and the sky was darkening quickly. Mary blew kisses to her family as they pulled out.

Jonas urged the horse into a fast trot along the downgrade that ran out of Gettysburg into the countryside. Rolling thunder echoed all around them, and on the horizon they could see the flash of lightning. It was getting dark, and the storm was almost on them. A gust of wind billowed Mary's bridal veil.

"I think I felt a drop," Mary said, moving closer to Jonas.

"We'll make it." Jonas said. "There's our house, just ahead."

In the busy week before their wedding they had found a house they could afford on the outskirts of town. It was a two-storied Pennsylvania Dutch house, deserted for years. The clapboard outside was now a weathered gray with only a few patches of flaking white as a sign that it had once been painted.

The rain was just starting to fall as Jonas turned into the dirt driveway alongside the house. He drove straight into the barn and unhitched the horse, covering it with a blanket. He lifted Mary down from the carriage and held her in his arms. Carrying her lightly, he dashed for the back door and into the kitchen. There was a huge stone fireplace, with its spit and hooks, and next to it a cast-iron stove. In the middle of the room were an old table and two upright chairs. Jonas carried Mary to the fireplace.

"Matches," he said, and Mary reached down to the fireplace mantel and picked up the box of wooden matches.

"Candles." With a grin she lit the candlestick and picked it up. She was enjoying herself, comfortable and warm in his arms.

"Ma sent over the table and chairs. And the bed upstairs," she said. "That's about all the furniture we have. So you'll just have to put me down one place or the other."

Jonas carried his new bride down the narrow hallway and up the stairs. The dim glow of her candle was the only light in the house except for the glaring flashes of lightning. The bedroom, directly above the kitchen, also had a fireplace. The ceiling had large beams, with a chiseled surface made by the adze that shaped it. The only furniture in the room was the same big brass bed that Jonas had slept in the first night John had brought him to meet the Hale family. The bed was made and turned down in the same way Mary had made it that first night.

Jonas carried Mary to the fireplace mantel and she placed the candle there. Only then did he set her gently down.

In the light of the candle they saw two miniature paintings on the mantel. The painting of Jonas was in an oval porcelain frame for Mary to keep near her on a table. The painting of Mary was in a leather case for Jonas to carry with him.

"My God, they're beautiful," Mary whispered. Jonas nodded, marveling at the feeling the paintings captured.

Mary picked up the note and read it out aloud. "I painted these from memory. They're for when the war keeps you apart. I hope you like them. Love, John."

They held each other a long moment. The wind howled outside and the dormer window strained at the latch. A branch tapped on the windowpane, sharp and insistent.

"I'll close the shutters," Mary said, moving away from Jonas. Suddenly the window burst inward, shattering the glass, hurtling shards at Mary. Startled, she cried out and her hand went to her breast. At that instant the wind blew out the candle, plunging the room into blackness. Jonas rushed to the window, and throwing his shoulder against the frame, he forced it closed. As he struggled with the window, a flash of lightning illuminated Mary for an instant. Just below her left breast, on her white wedding dress, was a vivid scarlet stain. With his back to her Jonas did not see it.

The room was black. "Stay where you are Mary." Jonas spoke sternly, but with an edge of tension. A match flared as he relit the candle. He turned to Mary. "Are you all right?"

She took a handkerchief from her cleavage and cradled her bloody finger in it. "Flying glass—it cut my finger. It's nothing."

But Jonas had seen the blood on her breast. He was ashen. "Your breast!" It was a hoarse cry.

Mary looked down and saw the bloodstain for the first time. "It's just blood from my finger."

But Jonas could only stare at the blood. This was the thing he feared above everything.

"I'm all right, Jonas! It's nothing."

"You've been hit!"

Mary reached for her bodice and tore it open. "Jonas! Look at me! There's no wound! I'm fine!"

Realizing that she was not hurt, the tension broke in him. He sank to his knees in front of her and put his arms tight around her. He buried his face in her soft breasts.

She held his head tightly, her fingers grasping his hair. "You'll never bring me harm, my darling. What you bring me is love."

They held each other and rocked gently in the candlelight as the storm crashed like the roar of cannons around them.

CHAPTER ELEVEN

The Peninsula Campaign, Virginia—April 4, 1862.

Jake and Malachy Hale marched with their company down a dusty Virginia road. Malachy's mind was dull and the dust choked him, filling his mouth and nose. By now he had learned how to march while asleep. With one eye barely open, he watched the feet of the men in front of him. He stumbled occasionally, and if the company halted, he usually walked into the man ahead.

Sergeant O'Toole walked next to Malachy and Jake marched beside a rookie who had joined the company when they moved south from Washington. The rookie, called Freddy, spoke up. "Hey, Sarge, fill us in, will ya?"

"Fill you in on what, rookie?"

"Where are we? Where we goin'?"

"Do ya remember bein' seasick?" Freddy nodded, his stomach turning at the memory. "Well, that boat brought you down the Potomac through the Chesapeake Bay to Virginia. This here's a peninsula. Yonder is Richmond. And all you gotta do is march fifty miles, take Richmond, and the war'll be over. Any more questions?" The rookie shook his head, frowning. It didn't sound too difficult. " 'Course you're liable to see the elephant a few times 'fore you get there."

Freddy turned to Malachy. "What elephant?"

" 'See the elephant' means to be in a battle."

"Have you, uh . . . seen the elephant?" he asked Malachy.

"Once. Over my shoulder."

Then they began to hear the booming of the cannon ahead and the scattered gunfire as the reb pickets and the Yankee forward units encountered each other. Malachy was suddenly fully awake with fear. They were marching into a fight. Through the spaces in the trees he could see the cannon smoke. Ahead of him he noticed men tossing playing cards into the ditch along the road. He asked one of them, "Why are you fellas throwin' away perfectly good cards?"

"If I get it, my stuff will all be sent home to my ma. I don't believe she'd like to get those cards. She says they're tools of the devil."

Jake and Malachy looked at each other. Jake didn't have any cards; he didn't play. He continued to look at Malachy. Malachy ignored his stare, but as soon as Jake looked away, Malachy quickly tossed his cards into the ditch.

Suddenly they heard the chilling whistle of incoming shells. They burst all around them, and the men broke formation, diving for either side of the road. Most shells exploded harmlessly in the rocky fields beside the road, but one scored a direct hit on a supply wagon carrying ammunition, and it exploded with a deafening concussion. The earth shook and rumbled, and the pieces of the wagon and bits of bodies fell down on them like

some hellish rain. Artillerymen wrestled with the
screaming horses as they worked to get their cannon off
the road and set up to fire. Jake and Malachy hugged
the ditch as more shells burst along the road they had
been standing on. The rebel artillery had them brack-
eted. An officer came riding back down the road and
ordered their company forward into battle. Crouching,
they ran as low to the ground as possible, moving
through the woods. They drew up with the other companies in a rough line along a creek at the edge of the
woods.

While they waited for more orders, they busied themselves loading their guns. Sergeant O'Toole walked
among them, checking them out. "Do you all have forty
rounds?" His men all nodded. "Firing caps?" They
double-checked. "Don't forget, aim low!"

O'Toole moved over to Malachy, who sat a little
apart from the others. "You all right, Malachy?"

"I ain't plannin' to run this time, if that's what you
mean." O'Toole grinned and slapped him on the
shoulder.

Jake sat on his haunches and listened to the quiet of
the moment. It was peaceful here. This little nameless
creek reminded him of home, of the woods around Gettysburg. He studied the beauty of the place for a long
time. He wanted to remember it later, long after he had
driven the memory of this war from his mind. And then
the bugle sounded.

In an instant the creek was filled with Yankee soldiers splashing across the shallow water. The reb infantry opened fire on them, cutting down a hundred men
before the first wave got across. The firing died down
as the rebs pulled back, leaving only a rear guard.
Jake's company swept quickly through the woods. Be-

hind them, at the creek, what had been a peaceful scene
was now a nightmare landscape. The trees were splin-
tered, many cut in half. Riddled gear littered the
ground. Yankee bodies floated in the blood-red water.
Others, wounded, too shattered to swim, rolled soundlessly over into the current and drowned.

Malachy's company safely reached the perimeter of
the woods. The standard-bearer stepped out into the
open field, and the entire Union battle line followed.
They moved across the field at a run, amid the whine
of minié balls and the exploding shells. Malachy fought
to control his fear as men fell around him.

After what seemed an eternity in the open line of
fire, they threw themselves behind the embankment of
a sunken road that crossed the field. The whole Union
line sank down behind the cover, panting. O'Toole
hoisted himself up for a look over the embankment.
The rebels had built a defensive line of dirt and timber
along the crest of the sloping field. It was well made,
and his practiced eye told him that it was impossible to
storm with the size force at hand. He also knew from
experience that that didn't matter; they would be ordered to do it.

Up on the crest, Major Welles sat on his horse and
waited for the Yankee devils to come to him. Today he
was wearing his black preacher's coat over a full dress
uniform. He had built this redoubt to withstand any
force, and he had well-trained, brave boys behind him.
He knew they were more afraid of him than they were
of dying. At this point in the Confederate line only he
and his men stood between the Yankees and Richmond. And he had sworn to God that they would not
pass.

Major Welles's son Homer stood at his place in the line. He was a small, round-faced boy with eyes like those of a puppy that has been whipped too many times—eyes eager to please, but afraid of the master's hand. Homer had never quite lived up to his father's expectations. He was not a leader of men—he had never been strong enough or tough enough. He was a sensitive boy, and in his father's eyes that made him weak. Homer wished to prove himself today more than anything in his life. He glanced up to see if his father was watching. Major Welles drew his sword and called upon Jehovah one last time. He sensed that the moment was coming.

A Yankee bugler sounded the charge. A standard-bearer broke cover and started uphill over open fields. The Yankee troops moved out behind him. O'Toole signaled his men to follow. "Let's not be late for the ball, men!"

On Major Welles's signal the Rebel line opened up a withering fire, and the shells rained down on the Yankees. Malachy emerged from the smoke, stumbling and coughing. He looked around, his eyes wide with terror. He had lost his squad. A shell exploded above him and he was thrown to the ground, stunned. He stayed there, his cheek pressed to the earth.

Up near the rebel line the standard-bearer fell. A comrade grabbed the flag and went on. The Yankees emitted a deep growl as they covered the last yard. They had paid for every inch of ground with a man's life, all the way from the embankment, and they wanted this one badly. The flag went down again, but this time no one picked it up. The Yankees had broken into the rebel line. The blue and the gray fought hand to hand in the trench, clubbing each other with rifles, even with their fists. Major Welles rode along the trench, using his sword like an executioner. It was an angry, bitter fight, but the Confederate line held. Not enough Yankees had made it all the way to the redoubt and they were driven back.

As the Yankees retreated down the slope, the men in gray jumped the earth works to pursue them. The counterattack was led by young Homer, who grabbed the rebel flag and led the rush down the slope, his flag streaming behind him. This was his moment of glory, and he knew it. He was more afraid of failing than dying. He ran so fast as he rushed into the smoke that he overran the retreating Yankees. Jake, who had made it all the way to the trench, turned and knelt to fire his rifle just as Homer emerged from the smoke running at full speed. Carrying the colors high, Homer looked back for an instant to see if his father was watching him. He never saw Jake or his gleaming bayonet. It plunged all the way through his chest and came out his back. He stood still for a long moment, his eyes now turned toward Jake, who knelt in front of him. He tried to speak, but only blood came out of his mouth. And then he fell, pulling Jake's rifle out of his hands.

Jake was horrified. Like all of the men he fought with, and against, he loathed the bayonet and would never have used it to kill anyone. He backed up, away from Homer's body. And then he turned and ran.

Malachy, his face pressed to the dirt, heard the rebel yell and looked up. He saw Yankees run past him toward the rear. He could see the rebel line coming at him. He summoned all the courage he had, raised his rifle, and pulled the trigger. It did not fire. He got up and ran, disappearing into the smoke.

When Malachy reached the woods, he slowed down and stopped to rest, leaning against a tree, panting. A mounted Union officer rode by him on his way to battle and Malachy quickly hid behind the tree. When he peeked around again, a squad of Yankee reinforcements came marching toward him, following the officer. He glanced around desperately. Near him a tree had been uprooted by cannon fire, leaving a large jagged hole in the ground. He dived in, landing directly on top of a Confederate soldier. Both men were so surprised that for a moment they merely stared at each other. Malachy had never met a rebel before—they were rumored to be vicious animals. The reb had never seen a Yankee either and was amazed that he looked so normal. But he wasn't taking any chances. He got the drop on Malachy. Leveling his musket at point-blank range, he pulled the trigger. Click. The gun was not loaded.

Malachy hesitated a moment, acutely aware that *his* gun was not loaded. Then, deciding to bluff it, he pointed his gun at the reb. But the reb had seen the hesitation and concluded correctly that Malachy's gun was empty.

The reb quickly began to load his musket. Malachy, his bluff called, did the same. It was a bizarre race: two men in the hole, standing three feet apart, loading their guns as fast as they could. The stakes were very high, and their hands were shaking. The reb put powder down his barrel and tamped it down with the ramrod. Malachy had paper cartridges, and he bit the end off and dropped the minié ball and powder cartridge down his barrel, tamping it down with his ramrod. The reb took a musket ball from the leather case at his belt and glanced over at Malachy. He saw that Malachy had the edge now, since his rifle took one step less to load. Malachy, sensing victory, tried to put the percussion cap on the nipple. With shaky, clumsy fingers, he dropped it. Kneeling, keeping one eye on the reb, he fumbled through the dirt for the cap. The reb saw his opportunity and hurriedly tried to jam the musket ball down the barrel. But he was keeping his eyes too much on Malachy, and he dropped the ball. It rolled right into Malachy's hands. It was a Mexican standoff. Malachy had no firing cap, the reb had no musket ball.

They both looked at their bayonets as if for the first time. Crouching, they began to circle each other, posturing as if to stab with the bayonet. But the idea of actually stabbing someone with the bayonet was repugnant to both men. Almost simultaneously, each man grabbed the barrel of his gun and held it like a club. Again it was a standoff. They glowered ominously at each other.

Finally the reb said, "Mebbe you 'n' me oughta talk, Yank." Malachy nodded tentatively, and the reb leaned his musket against the side of the hole. Malachy did the same.

"You was runnin' away, wasn't you?" the reb asked. There was silence from Malachy. The reb took it for yes. "So was I. Got lost."

There was another moment of silence. "How'd you know I wasn't loaded?"

The reb shrugged. "If you was loaded, you'd a kilt me."

Malachy sat down in the hole and leaned back against the wall. His hands still shaky, he took out his pipe and a small pouch of tobacco. The reb watched him press tobacco into the pipe bowl.

"Whose territory you reckon we're in?" the reb asked.

"Ours, I think. But your side was headin' this way." Malachy lit up his pipe. The reb took out his corncob and looked at Malachy pointedly. Malachy got the message and tossed him the tobacco pouch.

"It don't make no sense shootin' each other. I mean, they's too many folks willin' to do it for us."

Malachy nodded. "I guess they'd shoot us for runnin' away."

"Hell, they be glad to shoot us jes' for not shootin' each other." The reb grinned. "And if we wanna get shot real quick, there's that battle over there." He lit his corncob pipe and threw the tobacco pouch back. "What's your name, Yank?"

"Malachy. Malachy Hale. What's yours?"

"Darphus Teaberry. My folks got a little farm in North Carolina. Mostly sand and rocks though."

"How many slaves you got there?" Malachy asked suspiciously.

"Slaves?" Darphus laughed out loud. "Are you kiddin'? We don't even have no shoes!" They both laughed. "I don't even know no one who's got any slaves. I tell ya, my pappy was right. It's a rich man's war, but a poor man's fight."

They heard cavalry on horseback above them, coming through the woods. They huddled together against the wall of the hole to keep from being seen. The cavalry passed by the edge of the hole, but the two deserters were not seen. They looked at each other, trembling.

Darphus shrugged his shoulders. "Well, if we ain't gonna kill each other, how we gonna get out of this mess?"

Malachy sat down, thinking hard. "We gotta keep out of sight till the battle's over. Then one of us surrenders to the other."

"Which one you have in mind, Yank?" Darphus looked at him suspiciously.

"That's gonna be decided by who wins the battle." Darphus pondered what Malachy was saying. "I mean, come end of day, if you graybacks hold this territory, I surrender to you."

"An' if the damn Yankees win, then I go with you," Darphus said, nodding. "Seems fair."

Malachy held out his hand. "Is it a bargain?"

Darphus shook with him. "It's a bargain."

Leaning against the side of the hole, they puffed on their pipes and got to be friends.

Major Welles, his eyes wild, carried his son Homer in his arms into the Confederate field hospital tent. The surgeons were working frantically to save the lives of wounded soldiers. They worked on makeshift tables made from doors taken from a nearby farmhouse. The operations were mostly amputations; there was no time for anything else. If a soldier had been wounded in an arm or leg, they simply cut it off. The men who had been shot in the chest or stomach were left to die. The doctors knew from experience that they couldn't save them.

To prepare them for amputations, the men were given whiskey to make them senseless. Most passed out anyway when the saw cut through the flesh and hit the bone. The ragged incisions were often cauterized with a red-hot poker. The sounds that came from the tent were hideous.

Major Welles begged the doctors in the name of Jehovah to look at his son. When they told him he would have to wait, he ordered them to try to save his boy. Major Welles was in such a state of shock, he didn't even notice the pile of arms and legs next to him. One of the doctors left the amputation he was doing and, with the bloody saw in his hand, felt Homer's still heart. He looked at Welles impatiently. "This man's dead, Major." The surgeon turned back to the operating table.

Welles refused to believe the man. He slapped Homer's face, trying to wake him up. In shock and grief he carried Homer around camp in his arms for hours. He stumbled along like a sleepwalker, his eyes as glassy and lifeless as those of the dead boy he clung to.

By late afternoon, the sounds of battle had ceased. Inside their hole, Darphus was asleep and Malachy sat with his back against the side of the hole, dozing. He was startled awake by the heavy rattling of caissons being dragged through the woods. Malachy listened, his heart pounding. He tried to tell if they were Yankees or rebels by the sounds they made, but he couldn't, so he got up and peered cautiously out of the hole.

Malachy grinned. Yankee artillerymen were setting up their cannon about one hundred yards away. Picking up his rifle, he prodded Darphus with it. When the reb opened his eyes, the rifle was pointed at him. "You're my prisoner, reb."

Darphus jumped up angrily. "I never shoulda trusted no white-livered, blue-bellied Yank!"

Malachy put his rifle down, a hurt look on his face. "Why'd ya say that, Darphus?"

"Ya loaded that gun on me, didn't ya?"

Malachy cocked his rifle and pulled the trigger. It clicked. "We made a bargain." He pointed over the edge of the hole at the Yankee artillery. "You lost the bet."

Darphus looked over the edge and turned back to Malachy. He managed a rueful smile as he raised his hands to his shoulders in surrender.

They crawled out of the hole and started down the path toward the Union camp. Darphus had his hands up in the air and Malachy was behind him, his gun pointed at his back.

"Hey, Yank!" Malachy whirled at the hoarse whisper coming from the trees behind him.

"Don't shoot!" the voice cried out. A rebel sergeant stepped out into the open, holding his hands in the air. Malachy pointed the gun at him.

"Me and my men, we hafta surrender. We was fightin' rear guard, got surrounded. Half my squad gonna die 'less I get 'em a doctor."

"Can they walk?" Malachy asked.

"Them as can't, we'll carry."

"Glad to help, Sergeant. Fall in." Malachy was starting to like rebs—they seemed so accommodating.

At the edge of the Regimental Field Headquarters, Malachy and his gallant parade emerged from the woods and marched into the clearing. They were led by Darphus and the sergeant. Then came two walking wounded, supporting between them a badly wounded soldier. Two more rebels carried an unconscious soldier. Finally, two more wounded men emerged, hobbling along, helping each other. Behind them all was Malachy, carrying his rifle casually in one hand.

Malachy marched them all the way through camp,

followed by a large band of astonished Yankee soldiers, finally halting his parade in front of the general's tent. The general was drinking whiskey with the colonel while they studied a map. When the general looked up, he was so stunned by what he saw that the cigar fell out of his mouth and into his whiskey. Everyone stared at Malachy as he stepped to the front at attention, his rifle held in two hands across his body. "Prisoners halt!" he commanded.

There was a long silence. Finally the general said, "Who are you?"

"Private Malachy Hale, sir. Twenty-Third Pennsylvania."

"How did you take all those prisoners, Hale?" As Malachy spoke to the general, he absentmindedly pointed his rifle at the colonel, who glanced nervously at the gun.

"I kinda jumped on the first one by mistake, sir. And I stumbled on the rest in the woods. I really didn't do anything except . . ."

The colonel had had enough, and he pushed the gun barrel away from him.

"It's all right, Colonel. It isn't loaded."

The general burst out laughing. "He brings in ten rebs with an unloaded rifle! Son, I wouldn't want to play poker with you!" He turned to the officers nearby. "It's men like this win battles for us, gentlemen. Colonel, write this boy up a citation and give him a battlefield promotion." The general came over to Malachy and shook his hand. "Congratulations, Corporal Hale. You've done a good day's work."

Malachy knew there was nothing to do now but to play along, although he swallowed hard when the general talked about him winning battles. He saluted, turned smartly, and walked away with as much dignity as he could muster.

When he passed Darphus Teaberry, he stopped. They nodded to each other, both with a slight smile. Malachy handed Darphus the musket ball he had dropped. They had played it square.

CHAPTER TWELVE

The Peninsula, Virginia

It was a hot and lazy summer day in Virginia. Luke
Geyser sat on a log beside the Chickahominy River,
which wound down through the Peninsula. He was putting the finishing touches on a toy sailboat he had hol-
lowed out of a small log. It had a deep curving keel to
counterbalance the high mast, which was graced with
three sails made from old sheets. In all it was about two
feet long, crude but seaworthy. The Yankees were
camped across the river and Luke planned on doing a
little trading.

Luke, the youngest of Ben Geyser's children, was
nineteen. He had followed his brothers, Mark and
Matt, into the Confederate Army on his eighteenth
birthday. It had been all Ben and Maggie could do to
make him wait that long. Luke had always known
where the most excitement was to be found, and he figured that at the moment the war was it. He liked to tell
people that he was a lover, not a fighter, and for Luke

that was a truthful statement. When it came to fighting, he did his job, bravely and without complaint, but he didn't really like to fight. He considered it to be a waste, mostly because it interfered with the pleasure of just being alive—alive in a world where half the people were women.

During the entire first year of the war there had only been about ten days of fighting. The rest was idle time, and Luke was an expert at enjoying idle time. Unlike most of the other soldiers, he was never bored. Handsome, with blue eyes and sand-colored hair, he liked women and they liked him. He managed to spend more time on leave than any other man in the company, but no one really minded. He was blessed with an infectious sense of humor and was well liked by the other men.

With one last flourish on the miniature Confederate flag above the sails, he was finished. The men who were lounging around him had been watching him build the boat for two days. They had asked him what he was doing, but he had dodged the question. Their company was supposed to be on picket duty, guarding against a sneak attack by the Yankees across the river. But weeks ago they had come to an understanding with the blue-belly pickets on the far side: as long as no one showed himself on the river itself, they wouldn't bother each other.

When Luke jumped up and ran down to the river with his sailboat, a few of the men followed out of curiosity. At the bank he yelled out, "Hey, Yanks!" A shot rang out and a minié ball whizzed by his ear, tearing off a branch of the tree next to him. He hit the ground as the men behind him burst out laughing. "Hold your fire, Billy!" Luke yelled out, holding his head up. "I've got some tobacco for ya!"

A voice came from across the river. "Hey, reb, I got a question. How you gonna get it across?" There was some laughter from the Yankee side.

Luke smiled good-naturedly. "By boat!" he yelled back.

He loaded the well of the little boat with fresh Virginia tobacco, waded out into the current, and let it go. It sailed across with its load, the sails set just right to catch the wind moving on the river. When it arrived at the other end, the Yankees cheered. It was nearly impossible for them to get good tobacco. Several of the Yanks showed themselves on the bank of the river, peering across the water.

"What do you want from us, reb?" they shouted.

"Coffee!" Luke shouted.

The Yankees yelled back, "We got plenty!" They poured the coffee beans into the hull, turned the little boat around, put the mainsail on the other tack, and shoved the boat off for the other side.

As it sailed back, Luke called out. "You-all the Twenty-Third Pennsylvania?"

"They ain't supposed to know that!" one Yank said. He turned and called out, "Who told you, reb?"

"Abe Lincoln," Luke shouted, and the laughter of the rebs and Yanks floated over the water.

With both sides of the Chickahominy at ease, the Yanks enjoying their Virginia smoking tobacco and the rebs their fresh coffee, they became more bold. A Yankee soldier, stripped naked, climbed a big tree that hung over the river, and with a loud yell did a cannon ball dive into the water. Almost instantly, there were twenty Yanks splashing around in the water. The rebs,

seeing the fun, joined them in the river, and they bathed
and larked around to the strains of the company banjo
player. He made up a song just for the occasion: "If I
only had some likker/I'd get drunker'n a vicar/On the
Chicker, Chicker/Hom . . . min . . . eeeeee!"

When Luke sent the sailboat back across with more
tobacco, he pinned an envelope to the mast. It wasn't
for a sack of coffee beans that Luke had planned this
friendly collaboration with the enemy. True to his reputation, he had in mind a more reckless adventure, and
he wanted two Yankees to enjoy it with him. The envelope said, "Please deliver to Malachy or Jake Hale."

On the Yankee side, an entire encampment had
sprung up during the lull in the fighting. It was late in
the afternoon and fires were being started for the evening meal. There was a peacefulness in camp that came
from the sure knowledge of experienced soldiers that
tomorrow they might be fighting for their lives on some
nearby field or creek. These moments of quiet were
precious. There was time to write letters to the ones
they loved and thought about constantly. They had time
to think and to find themselves again among the scattered lives of war.

Malachy lounged contentedly in a homemade chair
in front of his tent, his new corporal stripes sewn to his
sleeve. He figured that, if they made him a hero for
running away and falling on a reb, then being a hero
didn't really mean that much. He wasn't a born soldier,
and he wasn't a hero either. But he knew that he would
do the best he could to see it through and would try to
stay alive so that he could go back home when it was
over.

Jake squatted in front of a wood fire, stirring a pot of

stew. John sat on a rock nearby, his shirt off, drawing
the scenes of camp life around him. Unlike most of the
other combat artists, he didn't try to make the life of a
soldier look romantic. He didn't make up gallant battle
scenes with stirring cavalry charges. He drew the truth.
That morning he had drawn a picture of the view from
inside a tent. He drew the meager possessions that a
soldier kept near him in the tent: the photo of his wife,
rubbed so many times the image was nearly gone; the
letter from his mother, read and reread countless times,
folded and unfolded until it fell apart; his cup; his cook-
ing pot and plate; his pipe; his clothes; his gun. John
drew the sad little flourishes and touches the soldier
created to make the tent more like a home. John
wanted the people back home to know what it was like
to be a common soldier.

When Sergeant O'Toole came by with the note from
the little sailboat, John was drawing Malachy and Jake
as they lounged around outside their tent and the other
men near them, who were playing cards, writing letters,
and reading the Bible. "This came from the reb side,
for you two," O'Toole said as he handed it to Jake. "By
boat, I'm told—whatever the hell that means."

Jake stared at the envelope while the other men
grouped around him. "Came from the reb side. Who
coulda written to us?"

Before Jake even got it open, John said with a slight
smile, "It's from Luke." They looked at him in amazement. "Well, who else do you know in the reb army
except my brothers?"

"Even so," Jake said, "there's three of them."

"Only Luke has that childish handwriting."

Jake took the note out and read:

Dear Cousins:

Meet me at ten tonight, at Munson's Landing. It is most gosh-awful important.

Luke Geyser

Jake turned to O'Toole. "Munson's Landing?"

"Ya, it's on my map. Just an unused, falling-down pier about a quarter-mile upstream."

"You comin' with us, Sarge?" Malachy asked, grinning.

"Not me. I got my pension to think about, 'n' my stripes."

The night fog rose over the river and flowed across the banks as though it had a life of its own. Malachy, Jake, and John emerged out of the dark mist, walking single file down the footpath along the riverbank. The rustle and sudden scurrying of the night animals startled them. They kept their rifles at the ready. It was past ten before they saw the rickety old pier looming out at them. They stopped and listened for a sign of Luke. They peered into the gloom. There was nothing.

Jake shivered a little. "Should we show a light?"

John shook his head. With Malachy in the lead, they crept stealthily out to the end of the pier. They looked down into the dark water of the Chickahominy. It slowly swirled and heaved, like a vast pool of slate-gray paint.

Suddenly Malachy snapped his rifle to his shoulder, pointing it down at the river. "Look! Down there!"

The bow of a rowboat glided slowly out from the blackness under the pier. As it drifted into sight, they saw Luke's body sprawled across the bottom of the boat. They stared at it in horror.

Jake whispered hoarsely to John. "Is it . . . ?"

"It's Luke!" John cried.

Jake was nearest the ladder that ran down the side of the pier to the waterline, and he scrambled down to the boat. Throwing his rifle into the boat, he jumped in after it. John and Malachy were right behind him. He knelt beside Luke's pale, still face. Frantically, Jake slapped Luke's cheek. "Luke, Luke!"

Malachy and John stood in the boat beside Luke. The boat began to rock from side to side.

Jake slapped him again. "Say something!" he pleaded.

There was a long pause. "Good evening, Jake," Luke said, opening his eyes. He laughed at the startled expression on Jake's face. Malachy stood next to Jake, also staring at the apparition. And then he saw John standing in the middle of the boat. "John!" He jumped to his feet. "If this don't beat all!"

Luke and John embraced, causing the boat to rock wildly beneath them. Losing their balance, they collapsed on top of Jake and Malachy. The four of them lay in a tangle at the bottom of the boat, laughing uncontrollably.

They heard distant voices on the Yankee side. Luke signaled the others to be quiet as he slipped forward and picked up the oars. While John, Malachy, and Jake huddled in the stern, Luke rowed the boat soundlessly out into the middle of the river through the heavy mist.

Luke was still rowing strongly as John glanced back toward the Yankee shore. "We can talk now."

"Yeah, slow down, Luke." Jake said.

"Can't slow down, we're late."

Jake peered over at the quickly approaching reb

shore. "Luke, rebs don't like Yankee soldiers on their side of the river."

"My friends won't mind. I've already told them you're kin."

Malachy looked over at Jake and then to Luke. "What's up, Luke? Where are you taking us?"

"To the dance, of course."

Malachy looked back to Jake. "Did he say 'dance'?" Jake nodded slowly. "He did."

Luke rested the oars a moment. "Ya see, I found this big ole barn, miles from nowhere, and we got good musicians in our outfit, so what could we do except give a barn dance?"

Jake wasn't sure he heard right. "You're takin' us behind Confederate lines to a barn dance?"

"Right," Luke said, rowing again. "I'll get you back to your side of the river before sunup."

Malachy was intrigued. "It's risky, Luke."

"S'pose it is? Look what you get for a little risk— music, whiskey—and women!"

"Women!" Malachy repeated the word, just to savor it.

"Wait'll you meet 'em. Belles from Richmond! Local gals, the pick of the crop! Beauties, all of 'em."

Malachy's eyes narrowed. "You tellin' the truth?"

Luke put his hand over his heart. "Word of honor."

"Move over." Malachy sat beside Luke and took one of the oars, rowing madly. After a while, he looked up at John and Jake. "You comin' with us, fellows?"

"How long you been in the army, Luke?" John asked, his eyes searching his brother's face.

" 'Bout a year." He averted his eyes. He'd known the same horrors they had.

"The war's not a game, Luke."

Luke smiled again. "There ain't no war, John. Not tonight."

The old barn leaned sharply to one side, silhouetted against the night sky. The farmhouse next to it had long ago burned down. The land was deserted and over-grown. Sections of the barn roof had caved in, and there were large gaps in the siding where people had taken the weathered boards for their own use. The light from the kerosene lamps inside shone through these gaps, making the barn look like a jack-o'-lantern with teeth missing. Music poured out of the barn, spilling over into the surrounding woods. The fiddle and banjo band whooped up the one-step; through the gaps in the barn, dancing couples could be seen whirling around.

Big Bear stood at the entrance to the barn, peering out into the darkness. It was past midnight, and he was worried Luke had been caught. He was a huge man, almost as tall and broad as a door frame. Like many of the reb soldiers, his uniform had been dyed with walnut shells, giving it a golden brown color. His mother had to send him homemade uniforms because the reb army didn't have any big enough. Big Bear was a local boy and was known in the area for his feats of strength. It was said that he could bend a silver dollar with the fingers of one hand and straighten a horseshoe into a rod. Coming from a poor sharecropper family, he could neither read nor write, and most folks thought he had the mind of a child. But Big Bear and Luke had become fast friends, and together they made an almost unbeatable team.

Finally Big Bear spotted them, walking up the old driveway to the barn, their blue and gray colors mixed. He grinned to himself as he heard their laughter. Stepping into the barn, he called to the other men. "Luke's here. He done it . . . he brung his kinfolk."

A group had gathered near the door when Luke strolled in. "Folks, I want you to meet my cousins, Jake and Malachy Hale."

"Howdy, Yanks!" they all called out, as if in a chorus. They were all anxious to see a real Yankee. "I never seen a *live* Yankee before," one man said. " 'Cept maybe their backside as they hightailed it outta Bull Run."

"Where you guys from?" Big Bear asked.

"Gettysburg, Pennsylvania," Jake said, staring at a wall of gray uniforms. "That's *southern* Pennsylvania."

"And this here's my brother, John," Luke said proudly.

Big Bear stared at John's civilian outfit, which John had adorned with touches from castoff uniforms of several different state militias. "Whose army you in?" Big Bear asked him.

"Nobody's. I'm a correspondent."

A drunken corporal pushed his way through the crowd with a belligerent swagger. "What the devil! Ain't those Yank uniforms?"

Big Bear stepped up to him, towering over his head. "I don't see no Yank uniforms, Stacey."

The corporal backed away from the huge man. "My mistake, Big Bear, my mistake . . ."

The lead fiddler held up his bow, stomped out the beat with his boot, and the little band launched into a waltz. John and Luke dipped their tin cups into the bucket of whiskey on the floor. Luke looked around at all the girls. "You sweet little critters," he said to no one in particular. "I have a special gal for you, John. Stay right here."

John watched the people swirling around him. There were at least twenty couples dancing on the hay-covered plank floor. Malachy waltzed by with a pretty girl, swinging her around in swooping circles and grinning from ear to ear. For tonight, all the differences of blue and gray were lost. For a while they could escape the strain and horror of the war. Still John could not help but realize that some of these men would be dead within a week.

He saw a few couples climbing the ladder to the upper loft, disappearing into the hay. He realized suddenly how much he needed a woman.

"Here you are, John. Meet Wanda Mae." Luke had two girls on his arm. One was easily the prettiest girl at the dance. John's eyes fell immediately on her, and he liked what he saw. He reached his hand out to her.

"How do you do, Wanda Mae?"

"No, I'm Francine."

"And Francine is all mine," Luke said, pushing Wanda Mae toward John. Luke swung Francine out onto the dance floor, grinning. John and Wanda Mae looked each other over. She was a big, buxom country girl, wearing a crazy-colored gingham dress. At the edge of her skirt could be seen bright red socks and men's ankle-high work boots. She had a big wad of something in her cheek.

"You're kinda purty," she said with a crooked grin.

"Just what I was going to say about you, Wanda Mae."

"A sweet talker too, ain't ya, Johnny? Do you wanna dance?"

"Sure."

Wanda Mae extended her arms. "Help yourself."

John gulped down his whiskey, took Wanda Mae into his arms, and they swung out onto the dance floor.

When the band finished the waltz, Wanda Mae tugged John over to the door. "Take me outside, Johnny. I'm sweatin' like a bull." Leading him off into the darkness, she sat down on an old abandoned hay wagon, patting the spot next to her. As they sat side by side on the wagon, Wanda Mae wiped her brow and fanned air up her dress.

She smiled at John. "Better out here—more air, less people. You said that you would of said I'm purty if I hadn't said it first to you?" John nodded.

"If you was to kiss me, I'd be mighty obliged," she said.

John smiled. He leaned forward and kissed her full on the lips. After a moment, he pulled his head back with a muffled cry. Spitting from his mouth like a man who had just gulped hot sauce, he pointed at his mouth. "Mouf . . . burning!"

"Shucks, I'm sorry, Johnny. It's ma chaw." She spit out the wet brown wad and wiped her mouth with the back of her hand. "I bet you don't chaw tobacco, do you?"

John shook his head. Seeing that he needed help, she hiked up her dress and groped around for the small flat bottle tucked in her garter. "This'll fix it. It's good stuff."

John quickly took a big swig from the bottle. His eyes bugged out and he opened his mouth as if trying to get air. It was his first taste of moonshine, and the tears rolled down his cheeks. His lips moved to speak, but no words came out; his throat was paralyzed.

"What's the matter?" Wanda Mae said. "Cat got your tongue?"

He reached out for something to hold on to as the world started to spin around. Wanda Mae took him gladly into her hefty arms and pulled him down to her.

Two Confederate soldiers rode up the old driveway toward the barn. A tough-looking Irish sergeant led the way, carrying a lantern to light the path. He was followed by Captain Randolph, a young Virginia officer from a fine old family. He rode with great bearing and grace, obviously conscious of his class. They stopped outside the barn, watching the couples through the gaps in the wall.

"Sergeant, I reckon we've located our missing men." As the two officers came into the dance, everyone had gathered around the band and, as a group, sang "Dixie." They were mostly drunk and tired, and they sang in a sweet, sentimental style. They didn't want the evening to end.

A couple of reb soldiers near the whiskey bucket saw the officers striding across the floor and they dove head first through the empty window frame. The captain pulled his revolver and fired a shot through the roof, causing hundreds of roosting birds and bats to fly around the high loft. Several half-dressed soldiers and their girls peered down from the loft. The music and the singing trailed off as everyone turned around and saw the officers.

"What the hell are these Yankees doing here?" Captain Randolph bellowed angrily. There was a long silence. "Who's responsible for this outrage! Step forward!"

Luke shrugged and stepped forward. Big Bear loyally stepped to Luke's side. "They're my kin, sir. My two cousins, and that's . . ." He looked around for John but couldn't find him. "I invited them."

"You invited the enemy behind our lines? Don't you know you could be shot for that?"

"It was just for a bit of fun, sir."

"Sergeant Boggs, arrest these two Yankees. They're prisoners of war!"

"Don't do that, sir!" Luke said. "I gave them my word of honor that I'd get 'em back to their side of the river, safe and sound."

"Bring the prisoners, Sergeant!" Captain Randolph turned on his heel and walked away. Luke stepped in front of him.

"You gotta listen, Captain!" Randolph paused. "I'm just a farm boy, Captain, but I'm a Southern farm boy, and I was raised to believe that a Southerner's word of honor can never be broke. If a Virginian's honor don't mean nothing in the army, then what are we fightin' for?"

The crowd of soldiers behind Luke mumbled their agreement. The captain looked at Luke and then at his men.

"Sergeant!" The captain took Boggs aside, and they talked in low voices. "You know the boy?"

"I do, Cap'n. Luke's just a lad, full of fun. The men love him. If you're askin' my advice, sir . . ."

"I am."

"If you want your men behind you the next time you walk into a fight, I'd back down."

The captain turned and pointed at Luke and Big Bear. "You two will be taken care of in the morning, and may God help you! In the meantime, get these damn Yankees back where they belong!" Captain Randolph wheeled and marched out, followed by Sergeant Boggs. As they went for their horses, they walked past the hay wagon. It was rocking and squeaking. They peered in. "Who in the hell are you?" the captain asked.

John looked up. "I'm Luke's brother."

Captain Randolph closed his eyes, a pained expression on his face. "I should have known." Sergeant Boggs led the captain away.

At dawn, the rowboat came out of the mist to the side of the rickety pier. John and Jake were rowing, while Luke and Malachy sat in the back drinking. They were trying to keep from laughing, but the harder they tried, the more the laughter burst out of them.

When they got to the ladder, Jake and Malachy climbed weakly up to the pier. John embraced his brother. He wanted to tell Luke how much he loved him, and how a war was the most dangerous place to look for fun. He wanted to tell him to take it more seriously, because it was going to get a lot more deadly. But he had known Luke too long to lecture him. Besides, he was a man now. He held Luke by the shoulders. "Take good care of yourself, Luke. Please."

"Sure, John." Luke smiled and nodded his head.

John stepped up the ladder and Luke got back to his seat and picked up the oars. "Hey, Malachy!" Luke yelled out.

"What?" Malachy whispered hoarsely.

"Did you see old John when Wanda Mae kissed him good-bye?" Luke started to laugh as he imitated Wanda

Mae. "Johnny, yer so p-p-purty!" Malachy fell down on the pier in tears.

Laughing, Luke rowed out into the river and disappeared into the night and the fog.

CHAPTER THIRTEEN

The Peninsula, Virginia

It was midnight. Dressed in civilian's clothes, his Spencer rifle across his lap, Jonas rode out of the darkness. When he reached the log barrier in the narrow winding road, he nodded at the Yankee sentry, who recognized him and saluted. Jonas turned off the road into the dense woods that separated the two armies.

Sergeant O'Toole and Malachy and a few others sat by the campfire sipping hot coffee. Jonas reined his horse at the edge of the campfire light.

O'Toole stood up. "Evenin', Captain."

"I'll have a word with you, O'Toole." Sergeant O'Toole walked over and stood at the side of Jonas's horse. "Where are they?" Jonas asked him.

"Johnny's on the far side of the crick. They know we're here, too."

"How far to the crick?"

"Quarter-mile, that way," O'Toole pointed with his thumb across camp.

"Pickets?"

"I got pickets posted every fifty yards, on the bank of the stream."

"Password?"

"Foxfire," the Sergeant said. Jonas nodded, as if to dismiss O'Toole. "You plannin' to go across the crick, Captain?" O'Toole asked him.

"Good night, Sergeant." Jonas moved on. Malachy got up from the campfire and came abreast of his horse as he went by. Jonas stopped, leaned down, and they shook hands.

"Jake drew picket duty tonight. He's with that rookie, Freddy."

"I'll look for them." They touched their hats as if to salute each other.

Malachy and O'Toole watched Jonas ride back into the darkness. "There'll be shootin' soon, if I read the signs right," the sergeant said. "Fightin' just seems to follow that man."

Major Welles also rode alone in the night, his horse moving slowly through the high brush along the Chickahominy on the Yankee side. He sang in a deep, rousing voice:

> "Mine eyes have seen the glory
> of the coming of the Lord . . ."

He carried his sword in his hand, the blade resting on his shoulders, weaving in the saddle as he sang. He seemed drunk, but it wasn't liquor that intoxicated Welles—it was vengeance.

Freddy heard the singing first. He listened in amazement. Cocking his rifle, he called out, "Who goes there?" The singing stopped. No answer. Then it started again.

"He has trampled out the vintage,
    Where the grapes of wrath are stored . . ."

Freddy peered into the darkness. In the night, with the mist rising over the creek, Welles was difficult to see. Occasionally the moon would break out from the clouds, lighting him for a moment.

"Halt. Who goes there?" Silence. Freddy was terrified now. The singing had stopped. Hearing a sound behind him, he turned. A sword flashed in the moonlight, its sickening thud ending Freddy's scream.

Fifty yards away, Jake stepped from the shadows of the trees into the moonlight. Tense and scared, he looked upstream, listening for another sound. He could hear nothing. He was sure he had heard a cry after the singing had stopped, and it was his duty to find out what it was. Staying within the shadows of the trees, he moved up the creek toward the sound.

The singing began again:

"He has loosed the fateful lightning,
    Of His terrible swift sword . . ."

As Welles rode slowing through the bushes, his singing mingled with the wind.

The bushes parted and Jake peered into the clearing where Freddy had been. "Freddy?" He whispered. Silence. Jake moved closer. "Freddy?" He looked around the clearing. Then he saw Freddy seated on the ground, his back against the trunk. Jake stood up and walked over to the tree. Kneeling, he grabbed Freddy's shoulder.

"Freddy, you idiot, you can be shot for sleepin' on . . ." Freddy slumped sideways and Jake saw the bayonet. It had passed through Freddy's heart with a ferocious thrust and was imbedded in the tree, holding the torso upright. Jake reached for Freddy's chin and lifted his face. His head had been slashed open, but Welles had carefully put Freddy's hat back on, at a jaunty angle.

"His truth is marching on. . . ."

Jake jumped back from the grisly sight, his rifle at alert, looking first in one direction and then another. Realizing he was in the open, he crouched in the shadow of the tree. He had never before been so scared. The singing had unnerved him, for the killer seemed to be everywhere at once. His heart pounded so hard he put his hand over it to keep the killer from hearing it.

Suddenly Jake heard a horse coming through the brush near him; he whirled and fired. The sound was deafening in the still night. He saw nothing. Backing up, he turned and ran.

He stopped at a tree and looked back. Again he saw nothing, and ran on. He stopped again, panting, and looked back. Nothing. As he turned to run again, an arm reached out and grabbed him by the throat. Jake struggled, but the arm held him like a vise.

"Easy, Jake! Easy!" Jonas said softly. Jake, recognizing the voice, turned and looked over his shoulder.

"Jonas!"

"A little quick on the trigger, ain't ya."

"Come here, I'll show you!" Jake was nearly hysterical.

When Jonas saw the corpse, he dropped the reins and slipped the Spencer from its holster.

"It's Freddy's own bayonet," Jake whispered.

Jonas took off Freddy's cap and ran his hand through the hair, clotted with blood. "The skull's damn near split in two. Looks like it was a sabre. Freddy was already dead when he got pinned to the tree. This don't have much to do with war, Jake. This is murder. And he wants us to know it."

"Why would he . . ." Jake's voice trailed off as the singing started again, about fifty yards further down the river. There was supposed to be another picket right there.

> "Glory, glory, hallelujah,
>   Glory, glory, hallelujah . . ."

"Don't move." Jonas told Jake, and he pumped a bullet into the Spencer. He moved quickly and silently to the bank of the river. Throwing himself on the ground, he looked downstream. He saw a ghostly figure on horseback crossing the river downstream, his sword raised in the air. The ghost rider reeled in his saddle as he sang, his face looking toward the heavens. Jonas raised his rifle to fire, but the spectral figure was swallowed by the darkness. Jonas felt a cold chill. In a moment of weakness he hesitated. He couldn't hit something that wasn't there.

The song came out of the darkness:

"Glory, glory, hallelujah,
    Glory, glory, hallelujah,
Glory, glory, hallelujah,
        His truth is marching on . . ."

Suddenly, for just an instant, the moon showed itself, shedding a beam of light across the water. Jonas fired. The bullet ricocheted off the sword that Welles carried, the ring of the steel echoing down the still river. Welles looked back, his eyes wild with madness. And then he disappeared into the mist.

BOOK III

CHAPTER FOURTEEN

The Peninsula, Virginia

"Thirty days! Fatique duty, digging latrines! When they're full, you bury 'em again! And then dig new ones!"

Luke and Big Bear exchanged depressed looks. Standing at attention in front of Captain Randolph, they looked at him with contrite expressions. Not taken in by the hangdog faces, Randolph would have drummed them out of the army if he hadn't needed as many men as he could get. Casualties had been terrible for both armies, but the Confederacy had very few men with which to replace them. Captain Randolph figured that the harsh punishment would be good for discipline. When the other men saw them at their fatique duty day after day, they would be less inclined to disobey regulations themselves. And since Luke and Big Bear were popular with the men, not discharging them was good for morale. The captain smiled at them grimly. The sentence made good military sense.

At the other side of the command tent, Major Fair-

burn looked up from his maps. He'd heard the tongue
lashing that Randolph had given Luke and Bear for inviting the enemy behind their lines for a barn dance.
Trim as an athlete, with a black handlebar mustache,
he was a man who liked to take chances himself. Like
Luke, he had a romance with danger. He turned to
Randolph. "Captain, may I ask your men a few questions?"

"Of course, Major. You can do any damn thing you
want with these two."

"Which of you is Private Grundy?"

Big Bear raised his hand as if he were in school.

"I understand you know the peninsula like the back
of your hand."

"Born and raised here, Major, sir."

"Good." He pondered a moment. "Do either of you
know anything about balloons?"

"Balloons?" Big Bear said, his brow knitting. He
wasn't sure he had heard right.

"You mean, like the Yankee observation balloons?"
Luke's mind was racing. He saw the light at the end of
the tunnel. "Yes, sir! I know all about them balloons.
Heck, we had gobs of 'em where I come from."

"Have you ever flown in one?" the major asked, intrigued.

"I don't know how many times, sir."

"Very good. As you know, the Fed balloons have
given the enemy an edge. We've been trying to hide our
movements from the Yankee observers for months. We
can't shoot them down—our cannon won't tilt high
enough and a rifle can't shoot far enough. So we did
the next best thing. We formed the Confederate Balloon
Corps."

"We have a balloon corps?" Big Bear was deeply impressed.

"We have a start. We've built one balloon so far, in Savannah. It just arrived. I need two volunteers. The duty is risky, but I have a hunch about you two. If you see fit to volunteer, I'm sure Captain Randolph will consider suspending the thirty-day sentence."

Luke's eyes were shining. "You mean, we get to go up in it?"

Major Fairburn grinned. "Of course."

Luke and Big Bear glanced at each other. Then they looked over to Captain Randolph. He nodded reluctantly. He wasn't reluctant about suspending the sentence—he just hated to lose two good men. It was common knowledge among the officers that balloon observers had very short life spans.

Luke and Big Bear snapped to attention and saluted. "Volunteers for the Confederate Balloon Corps reporting for duty!" Luke said, trying to keep from smiling too broadly.

"Glad to have you, men," Fairburn said.

Big Bear leaned forward. "Is our balloon a big one, like the Yanks have?"

"Bigger, I think. And much, much prettier."

The Confederate balloon floated triumphantly against the blue sky. Although tethered to the ground with ropes, it towered above the crowd of soldiers and civilians that had gathered to watch its maiden flight. No one could quite believe what they were seeing. The balloon was as colorful as a silk patchwork quilt waving in the breeze.

Luke and Big Bear stood in front of their tent in the middle of the field. Above them a handmade sign read: THE CONFEDERATE BALLOON CORPS. They stared up at the balloon in awe.

"It's beautiful," Luke said, his face filled with wonder.

Big Bear turned to Major Fairburn. "How come she's made of such little pieces?"

"When we went to make her, we found out that there's just no silk left in the South. The blockade cut off all our supplies from Europe. The good ladies of Savannah volunteered their silk dresses and petticoats and . . . other items of apparel." He smiled. "All colors, all sizes."

"Plain ole dress silk!" Luke said. "How does it hold the gas?"

"We dissolve gutta-percha in naphtha and coated it . . . do you hear that?" In the far distance they could hear the booming of cannon.

Big Bear cocked his head like a hunting dog listening for game. "Reckon it's up by Gaines Mill."

"Well, gentlemen. Let's do our job." Major Fairburn took off his military cap and pulled from his shirt a civilian tweed cap, placing it rakishly on his head. Then he took a pair of homemade goggles from his pocket, cleaning the lenses with his silk handkerchief. The lenses were dark, rimmed with metal circles, and held together by half-inch strips of black leather, with an extra loop to go around the head. Luke watched with envy as Fairburn put the glamorous goggles on, tying the silk handkerchief around his neck.

"Bear, you man the windlass. Luke, you come with me."

They strode manfully through the crowd toward the

balloon. Without losing his brave smile, Luke spoke softly to Major Fairburn. "Major, I think you oughta know something before . . ."

A beautiful woman stepped out of the crowd with a bouquet of roses. Mrs. Binford had been sent by the ladies of Savannah to represent them at this historical occasion. The young widow handed the major a rose, wishing him well, and he, of course, gallantly kissed her hand. She seemed a little disappointed. As the major took Big Bear over to the windlass, she presented Luke with a rose and kissed him on the cheek. Luke, who had never been a gentleman, kissed her full on the mouth. She blushed, but smiled at him radiantly.

"You're terribly brave to fly our balloon," she said breathlessly. "I've brought along some more petticoats, in case you need more. Maybe you'll help me with them later."

Luke was in familiar territory. "I'd be glad to, ma'am. Anything to further the cause. Where are they?"

"I'm wearing them," she said with an angelic smile.

"Yes, ma'am." Luke knew that he had found his true calling . . . as an aeronaut. He walked backward to the balloon, not wanting to take his eyes off her.

The two men climbed into the basket. Major Fairburn cupped his hands and shouted, "Release the guide ropes!" The three ground crew teams, each holding a rope, allowed the balloon to drift upward.

Luke watched the ground fall away and his stomach went with it. "Major, I ain't really gone up a whole lotta times in one of these things. In fact, if truth be told, I never did once."

"Unlock the windlass!" the major called down. Big Bear threw the lever on the windlass, and the ratchet clicked as the cable played out. The rope cable, coiled at Bear's feet, snaked off the ground and through the ratchet.

"I know that, Luke. If truth be told, I needed two innocent volunteers. One that knew the lay of the land, and one that was crazy." He threw the last sandbag out and looked over at Luke. "You'll do."

The lovely patchwork balloon rose gracefully into the sky, taking its place among the majestic white clouds. The citizens cheered, the soldiers gave a rebel yell, Mrs. Binford blew a kiss, and Luke waved his red rose as he sailed away.

On the ground Big Bear stared intently at the coiled rope by his feet. When two thousand feet had passed through the windlass, a red handkerchief appeared from the coil. Just before it reached the ratchet, he threw the lever, freezing the windlass. That was the height from which they would take their observations.

From two thousand feet the land below them spread out for fifty miles into the distance. The Chickahominy River ran southwest as they looked out. The gently rolling land was a tangle of plowed fields, clumps of dense woods, and lush meadows. Roads appeared to meander aimlessly. Just a few miles ahead of them they spotted Gaines Mill, sitting along a stream that came off the Chickahominy.

They could see a battle taking shape at the mill. The Yankees were dug in along a three-mile slope, first behind a split-rail fence and then in lines up the slope. Their artillery was massed behind them on the plateau. All along the front of their lines was a swamp, which acted as a sort of moat that the rebels had to cross under fire. The Yankee position looked too strong to attempt to assault.

The aeronauts watched as the rebels attacked first the left side of the Yankee line and then the right. Through the binoculars they could see the mass of gray infantry move forward into the smoke only to be driven back both times, leaving the ground sprinkled with gray shapes. They watched in disbelief. It seemed so clear from this perspective that the Yankees were too strong to storm from the side.

Major Fairburn had a map spread out in front of him. He marked the positions of both armies, carefully noting the movements on the roads and the shifting Yankee defense. "Our boys are getting butchered by these piecemeal attacks. Do you see those Yankee columns splitting off to both flanks? They are reinforcing the two flanks from attack. If General Lee hit the center of their lines now with everything he's got, every man jack of them, he might break through."

"The Old Man must be reading your mind, Major. Look there!" Lee had ordered all sides of his army to converge on the center. They wheeled around in formation and in one massive push stormed across the swamp. In a nearly suicidal frontal charge, they breached the Yankee line. Bursting across the rail fence, the rebels drove the Yankees back up the slope. Yankee cavalry smashed at their flanks in a countercharge, driving through in an effort to plug the hole in their lines and stop the flow of rebels into their center. But it was too late. The rebels had split the Yankee line. The aeronauts were frantically recording the shifting tides of blue and gray on the maps in front of them.

"Column of Yank cavalry retreating toward Bosun's Swamp," the major called out, and Luke penciled it on the map.

"Yank infantry running through the fields, away from the mill," Luke said, looking through his binoculars.

"Show me!" Luke pointed out the massive wave of retreating blue as they surged back to the bridge at the Chickahominy.

"Also, Yank supply wagons on this road, sir." Luke drew a line on his map.

"What's it look like to you, Luke?"

"Like we're pinnin' their ears back, sir."

"I think you're right. The whole damn pack of 'em is moving back to the river. McClellan might fall all the way back to the James River. We've got the Yankee line of retreat pinpointed on this map."

Major Fairburn grabbed the red flag at his feet. "Here, Luke, signal them to bring us down. This can't wait."

Luke leaned way out of the basket and waved the flag like mad. Looking down, he could see Big Bear running around gathering men to crank the windlass. Almost immediately the balloon began to descend.

Luke marveled at the silence around them. He couldn't hear any wind—only a faint whispering of air as it moved over and around the patchwork balloon. There was no real sense of movement, just the sensation of floating free—free from gravity and free from all the pain and all the rules. This was what he had been looking for all his life. If for only a few moments, he had broken free. "Peaceful up here," Luke murmured. "I kinda hate to go back down."

"Right now we're above firing range of the Yankee artillery on that plateau. From fifteen hundred feet on down, we're sitting ducks. They'll make it hot for us."

"There wasn't no shooting on the way up," Luke said.

"They weren't ready. But you can bet your bottom dollar they're waitin' for us now."

On the ground the crew of soldiers toiled at the windlass. Big Bear stared intently at the balloon. "Now! Fast as you can! They're under fire!" Big Bear grabbed part of the handle and the ratchet clicked furiously.

Shells were bursting all around the balloon, leaving puffs of white smoke. A shell exploded next to the basket, and Luke shook his fist at the artillerymen below.

Another shell exploded behind them, and a piece of shrapnel the size of a silver dollar tore through the major's arm at the bicep, shredding flesh and muscle, smashing into the bone. Luke grabbed him as he almost fell out of the basket, using all his strength to pull him to the floor. The major had his hand clamped over his arm, the blood pouring out from between the fingers.

"Let me see it, Major," Luke said.

The major hung on grimly. "It's nothing!"

Luke yanked the major's hand away. The arm was nearly severed. Luke tore the silk handkerchief off the major's neck and tied it around his shoulder as a tourniquet. They both knew the war was over for the major.

With his good hand Major Fairburn slipped the goggles off his head and handed them to Luke. They looked at each other a long moment. Now it was Luke's job.

When Big Bear and the ground crew had pulled the balloon down to fifty feet, Luke threw out the tether ropes and the basket was brought to earth. Luke helped them lift the major out and then he jumped to the ground, knowing what he had to do now.

Captain Randolph and his men were waiting for the reconnaissance information on the battle. Luke saluted and handed the map to Randolph, who looked it over. "Judging from the map, I'd say the Yanks are in retreat. Is that your impression?"

"Yes, sir. Looked to me like a big skedaddle."

The captain handed the map to the lieutenant at his side. "Take this to General Lee's headquarters. Tell him that from here it looks like a big skedaddle." He turned back to Luke. "You did well . . ."

"I'm going back up," Luke said, climbing back into the basket. "We need to know exactly where to hit their flank as they retreat to the James. We may have a chance to smash the whole damn Yankee army!"

Randolph smiled. "I'm glad you volunteered. I was wondering how I was going to ask you to go back up with me."

"Sir, I need Big Bear. He knows the land better than either of us. He'll be able to find them on the map." Captain Randolph nodded reluctant agreement. Big Bear lumbered into the basket, his face gleaming with a wide grin. Luke had done it again, he thought. They were going up to the sky together.

"Release guide ropes!" Luke yelled with an air of authority. The balloon began to ascend.

"Unlock the windlass!" He pulled on his goggles and adjusted the tweed cap. Facing Captain Randolph and his men, Luke and Big Bear saluted as they rose into the sky.

Their work done, the ground crew stepped back from the windlass to admire the patchwork colors in the setting sun. As they stared up at the balloon, a soldier inadvertently stepped into the coiled cable with one foot. One of the loops lashed itself around the man's leg as it snaked out of the coil. He cried out as he was dragged by his leg toward the huge iron gears of the windlass. "That machine'll take his leg off!" a soldier shouted, grabbing the man by the arm. But the force of the balloon was too great, and the ensnared soldier was ripped from his hands.

Another soldier, standing near the tent, grabbed the wide-blade ax that was kept in case of fire and ran to the windlass. The ensnared soldier screamed in terror as he was smashed against the windlass. At the same instant, his eyes widened in horror as the ax came down, severing the rope with a terrible clanging of steel against steel, only inches from his foot.

The soldier wept in relief, as the severed rope passed instantly through the windlass, leaving the ratchet silent. The dangling rope soared upward. The balloon was adrift.

In the basket Luke and Big Bear were immediately aware of the increase in ascent speed. Looking down, they could see the crowd waving up at them, pointing at the rope trailing through the air beneath them.

"We've broken free somehow! We're drifting!" Luke yelled.

Big Bear looked at him. "Wadda we do about it?"

"How should I know?"

"You're the man with experience." He mimicked Luke. " 'We had gobs of 'em where I come from.' "

Luke didn't want to be reminded. "Which way are we drifting?"

Bear looked below them at the land sailing by. "We're coming up on Savage Station. We're headin' for the James River, Luke."

They both knew what that meant. They would come down on the entire Yankee army, beat and angry, their

backs to the James. "The major told me that to get
down in an emergency I should pull the rope with the
red handle." Luke found the handle and pulled down
with all his strength. "Hold on to this, Bear. Keep it
pulled down tight." While Bear held it, Luke peered
up over the side of the basket.

"What does it do?" Bear yelled.

"It lets the gas out," Luke called back. "We gotta get
down before we reach Yank territory."

The once proud patchwork balloon, now slack from
loss of air, just barely cleared the treetops as it drifted
down to the riverbank.

"It's the James," Big Bear said simply.

A Yankee cavalry unit moving along the river, seeing
the balloon from a distance, dismounted at the edge of
the woods. The balloon was only fifty feet off the
ground when the cavalry kneeled and opened fire. They
were easy prey. Minié balls smacked into the wicker
from all angles, tearing the sides off the basket.
"Damn!" Luke released the railing and pulled back, his
hand smashed by a bullet.

Beside him Big Bear grunted and, holding his belly,
sank to his knees in the bottom of the basket. A red
stain spread across his gray shirt and down his pant
legs.

"Bear!" Luke cried, and as he reached out to Big
Bear the basket crashed to the ground, spilling both of
them out onto the grass. The Yankees stopped firing
when they saw Luke crawling and stumbling over to
Big Bear. Lying on his back, looking up at the sky,
Bear had a startled look on his face.

When Luke reached his side, Bear looked over at
him. "What happened, Luke," and then the pain hit

him. "Oh, Jesus! Jesus! Luke don't wait on me. Run! Luke, run!"

Luke got up and dashed away. But after a few steps, he stopped. He turned slowly and walked back, sitting down next to Bear.

"Luke, you fool. I'm gut shot, I'm killed."

Luke could hear the Yankees coming. He knew Bear would die. He wanted to run; he had never wanted anything so bad.

Big Bear reached up with both hands and tore his bloody shirt wide open, exposing his wounded belly. "Those blue boys are downright serious today. I'm thirsty, Luke. Oh, Jesus, I'm thirsty."

"You're gonna be okay, Bear. It ain't that bad. You and me, we make too good a team. They can't lick us. I'll get you back, and we'll fix that damn balloon with all those bitty pieces." He lifted Bear's head, avoiding his own useless bloody hand. "We got it made now, Bear. We just gonna float around all day. Up there, Bear. Way up there." Bear looked up at the blue sky.

The Yankee cavalry surrounded them, the horses stamping the ground all around. Luke pleaded for a canteen, and the Yankee captain got off his horse and handed him one. When Luke turned back, Bear was still staring up at the sky. For a long moment, Luke just looked at Big Bear's hopeful face. And then he reached out with his bloody hand and placed it gently over Bear's heart. It was silent.

"Your friend's dead. Get up, soldier." Luke brushed aside the captain's hand and stood up by himself. He never took his eyes off Big Bear. There was a bloody hand print over Bear's heart.

"What were you doing, flying over this sector?" the captain demanded.

"Watching bluebellies skedaddle," Luke said with a half-smile.

"Cocky little bastard, ain't he?" a soldier said, grabbing Luke by the collar.

The captain mounted up. "They'll beat that outta him in prison camp."

As they led him off, Luke reached up and pulled the goggles down over his eyes.

CHAPTER FIFTEEN

Vicksburg—June 1863

Stripped to the waist, the Yankee gunners loaded their cannon with another explosive shell. After a long hot morning of work, they were grimy with black powder and sweat. The enormous siege guns were dug low into the ground behind earth breastworks, safe from rebel sniper fire. The ground shook as it absorbed the recoil of each booming shell. They lit the fuse on the shell and fired it into the sky. The shell arched high over both Yank and rebel trenches and came down on target on a row of stately homes in Vicksburg. The explosion rocked the neighborhood, demolishing a house in the middle of the block.

John sat behind the battery of guns and sketched the gunners in action. In his drawing he placed the battery of Yankee seige guns in the foreground, the Yankee trenches in front of them, and then the trenches of the rebel defenders a hundred yards away in the middle of the drawing. He drew a high arching shell coming down on the city of Vicksburg in the background, exploding on the big courthouse that sat prominently on the highest hill with its tower and cupola. He could see several buildings ablaze in the city, and he drew them also.

The lieutenant in command of the battery took out his pocket watch. "Cease fire!"

The artillerymen wandered off to sit and relax; this was a familiar routine in the day. The artillery fire from all sections up and down the line died out, and the rifle fire between Yank and reb trenches stopped. After the constant roar of cannon fire, the silence was strangely ominous.

John hopped off the mound of dirt and trotted over. "What's up, Lieutenant?"

"The men have to eat. I'm suppose to stop three times a day. For an hour. The rest of the time we lob explosives into the city, night and day."

"I just got here today. How long's it been goin' on?"

"Over a month." The lieutenant looked back toward the city. "Vicksburg's full of women and children, surrounded, starving, in a city that's being blown apart. What the devil makes them so stubborn." He turned back to John. "I forgot. You want to go down to the trenches." John nodded. "Now's the time. During the lull."

The Yankee trenches were built in a zigzag pattern. The long slanting points were methodically excavated and extended, foot by foot, toward the reb trenches. Gradually they were tightening their stranglehold. In some places the two trenches were separated by only a thin wall of earth.

John made his way along the inside of the trench, passing the Yank soldiers, who glanced curiously at John's civilian clothes. John slogged through filthy water that stood stagnant in the trenches, the flies thick all around him. Despite their discomfort, the men were in good spirits. They knew instinctively, as all veterans did, that although this siege was dull and boring, it was a lot safer than a frontal assault. As long as the trenches meant living a little longer, they would stay in them without complaint.

John came upon a couple of soldiers from the Engineer Corps extending the slant of the trench toward the rebel trench only a few yards away. As he went past them, a reb voice called out. "Hey, Yanks!"

The Yankees stopped digging and leaned on their shovels, grinning. "What's on you mind, reb?" the corporal yelled back.

"Why you comin' at us with that new ditch?"

After living for weeks only a few yards away from each other, both blue and gray had become friendly. During the lulls in shooting, they competed with each other for the best insult. The corporal stepped up to the breastworks. "That's a military secret."

"I know, I know, but you can tell *us*."

"Well, okay. When we get it dug, we gonna flood it. Then we can sail our gunboats up here and blow hell outta ya!" There was laughter from the rebel trenches.

The corporal tried another tack. "Hey, reb! It's been a real fun picnic, but we're gettin' bored with this crap. When ya gonna give up?"

"Damn, boy, we been waitin' for *y'all* to give up!"

"Mind if I talk to the reb?" John asked the corporal.

"Be my guest." The corporal and his men went back to digging.

"Hey, reb!" John yelled.

"Yo!"

"Is that General Stevenson's division?"

"What of it?"

"I gotta talk to Corporal Matthew Geyser, artillery-man. He's with the Virginia battery."

There was a long pause from the reb trench. Then a rebel officer called out. "Who wants Matt Geyser?"

"John Geyser, his brother."

"Stay where you're at."

John sat down to wait. Lighting up his pipe among the soldiers, he listened to the stories they swapped about their sector of the line. One soldier claimed that one night they had been digging the trench at an angle out toward the reb trench when suddenly they pushed through the wall of earth that separated the two armies. The rebs that were on picket duty were furious at the infringement of their territory. The rebel officer told the offending Yanks that he was outraged at the breach and that they were trespassing on Confederate soil. The Union officer apologized for the intrusion, but said he was under orders to dig in this direction, reb line or no. Of course, the reb officer knew what it was like to have orders, so they came to an understanding. The Yanks could continue digging, but at a slightly different an-gle—one that would parallel the reb line but not cross it. They shook on it, and the Yanks went back to dig-ging.

Another soldier, older and grizzled, felt obliged to top that story. He said he belonged to the Engineer Corps, assigned to dig tunnels under the Confederate lines, plant explosives, and blow them up. Each time they blew one up, the rebels would have to move to a trench further back in the rear and the Yanks would move in. One time they set off a bomb under a trench and blew a Negro cook up into the air and over into the Yankee trench. He wasn't hurt at all, and the delighted Yankees who had captured him put him on display in a tent nearby, charging five cents a head to see the "nigger who flew into the bosom of Abraham."

The firing resumed at the end of the rest hour. Each side fired sporadically at the other, shooting through slits made between the sandbags. The constant racket of rifle fire was nerve-racking to John, but the soldiers around him talked and moved around as if the gunfire was the most normal thing in the world.

"Hey, Yank!" the reb officer yelled out. No one heard him above the din.

"Yank!"

"Hold the fire!" the Yank corporal called out. The rifle fire died down.

"Matt Geyser's here!" the reb yelled out.

"John Geyser's ready!" the Yank corporal said.

Everybody up and down the line within earshot heard them and knew what was going on. The soldiers in both trenches leaned their rifles up against the mud wall and lit up their pipes or played cards.

"What goes?" one rookie asked the soldier next to him.

"Brothers."

John looked at the corporal, and the officer motioned John over the top. John clambered up into the no-man's-land that separated the two armies. The strip of ground was burned and cratered, a barren, scarred landscape.

John saw Matt climb up out of the reb trench. They walked slowly toward each other, the only living things standing above the ground for miles around. They stopped when they were a few feet apart, neither man reaching out his hand to the other. They stood for a moment and stared. Matt was a ghost of the brother

John remembered—the easy, slow manner, the thoughtful gentleness seemed to have been worn away. Matt, who had always had a rumpled look about him, appeared more than merely ragged. The parts of his uniform didn't match and he wore no shoes. He had a mangy beard, which he stroked nervously, and his eyes had that hard, haunted look common to all veterans.

John was a veteran, too, and he traveled light. His satchel, slung low over his shoulder, held everything he needed for his work. He wore the only clothes he had. He was no longer the idealistic kid that Matt had known. They had both changed. Like the scarred and desolate land around them, they showed clearly the terrible effects of war.

Matt finally spoke. "You come lookin' for me?" John nodded. "How come?"

"We're brothers," John said simply.

"Last time I saw you I named you traitor."

"I remember." John looked away for a moment. "How's Emma?"

"I seen her once in Vicksburg, before the shelling got bad. Went to her house. Real nice big ole thing. Lester made a lotta gold tradin' cotton with the Yanks."

"Emma, the big patriot, letting her husband trade with the enemy?"

"Ya, that's what I said. But she says he'd buy medicine and stuff with the cotton money and smuggle it back to Vicksburg. We do need the medicine."

"All at a nice profit, I bet." John never did like Lester.

"Ya, well, it don't matter now. I heard later he got hisself killed."

"Does that mean she's alone in that city, or what's left of it?"

"She's alone, 'cept for the baby. She had a boy, named him Jesse."

"Jesse." John seemed surprised for a moment. He had seen so much death that he had almost forgotten that life was still possible. "They may be starving."

"Emma's a strong-willed woman. If anyone can make it in that city, she can. Besides, ain't nuthin' *I* can do. We're spread out so thin up here, nobody can leave the front lines."

"Do you remember her address?" John asked.

"Newlet Street—eighteen, I think. How you gonna get into the city?"

"Don't know yet."

"You could do me a favor," Matt said as he reached into his pocket. He handed John a small roll of bills tied with string. "I saved some money to send Ma and Pa. They'll probably need it—they're just gettin' by. But we're surrounded, so there's no way I can get it to 'em."

John shoved the wad into his pockets. "I'll see it's mailed."

"You artists really get around. What you doin' out here anyway?"

"Vicksburg is an American city under siege. Nothing like this has ever happened before. People want to know what's going on."

Matt's anger showed for an instant. "Folks are starving to death, that's what's going on."

John nodded. "What about you? You're a long way from Virginia."

"My outfit got transferred. They needed artillerymen. But now we ain't got nothin' to shoot with." There was an awkward pause. Matt looked around. "We're holdin' up the war."

John smiled sadly. "I'm glad I saw you, Matt." Matt said nothing. John turned and walked back toward the Yankee trenches.

"John . . ."

John turned and Matt stepped toward him. "We've about run outta food and everythin' else. I don't think this'll last much longer. Either we give up or we'll have to break out. A whole lot of us won't make it. I just wanted you to know . . . in case . . ." He couldn't find the words.

"You still think I'm a traitor, Matt?"

Matt slowly shook his head. "Not anymore. You followed your heart. I know that now. We all did. But . . ." Matt tried to blink back the tears, but he was just too exhausted to try. "We've lost so many. I don't wanna lose you."

John reached out for him. In the middle of no-man's-land, the two men embraced and held each other.

John spoke softly to his brother. "You are the best one, Matt. Of all of us, you are the one to spare."

With one last look they both turned and walked back to their trenches. When John was safely below ground the Yankee corporal cupped his hands to his mouth. "Get your head down, rebs!"

After a moment, the Yankees opened up with a roar of rifles. The reb line returned the fire. The war was on again.

CHAPTER SIXTEEN

Gettysburg—July 1, 1863

From their trim white houses and shops the townsfolk looked out at the ragged gray shapes as they passed by. They didn't look at all like an army. They looked more like a mob. Lean, tanned dark by the sun and constant exposure to the weather, the men in butternut slouched through the little farm towns of Pennsylvania. They had no uniforms to speak of—handmade shirts mended themselves, blue coats and shoes stolen from the Yankee dead who had fallen before them. Some were dressed in civilian clothes with no military look at all except for a gun.

They didn't look like much of an army, but they were to be reckoned with when it came to a fight. They called themselves Marster Lee's boys and they thought themselves invincible.

The people of the little village of Gettysburg had heard the rumors but had not believed them. It sounded ridiculous. It was said that Robert E. Lee and his army had invaded the North. They had read many times in Jacob Hale's newspaper about the ravaged farms and towns of the South—places with names like Bull Run, the Peninsula, and Chancellorsville in Virginia, Shiloh in Tennessee, and Vicksburg in Mississippi. They knew about these places from the stories and drawings of John Geyser; to them the war was fought in those distant places. But now they were told that Lee was going to bring the ravages of the war to the North and feed his mob on the fat and prosperous land of Pennsylvania. For the people of the North, the war was coming home.

The rebel cavalry came to Gettysburg to find shoes. They had seen an advertisement in Hale's newspaper:

> Boots and shoes, comprising men's fine calf boots . . . all of which will be sold as cheap as the cheapest. Let all who wish to supply themselves with good and substantial work call and examine our stock.

When the rebs got to Gettysburg, they ran into the Yankee cavalry who had come looking for them, with Jonas scouting at the head. The two armies had found each other at last, not out of design, but simply because the roads led them there. Jonas and his men formed an arcing shield between the reb army and the strategic hills beyond Gettysburg. With the tremendous firepower of their Spencer rifles, they held the sea of gray soldiers back, while General Meade rushed his Union army onto the high ground beyond town, where they entrenched themselves.

Jonas moved coolly among his men, reassuring them, holding their fire until the rebs were nearly on top of them. And then, as the enemy emerged from the woods like a moving gray wall, the Spencers spoke. The rebs had never faced the Spencer rifle in such force, and from the continuous roar of Yankee fire they assumed they must have charged the whole Yankee army.

On they came, slowly but with gathering strength, forcing Jonas and the cavalry to fall back before their overwhelming numbers. The Yanks fired and dropped back in precise order, holding back the tide as long as they could. Every time they moved back toward town, they left a row of men on the ground. Finally the Yankee infantry arrived to support them, but it was too late. The rebel army swarmed over them.

The Yankees poured through Gettysburg in retreat, surging toward the hills beyond town. In the confusion of streets and alleys the fleeing Yankees and the pursuing rebels got all tangled up. It quickly became a giant brawl of ten thousand men. Yankees dove over fences, hid in cellars and pigsties, sprinted down alleys and sidewalks. In the chaos many lost their direction completely and ran around in circles. The Yankees fled into houses, hiding under beds and in kitchen pantries. The rebels started at one end of town and broke into each house looking for them. Companies of blue got separated and then later would run by each other in the same alley. The ragged rebels hunted them down and picked them off in dead-end streets and backyards as if Gettysburg were a carnival shooting gallery. From the hills beyond, where the main Yankee army had dug in, the streets of Gettysburg looked like a lunatic asylum.

Jonas led his cavalry through the back streets of town and safely to the Union lines beyond. Then he rode for home. All he could think about was Mary alone in their house at the edge of town. He knew that the rebs would have to stream by his house to strike the Union lines.

When Jonas rode into his driveway, he could see the rebs already coming over the hill from town. As he came in the back door, Mary flew into his arms. He crushed her against him for a long moment, losing himself in her softness and her warmth. He could feel her strong heart pounding against his chest.

He pushed her away from him by the shoulders. "Are you all right?" She nodded, smiling bravely. "Mary, when I'm gone, lock the doors and go down to the cellar. Bolt the cellar door. Take some food and water. Stay there till you're sure it's safe." Mary nodded. "Promise me!"

They could hear the reb soldiers out on the road. Her eyes filled with tears. "Go now," she said. "Before it's too late."

He didn't want to leave her. "I won't be far away. Don't cry." He felt helpless, torn between his duty and the dread he felt in leaving her alone.

She reached up and held his face in her hands. "I love you. Lord, I love you," she whispered.

Jonas touched her hair. "You're the best thing that ever happened to me." For one long moment they looked at each other. He kissed her gently on one cheek, and then she urged him toward the door.

Mary watched as he leaped to the saddle, his Spencer in his right hand. She locked both doors and, grabbing a few things to eat, went through the closet and down to the cellar. She heard the rebs shooting at Jonas, the bullets smashing into the house. She flinched each time they fired, listening anxiously for a cry from Jonas.

When he reached the end of the driveway, Jonas

plunged into a company of rebels, who turned in surprise and fired on him wildly. The road back to the
Union lines was blocked off. He turned and raced back
down the driveway and through the fields toward the
edge of town, leaping the rail fences in his way.

Ahead of him he could see the Yankees boiling out
of town on the only road still open. Wagons, cannon,
and horses lay sprawled all up and down the streets.
Jonas rode among them, organizing the men as best he
could and directing them to the cemetery on the hill
beyond town. For the first time since they had entered
the other side of town, these Yanks knew where they
were going.

He sent them off at a run down the road toward their
lines, staying behind to cover their retreat. Hundreds of
Yankees streamed past Jonas for safety. Suddenly a reb
unit emerged from a side street and opened fire on him.
His horse was killed instantly, dropping beneath him
like a sandbag. He lept from the saddle as the horse
fell, cocking his Spencer as he whirled. He fired three
times in a continuous roar and three rebs fell. Firing as
he ran, Jonas drew four more reb soldiers away from
the retreating blue army by racing back into town and
darting down the first alley. The four rebels chased
after him with a whoop. For them shooting these hightailing Yankees was just like a squirrel hunt. Rounding
a corner in the alley, he found himself facing a high
fence. It was a dead end.

The four rebels came scampering around the corner
and stopped in their tracks. Jonas stood facing them,
his back to the wall. He had his Spencer in one hand
and his pistol in the other. They stood face to face, siz-
ing each other up.

"What do we got here," the rebel sergeant said. This bluebelly wasn't like the others they had chased down; he wasn't pleading to surrender or trying to scramble over the fence. This Yank was deadly with that rifle. They had all seen that. But he had already fired it four times, and there wasn't any time to load it again.

"I'll be wantin' that peashooter, Yank," said the burly Irish reb standing next to the sergeant. He eyed the repeating rifle greedily. The Irishman figured one of them might get hit, but this Yank was a dead man. He grinned at Jonas.

The third reb was just a boy of fifteen. The gun he carried was longer than he was. He stood near the sergeant, not knowing what to do. To him this didn't seem to have much to do with soldiering.

The fourth reb, a small lean man, well poised and handsome, was a marksman. He recognized the Spencer and he knew it still held four shells. He also knew that Jonas was no ordinary soldier. He moved off to one side. He wanted lots of space between him and the others. He waited for one of the other rebs to move first.

Jonas stood and watched them impassively. He noticed the shooter immediately. Jonas smiled to himself slightly as the reb shooter stepped to the side slightly. It was the right move. Jonas knew that the shooter would not fire first, but would shoot best. He turned his shoulder slightly to the shooter, giving the reb less of a target.

He watched the eyes of the sergeant. These infantrymen would wait for their sergeant to make the first move and Jonas would see it in his eyes. The sergeant and the Irishman were old pros. They would stand their ground when the shooting started. And they would go down hard.

Jonas hoped the kid would not move at all.

"Now!" The sergeant and the Irishman jerked at the same instant, quickly raising their rifles.

Jonas saw the sergeant blink before he spoke, and he fired both of his weapons at once. The slug from the Spencer hit the sergeant between the eyes before he had his rifle to his shoulder. With his arms flying above his head, he fell straight back into the dust.

The slug from Jonas's pistol hit the Irishman square in the chest just as he fired. His minié ball went wild, missing Jonas and smacking into the wooden stock of his Spencer, splintering the end of it. The Irishman was knocked backward, but almost immediately he charged Jonas, his rifle in his hand.

The shooter aimed perfectly and fired at Jonas's heart. But the impact from the Spencer being hit had spun Jonas even more to the side and the reb shooter's bullet tore into his shoulder. As Jonas fell, he fired the pistol again, hitting the shooter in the belly.

The Irishman came bellowing at Jonas with his rifle raised high over his head like a club. Jonas shot him with the pistol, hitting him again in the chest. Still he came on. In the split second it took the Irishman to swing the rifle down to crush Jonas's head, Jonas cocked his pistol and shot him carefully in the mouth. The Irishman, moving with the force of his swinging club, fell dead on Jonas.

Jonas pushed the huge man off him and staggered to his feet. He slammed another shell into the Spencer. The shooter was lying on the ground, still alive, but mortally wounded.

The kid had frozen, his rifle leveled at Jonas but not raised to his shoulder. The roar of the gunfire in the alley had been deafening. Jonas walked slowly toward the kid. "You don't have to do it, soldier," Jonas said. "Ain't no one gonna care."

The kid's face reflected a tormented mix of fear and duty. He looked as though he was going to cry. Suddenly he raised his gun to his shoulder to fire. Jonas was only fifteen feet away. "Don't," Jonas said. Then he shot the boy in the head.

Jonas looked over at the shooter. The reb was trying to die quietly. They looked at each other, respectfully, both knowing that if the reb had had a Spencer Jonas would still be lying back at the fence. Jonas turned and walked away.

Jonas had gone ten feet when he heard the click of the hammer. Damn, he thought. I should have finished him. Jonas waited for the slug, wondering where it would hit him, knowing the shooter would make it clean. In that instant he thought of Mary.

The reb held the pistol steady on his knee. He had always carried a pistol in his boot; he had needed it before. The reb hesitated a moment, and then another. Finally, with a grim half-smile, he lowered the gun. The shooter knew he was going to die, and they don't give medals in hell. He looked around at the others. The Yank had done well.

Jonas got tired of waiting and started to turn. At that instant the pistol fired. Jonas flinched at the sound. I'm still alive, he thought. When he turned around, the reb still had the pistol to his temple. But the top of his skull was blown away.

Working his way carefully along the alley, moving in the shadows, Jonas made it out of town and up to the safety of the hills.

* * *

From the dark cellar Mary listened fearfully as someone struggled with the doorknob. The door rattled and shook on its hinges as someone pounded on it. Then there was silence. Mary sighed in relief. Suddenly she heard the crash of a rifle butt on the door and a splintering sound as it gave way. She shrank back in fear.

She heard footsteps above her, as someone staggered across the floor. She crossed the cellar, staring upward, following the sound of the heavy footsteps. With a crash of furniture a body fell on the floor above her. There was silence. And then she heard him moaning.

"Help me. Somebody, help me."

Standing directly below the man's body, Mary heard his moaning strongly. She put her hands to her ears.

"Please. Help me." His voice drifted down into the cellar.

Mary hesitated. And then she quietly walked up the stairs. Lifting the latch silently, she opened the door a crack and peeked in.

A reb soldier was lying on the kitchen floor. He was shot in the head, the blood flowing all over his face. Mary stared at him in horror, not knowing what to do.

She opened the door a little more, and it squeaked. He looked over at her with blank eyes. "Water— please."

Throwing the door open, she rushed to the sink, pumping water into a glass. Kneeling at his side, she put the glass to his lips. He drank it greedily. Gently she turned his head toward her and wiped his face with her skirt.

Mary saw that part of his face had been blown away and had to fight to control her urge to turn from him, fearing he would see her revulsion. Then he reached out for her hand, his blank eyes staring up at her. Mary saw that he was blind.

"Your hands . . . are gentle. A woman's hand."

He looked like any young man from anywhere, she thought. A boy really. There was nothing special about him—except that he was dying in her lap, on her kitchen floor. Somewhere back home his mother worried for him, his girl friend missed him. They waited for him to come home.

He was bleeding heavily. She started to get up to bring a towel, but he clung to her hand. "Let me . . . hold it." She held his hand tightly. "I can't see a thing," he said softly. "I can't see a thing." His blind eyes were crying. "I wish I could see you . . ."

His head fell slowly forward, and then he was still. She sat with him for a long time holding his hand. The blood stopped flowing from his wound and his hand began to lose its warmth. She could still hear sporadic firing outside. How can they still be fighting? she thought.

Finally, after letting him down gently, she stood up. She thought of Jonas and worried for him out there. And then, for a moment, the firing stopped, and everything was very quiet. The sun slanted in through the windows onto the kitchen floor.

The musket ball crashed through the door, blasting loose wood splinters that gleamed momentarily in the sun's rays, tracing the line of the bullet.

The bullet hit Mary in her left breast, exploding softly under her heart, knocking her to the floor. As she fell, Mary grabbed for the table, and as she pulled it down with her, John's small painting of Jonas slid from the table onto the floor. She saw his face near hers. She reached out and curled herself around it as if to hold on to him longer.

"Jonas . . . oh, Jonas . . ." She was still looking toward the painting of Jonas when they found her body.

July 4, 1863

The church bells rang out joyfully in celebration of the great Union victory at Gettysburg. The battle had lasted three days, but its outcome had really been determined in the first hours. Jonas and the cavalry with their Spencers had held the rebels long enough for the Yankees to take the hills above town. General Lee sent wave after wave of reb soldiers up those hills, but the Yankees repeatedly beat them back. On the third day Lee sent General Pickett and fifteen thousand men up a long sloping field to hit the center of the Yankee line. They were butchered. Only half came back. The flower of the South was killed at Pickett's charge. It was the last sunny day for the Confederacy, for its back was now broken. The time of gallant men and of the romance and pageantry of war was over. Only killing mattered now. The rebel army turned and limped for home.

The church bells rang out over the valley and across the fields. More than fifty thousand men were dead, maimed, or missing. Many still lay in the fields, their bodies black and bloated in the sun.

Jonas rode through them as he headed home. He followed behind an ambulance laden with wounded men, piled inside as though in a meat wagon.

The battlefield was a vast junkyard of smashed machines. The barrel of a blasted cannon pointed at the sky. Thousands of dead horses lay scattered around the field. Souvenir hunters moved over the bodies like vultures. And then the rain started, slowly washing the blood off the grass.

The townspeople of Gettysburg lined the street and cheered as the exhausted Yankee infantry marched in from the fields. The drizzling rain streaked their faces, blackened from the gunpowder and smoke; their shoulders sagged—they did not look like a victorious army. But they were. Under direct attack they had defended their own soil as ferociously as the Southern men had defended theirs in the last two years.

Jonas rode past the infantry column. He was numb and weary from the killing. His bandaged shoulder throbbed constantly and he was flushed with fever. A girl ran out of the crowd and threw a bouquet of flowers up to him. He held them, looking at them as though he had forgotten that flowers existed.

Riding up his driveway, Jonas felt a chill of fear. He instantly sensed that something was wrong. Jumping off the horse he ran to the back door. The first thing he saw was the bullet hole in the door. He burst into the house, staring wild-eyed at Evelyn and Jacob, sitting at the kitchen table. Evelyn was crying. Jacob's face was drained of all color. He looked up at Jonas with empty eyes, not knowing what to say.

Jonas didn't need to hear anything. He knew already. He dashed through the kitchen and into the parlor. He stopped still at the door. Mary was lying in an open coffin, clothed in her wedding dress. The bloodstain was still on her left breast from their wedding night, when she had cut her finger in the storm. The miniature paintings of Jonas and Mary rested on the edge of the coffin.

He walked slowly across the room and stood at her side. His grief was terrible. He wanted to cry, but he could not. He only felt the black thing that had always existed inside of him begin to rise. It spread across his guts and into his heart and blood. Everything was suddenly very simple.

He lifted the painting of Mary from the coffin and put it in his pocket. Placing his hand on the edge of the coffin, he leaned over and kissed her cold cheek. And then he whispered in her ear.

"I will join you soon."

CHAPTER SEVENTEEN

Vicksburg—July 1, 1863

"Please! No! Oh, God! They're dead. We're all dead . . ." In the grip of another nightmare, pale and sweaty, John mumbled in his sleep. It was late in the afternoon, and he was alone in the tent. He had not slept well in the months since Antietam and he had been glad when *Harper's Weekly* sent him to Vicksburg, for he wanted to escape the memory of the carnage he had seen. On a sunny afternoon in September he had walked through the cornfields near Antietam Creek, where twenty-five thousand men lay dead and wounded. He wanted to get the smell of thousands upon thousands of rotting bodies out of his mind. But he could not forget. He could not simply go blank and numb as the others could. He had realized on that sunny day in September that in this war there would be no mercy. And the nightmares came every night.

Captain Harrison entered the dim tent. The air was stifling. Standing over his bed, the captain watched as John cried out in his dreams, whimpering like a lost child, gasping for breath as if stricken with asthma. The captain picked up the drawings John had been working on. Several were of the Yankee gunners at Vicksburg and of the men in the trenches. But one was different, and he recognized it immediately. No one who had been at Antietam could forget the cornfield and the torn, broken bodies of the men who fell.

Captain Harrison held the drawing up higher to catch the light. There was something else in the drawing, something that John had added. There were faint outlines of ghostly forms and faces floating above the dead—angels with lovely smiles, grotesque beings with tortured expressions. His drawings were beginning to change. The precision and richness of detail, the beauty and sensitivity of the people were gone. These drawings were the work of a man standing on the edge.

Captain Harrison sat on his bunk and watched John tossing back and forth. They had known each other for only the few weeks John had been in Vicksburg. The captain was a devout Christian, finding Jesus on the same battlefields where John had lost Him. Nevertheless, they had become friends. He had seen John like this before, and he never knew what to do. If John were a soldier, Harrison would have ordered him home. But John was an artist, and he didn't even have a home. So Captain Harrison did the only thing he could do—he prayed.

Suddenly, John sat straight up with a jolt, as if to cry out. He looked around, startled, breathing hard. Seeing that he was safe in his tent and not alone, John smiled sheepishly as he tried to regain his composure.

"Hi, John," the captain said. "You look awful."

"Thanks."

"How about a drink?" Captain Harrison didn't drink whiskey, but he poured John a glass from John's bottle.

John rubbed the sweat off his face. "Good idea."

On the crate next to his cot was a package of John's best drawings, wrapped with brown paper and addressed to *Harper's Weekly.* Forcing his mind to wipe away the dreams, he began to tie some string around the package. Then he took the roll of bills that Matt had given him, smoothed them out, and tucked them into the envelope he was sending his folks. He had tried to write a letter to go with the money, but he couldn't find the words to say he was sorry. He didn't even know if they would read his letters. He stuffed most of his own money into the envelope and sealed it.

He turned to Captain Harrison. "Fred, I've got some mail. Can you put 'em in General Grant's pouch?"

"Sure can."

John got up and tossed the mail on Harrison's cot. "Kinda spruced up, aren't you?"

"Just came from a staff meeting. The news is good." He handed John his drink. "Grant just got word that as of yesterday the rebs were cut to quarter rations. And that will only last six days. Water's short and there are no drugs left at all. Thank God it'll be over soon."

"Where does Grant get the up-to-date information?"

"Our courier."

"Courier?" John asked, suddenly very interested.

"Lamar. He's a Vicksburg man. Courier, spy, smuggler—a little of each, I suppose. He runs back and forth on dark nights in a dory. Peddles us information. We pay him off in flour, drugs, sometimes whiskey."

John pulled on his jacket and checked his wallet for money. "Where is he now?"

"He's loading up at the supply tent."

John picked up his two satchels, threw some stuff into them, and headed out the door.

"Where are you going?"

"To make a deal with Lamar."

"John, the man is a scoundrel. Probably spies for both sides!"

John paused at the door and grinned. "Just the man I need."

With his oars greased and muffled, Lamar rowed soundlessly through the tall reeds near shore. They had crossed the wide Mississippi without being spotted by the ominous gunboats the Yankees used to patrol the river. They were lucky. The dim sliver of a moon cast almost no light on the sluggish brown water.

The front of the dory was filled with Lamar's cargo, mostly medicine and whiskey. John sat on the back seat, facing Lamar, never taking his eyes off the nervous little man. With his black greasy hair and tiny, mean black eyes, Lamar had the face of a cornered weasel. John knew that Lamar was a dangerous man, and he kept himself coiled inside, ready to leap into the muddy water if Lamar lunged at him.

Lamar sat hunched over the oars, his eyes darting along the shore and out into the river. It was an hour before dawn and he was running out of time. If he didn't make the wharf before sunrise, the gunboats would surely see him and blow him out of the water. He glanced quickly over at John. He was wasting too much time on this man. It would be a lot simpler just to stick him with his Bowie knife and take his money.

Lamar turned the dory toward the dark shoreline

and let the boat drift in while he rested the oars. He beckoned John toward him. John braced himself. Both men leaned forward so that their heads were close together. Lamar spoke in a low, guttural tone. "Git the other half of the money ready, mister. Ah'm pullin' into . . ."

With a thundering boom a gunboat only about one hundred yards ahead of them fired a shell. In the blackness they could see the glowing fuse of the mortar as it arced over the shoreline toward the wharf. The explosion lit up the night sky, and in the flash of white light John could see Lamar grimace in animal fear, his wet lips curling back. And then they were plunged into darkness again.

Lamar's voice came out of the night. "Ah'm pullin' inta the bayou. Gon' drop you off in a coupla minutes."

John nodded, watching him row into the narrow bayou. He adjusted the two satchels he had crisscrossed on his back. They were bulging with food.

The dory's prow hit the muddy bank with a jolt. "Go a quarter-mile yonder—ya gon' come to a road. Turn right. It'll take ya into town."

As John took a few bills out of his wallet, Lamar noticed that more bills were left. His hand reached for the bone handle of his knife. John started to hand him the money, but suddenly held it back.

"Why here?" John said suspiciously. "Where do you land?"

"The city wharf."

"The city wharf! What about the authorities?"

"Smugglin' food, I got no problems. Smugglin' a spy . . . that's another kettl'a fish."

"I'm not a . . . !"

With a lightning move Lamar snatched the money from John's hand.

"Mister, I don't give a damn what ya're, long as I get this!" The Bowie knife appeared in Lamar's hand, held low and ready. Lamar knew that this would have to be the moment. John sat steady and solid, showing no fear as the two men stared at each other. Lamar saw that it would not be easy—he had hesitated too long.

"Now git!" Lamar finally snarled. John stepped carefully out of the boat into the knee-deep water, watching Lamar's dory slip away into the reeds.

The streets of Vicksburg were strewn with bricks and rubble. Homeless, starving civilians wandered by, carrying their meager possessions on their backs. Their hollow eyes searched the streets constantly.

For them blind chance was the only reality. No one bothered to ponder why one house stood proud and stately while the one next door was a shell filled with rubble. Carrying his two satchels, worn and dirty, John blended in with all the other haunted people.

A reb cavalry officer rode by John, his horse picking its way around the rubble, halting in front of one of the few intact buildings on the block. Leaving his horse tied to a lamp, the officer limped into the house. When John got within a few hundred feet of the rebel command building, he heard the whine of an incoming shell. The people around him froze for a moment, listening to the dreadful sound. And then they all dove for cover in the same direction. John dove in the opposite direction, closer to the impact. The shell exploded in the middle of the street, blowing open a huge crater.

When John got up, he heard the horse screaming in

pain, his hind leg blown off. The animal struggled to get up on three legs but its hoofs kept slipping on the blood pumping out of its severed leg. The reb officer came out of the building, drew his pistol, and shot the horse in the head. It lay still. The officer limped back into the house.

Almost instantly, two wounded rebel soldiers appeared from nowhere. One had a filthy bandage wrapped around his head, covering one eye. The other soldier walked with a handmade crutch, his leg stiff, unable to bend at the knee. They took knives from their belts and plunged them into the still quivering horse.

John stood and stared at them. The street all around the horse looked like a slaughterhouse, as the two soldiers made off with an entire hind quarter.

John heard footsteps behind him. He turned to find a little old lady coming toward him as fast as her hooped skirt would allow. Unlike the rag-tag civilians he had passed on the street, this Southern lady seemed to be on a Sunday stroll, her lace parasol shading her from the morning sun. Her Sunday best dress looked unreal amid the rubble and carnage—ruffles at her throat, a silk bodice pinched in at the waist, a flaring skirt to her button-down shoes, and a flower-filled bonnet gracing her head.

John, who stood between her and the butchered horse, hoped she hadn't seen the gruesome sight. He stepped into her path. "Good morning, ma'am." John tipped his hat. Now that she was close to him, he could see that her outfit had been mended and patched many times. "Can I suggest you use the other side of the street?"

Mrs. Lovelace tried to peer around John. "What are you hiding, young man? Is that a dead horse?"

"Yes, ma'am. And it's not a sight for the eyes of a lady . . ."

Mrs. Lovelace whipped a butcher knife out of her embroidered bag and leveled it against John's stomach.

"Are you trying to do me out of my share?"

"No, ma'am, no! I just thought . . ."

"Step aside, young man!"

John immediately moved out of her way. This is the second time this morning, John thought. Do *all* these people have knives?

Mrs. Lovelace stooped over the carcass and shoved the knife into the side of the horse. Steam drifted off the hot blood. John continued on, tipping his hat as he passed her.

A little further down the block John passed a partially wrecked house, the front wall smashed and scattered on the street. Inside the living room the plaster and rubble had been cleared from the piano. An earnest little girl was seated at the piano, playing a lilting, soothing lullaby. As John stood and listened to her play, a parade of little kids walked by, all in a row, led by an old man in a uniform, his chest filled with medals.

None of the things he saw and heard fit together; none of them made sense. Maybe he was losing his mind, he thought to himself. Shells flying in at random, horses butchered almost before they hit the street, little old ladies with butcher knives in their dainty bags. Then John realized this was a city of sleepwalkers, like himself, living the same strange nightmare.

He heard the whine of an incoming shell, becoming a roar as it passed over. The children and the old man disappeared around the corner, but the little girl playing the piano didn't miss a note. She just kept right on playing her lullaby. John vaulted a low garden wall, diving headfirst into a tomato patch, squishing several ripe tomatoes. The shell burst on the roof of the house next door, smashing the chimney and showering John with bricks and tile.

He lay there for a while, not wanting to get up and go through the whole thing again. Suddenly, he felt a sharp pain in his side. It was Mrs. Lovelace prodding him with her parasol.

"On your feet, young man! You're not hit." John picked himself off the ground, spitting out dirt. He felt himself all over to be sure he was all right.

"Is it your wish to stay alive?" Mrs. Lovelace asked him. John nodded. "Then the next time you hear a shell coming at you, run toward the sound, not away from it! If it bursts directly overhead, stand still!"

"Yes, ma'am, I forgot. A little panicky, I guess." John lumbered over the garden wall. "Did you follow me?" he asked her nervously. The last thing he wanted was to appear out of the ordinary in Vicksburg.

"I came after you to apologize. It came on me all of a sudden. You were just being polite back there." John shrugged his shoulders. "I'm Mrs. Lovelace. Anything I can do for you, young man?"

"I'm looking for my sister. Newlet Street." She beckoned him to follow her, and they walked off together.

Newlet Street was the center of a very old and stately neighborhood with big fine homes. John had to smile to himself. Emma always did say she was going to marry the richest man she could find and live happily ever after.

"Newlet Street," Mrs. Lovelace said. "What number?"

"Eighteen."

The elegant homes they passed were scarred but intact. Mrs. Lovelace counted the house numbers as she went. "Ten . . . fourteen. Eighteen must have been there."

John felt a wave of icy fear in his stomach. The houses on both sides of eighteen were untouched. But eighteen was a shell, filled with rubble.

John walked through the space that was once Emma's front door and parlor. The fireplace and part of the chimney still stood in the living room. A grand flight of circular stairs led nowhere. John looked around him for some sign of Emma's fate. Almost at his feet, he saw a baby rattle. He sat down numbly on the stairs, clutching the toy.

Mrs. Lovelace had been watching him carefully. "What's your sister's name?"

"Emma. Married a Vicksburg man, Lester Bedell."

"I don't trust you yet, young man. What are you doing here? You just arrived in Vicksburg, didn't you?"

"Just before the siege," John mumbled. He was a lousy liar.

"Piffle. You must've arrived yesterday or this morning. You don't know how to dodge a shell. Can't even find your sister's house. You're new here, all right." She drifted off into her imagined scenario. "You must've floated in on a log—others have done it. Let's see— you ran the blockade, toting that pack of food . . ."

"Who said it was food?" John said, startled.

"Nose like a beagle. Starve awhile and you can sniff food a mile away. So you ran the blockade, bearing food for your sister and her baby. Leastways, that's how *I* see it."

John smiled and shook his head helplessly. This little old lady had him cold.

"Young man, do I have your word as a Southerner that you are not a spy?"

"Mrs. Lovelace, I am not a spy."

"Just as well—you couldn't fool a dead mule. Of *course* I know Emma! I know everyone around here!"

"You *know* her?" John said hopefully. "You mean she's alive?"

Mrs. Lovelace nodded. "She's living in the caves."

When John looked out over the edge of the limestone cliffs, down to the Mississippi River below, he saw no caves. But when he began the steep descent down the zigzag paths toward the river, he began to pass them. They were dark gaping holes in the raw earth, the mouths of the caves supported by rough-hewn timbers. The cliff was dotted with them.

A woman and her children were moving around just outside one of them. It was lunchtime, and the Yankees had ceased firing for their midday rest. When the woman saw John coming by, she rushed out to him. Like her pale children, she was gaunt and pinched with hunger. Her hollow eyes pleaded with John. "Do you have any food? We're desperate. I'll pay you whatever you ask." She paused, summoning her courage. "I'll *do* anything you ask."

"I have a little," John said softly. "But it's for my sister and her baby. I'm sorry."

The woman sagged and slowly turned away.

"Do you know her—Emma Bedell?" The woman pointed just down the path.

John peered inside the next dark cave, unable to see beyond the daylight's penetration. "Emma?"

A voice came out of the dark. "Who is it?"

The cave was about the same size as a small room, about eight feet wide and just over six feet high. The hole had been chopped out of the hillside, and the ceiling and walls were uneven and crumbling. The roof was supported every few feet by old timbers. As his eyes became accustomed to the darkness, John could see the dim glow of an oil lamp at the back of the cave. A few pieces of furniture had been salvaged from Newlet Street—a mattress, a table and chair, and a crib for the baby.

Emma appeared from the shadows at the back of the cave, stepping into the light. Her eyes were wild, blazing out from behind her matted tangled hair. Her hollow cheeks and pale gaunt body told John more than she could ever say. The dress she wore was a filthy rag, and she scratched herself spasmodically, no longer even aware of the lice.

Unable to even speak, John held out his arms to her. She jumped aside with a snarl. "Stay away from me!" John stepped back. "How did *you* get here, bluebelly?" Her eyes widened. "We haven't surrendered?"

"Not yet," John told her.

"Thank God for that!"

"How's Jesse?"

"Asleep."

"I heard about your husband."

"Lester? Lester's dead."

"I'm sorry, Emma." John was trying to make contact.

"You're *sorry!*" She was suddenly screaming at him. "You killed him!"

She raised her right hand, which had been concealed in the folds of her dress, and pointed a small revolver at John's chest. "Get out of here!"

"Emma, it's me. John."

"I know you, all right! You're the enemy! You killed Lester! You blew up my home! You forced me to live underground like a stinking animal! You're starving my baby to death!"

"Emma, put away the gun." He showed her the satchels. "I brought food."

"I won't take it!"

"There's milk for Jesse. Fresh, only two days old."

"He'll die before I give it to him!"

John looked at her wild eyes and then at her gun. She seemed crazy enough to use it. He spoke to her with a quiet, gentle voice. He wanted to reach her, to make her understand. "I'm not the enemy. I haven't fired a shot against the South."

"Or against the North either!" Her teeth were clenched. "Get out, traitor!"

"I'm going to see Jesse. You'll have to shoot me to stop me." He started to step around her, and she blocked him. He moved again and she cocked the gun. The click was very loud in the cave.

John never did find out if she would have shot him because at that moment the baby began to cry with hunger. Suddenly Emma seemed to snap out of her crazed trance. She put the revolver on the table and lifted the baby into her arms. John could see that Jesse was dying of starvation. The baby's bones were starting to break through the skin. His eyes were huge and sad in his tiny face. John slowly reached out his hand and tucked the rattle into the baby's arm. Jesse stopped crying a moment and looked at John.

"You've had your way," Emma said. "Now go."

John looked at her, and all of the terrible hurt and loneliness of the last three years was there in his eyes.

"I hoped we could help each other," he mumbled, almost to himself.

Emma, holding the baby to her protectively, stared at him with cold hatred. She had always been the most like their father, hard as a stone. John gave up. Putting the satchel of food on the table, he backed out of the cave into the glaring sunshine.

As he turned back to the path, he heard the loud whine of an incoming shell. They were right on time, he thought. But he didn't even stop walking. He knew from the sound that this one would hit somewhere else.

John sat on a rise across the road from the courthouse, sketching the entire scene. He had drawn the courthouse before from the viewpoint of the Yankee gunners. Now he was here in front of it. Mrs. Lovelace came bustling down the road toward him, distraught. She hurried past a line of civilians who stood silently by the road near John. When she recognized him her curiosity forced her to stop long enough to peer over his shoulder.

"I declare, young man, I'm glad to see there's *something* you're good at." John grinned. He was starting to like the old lady. "Did you find your sister?" John nodded without saying anything. She leaned toward him and whispered. "Have you heard the terrible rumor?"

"It's true, Mrs. Lovelace. Vicksburg has surrendered."

"No!"

"They've stopped the shelling."

"We'll never surrender!"

"Listen." John pointed off toward the approaching sound of drums.

"I just don't believe it!" Mrs. Lovelace hurried off in the direction of a marching column of soldiers.

John continued his drawing. Suddenly the cavalry of Yankees he had been expecting galloped by him, turning off the road to the courthouse. John knew that for months the Yankees had been looking with frustration at the reb flag flying proudly on top of the courthouse. Like the people of Vicksburg, it had defiantly refused to be crushed by Yankee shells.

John watched as they hauled down the rebel flag. Then the stars and stripes quickly rose to the top of the flagpole, and Vicksburg belonged to the Union again. John bent over and drew in the soldiers raising the red, white, and blue flag. He held the drawing up and compared it to the scene before him. In the drawing he had included the ragged line of civilians. They watched as the advance troops of Yankee soldiers marched into Vicksburg with colors flying and drums beating. To the sullen, proud, unbroken people of Vicksburg, the Yankee band played only hateful tunes.

And he had drawn Mrs. Lovelace, standing alone in the road. The fiesty old lady had endured the long siege without a whimper, and she had survived. But now her city had fallen, and she stood in the middle of the road with tears running down her face.

John closed his sketchbook and put it into his satchel. Walking in the opposite direction of the Yankee parade, he shuffled down the dusty road out of Vicksburg, heading east.

CHAPTER EIGHTEEN

Washington, D.C.—May 1864

"Jonas, I know how tired you are of this place. How was it you described us politicians—'always flapping their gums just to hear their tonsils rattle.' " Lincoln chuckled to himself. He was very tired of Washington himself. "Now that your shoulder's mended, why don't you head south and give Grant a hand. He'll need someone he can trust. And don't feel like you have to hurry back."

Lincoln paused a moment. "Tell me, Jonas. What do you make of our General Grant?"

Sitting quietly in the corner of Lincoln's office, Jonas had been able to watch the President. He could see the war's terrible effect etched into his face. It seemed to deepen every time he saw him. Lincoln looked very different from the strong man Jonas had first met in Illinois. There were large, dark pouches under his eyes. One eye tended to wander off to the side slightly as he

grew tired. His skin was pale and yellowish, his beard
scraggly and untrimmed, and his dusty clothes hung
loosely on him, flapping as he moved. It was as though
his face had become another battlefield of the war,
showing the burden on his mind and heart.

Jonas smiled slightly at the President's question. One
of Lincoln's few pleasures was to fish around for opin-
ions of other people. It was a hobby he had picked up
when he was a country lawyer sitting around the stove,
chewing the fat with his neighbors.

Jonas thought for a moment. "For three years we've
been marching down there to Richmond. Every time
Lee sends us back North with our tails between our
legs. But now we've got Unconditional Surrender
Grant. He ain't interested in Richmond. That's just real
estate. And politics. Taking Richmond would sound
real good in the newspaper. But not to Grant. Grant
wants to find Lee and *hit him*! Until something
breaks." Jonas puffed a little on the cigar some politician had given him. "I like him."

Lincoln smiled. "Jonas, you're a man after my
own heart."

He picked up a newspaper clipping from his desk. It
was one of the humorous pieces by Artemus Ward.
"Let me read you a bit of this. It's a story about the
Republican Nomination Committee, chosen to notify
'Old Abe Lincoln, the Gorilla.'

> "There stood Honest Old Abe in his shirt-sleeves,
> a pair of leather-home-made suspenders holding
> up a pair of home-made pantaloons. . . . 'Mr.
> Lincoln, sir, you've been nominated, sir, for the
> highest office, sir.' 'Oh, don't bother me,' said Hon-
> est Old Abe; 'I took a stint this mornin' to split

three million rails afore night, and I don't want to be pestered with no stuff about no Convention till I get my stint done.' "

Jonas and Lincoln laughed together. "I read that to those senators, and they didn't laugh. I think they disapprove of my laughing during such dark times." He paused a moment, lost in sadness. "If I did not laugh, my heart would break. I'd die."

Virginia—The Wilderness

Following a narrow footpath, John and Jonas rode slowly along the north bank of the Rapidan River. John rode ahead. The air was heavy with the sweet smell of honeysuckle blossoms. The fragrance reminded him of home, and he thought of the times when he would just lie in the tall grass by the creek and draw the blue herons.

Jonas rode behind, with his hat tilted down over his eyes, dozing. It had only been two days since his talk with President Lincoln. He had wasted no time in fleeing Washington.

The footpath led to the riverbank, where a crude raftlike ferry was tied. It was nothing more than a flat, square platform with logs as floats. The ferryman, a dour old man with gleaming eyes, sat on the end of the ferry. His eyes narrowed as he looked up at the two men on horseback. "You aimin' to cross?"

"We're makin' for the Germanna ford," John said.

"Three miles downstream. Whole Fed army's crossin' the river down there. Headin' south."

"Much obliged." John turned his horse.

"Wanna spend fifty cents? It'll save you a couple of hours."

John thought about it a moment, then nodded. He slid out of the saddle. "Hey, Jonas, wake up. Spring is here." Jonas looked down at John with vacant eyes.

With John and Jonas aboard the ferryman poled his raft across the river. John stared at the dark, gloomy shoreline. Dense tangled underbrush crowded the river's edge. Old dead trees stood black and barren in silhouette against the sky.

"Look at that shoreline up ahead. Christ, it makes your hair stand up on end," John said. Jonas stared impassively at the shore.

The ferryman had been watching John staring at the woods. "That be the Wilderness, mister. Worst soil in Virginia. A man can break his back tryin' to raise a crop. Nobody tries. Not anymore. Seventy square miles of it. Satan's country."

The ferry slid onto the bank in a small clearing the old man had hacked out of the woods. John and Jonas mounted their horses and rode off the ferry. "There's a path, if your eyes are good. You'll come out on the wagon trail," the old man said, leaning on his pole. He watched them ride out of sight into the dead trees, and slowly he shook his head.

Jonas spotted the narrow path, and they headed down it. All around them the land had been cleared of all timber long ago, and the second-growth brush clogged the land on all sides with thorny blackberry vines, dead scrub pine, saplings, and moldering stumps. The ground was low and swampy, pitted with black sluggish streams and endless stagnant pools of stained water. It was very still; not even the birds sang.

John shivered in the dank air. "Satan's country, he

said. It's like descending into hell." He looked over at Jonas, who had a strange grim smile. "You're mightly gloomy yourself, friend. I haven't heard more'n a grunt out of you in days." Jonas was silent. "Jonas, it's almost a year since Mary was killed." In reply Jonas pulled his hat down over his face.

As they penetrated deeper into the woods, they came to a clearing where the two narrow dirt roads that wound through the Wilderness crossed. On one corner was the long-deserted Wilderness Tavern. It had been shelled a year ago in the Battle of Chancellorsville, which had been fought in these woods. The roof had mostly fallen down into the crumbling stone frame. The yard was overgrown with tangled weeds and under-brush, as the dark woods sought to reclaim the space. Snakes slithered through the high weeds and into the tavern doorway, disappearing inside.

In the clearing across the way General Meade and General Grant had established their command head-quarters. Several officers sat around a table outside the main tent, among them Captain Harrison. When he saw John and Jonas dismounting, he leaped to his feet. "Hey, John!"

John had not seen Harrison since the day Vicksburg was taken and smiled broadly when he shook his hand. Harrison introduced everyone at the table as John and Jonas sat down. It was getting dark, and the lamps were turned up.

John turned to Jonas. "Jonas, you know Fred Harrison, of General Grant's staff."

"We've met," Harrison said, when Jonas said nothing. Jonas was feeling mean-spirited today, and he looked hard and cold. When someone shoved a bottle in front of him, he drank heavily. His dark mood was so intense that people near him eased away slightly.

"Is General Grant here?" Jonas asked Captain Harrison.

"He's camped back at the ford. I'm here as his liaison."

"Why'd he bring the whole damn army into this hellhole?"

Harrison was taken aback. The talk died down as the other officers around the table listened in. Jonas was known as a loner and a very tough character.

"It's a matter of overall strategy, Captain. We're out to win the war this summer. We're pressuring the rebs everywhere, from the Shenandoah to Mobile. General Sherman's in Georgia, starting down the slope. Butler's on the south bank of the James, threatening Richmond. And we"—Captain Harrison lifted his glass—"the grand old Army of the Potomac . . ." Everyone around the table joined in the toast. "Our job is to engage General Lee and the Army of Northern Virginia."

Jonas grunted. "Here in this mire?"

"Nobody starts a battle in a jungle like this, Captain. We're just marching through. Six miles further on its open territory. That's where we'll crush Lee!"

Jonas tossed down a stiff drink. John looked at him, worried. He had never seen his mood this ugly. These dark silent woods had affected Jonas, and John sensed that at this moment he was very dangerous.

Harrison went on. "Lee's running short of manpower. We have more of everything than he does."

"Except maybe brains," Jonas said darkly. Harrison, angry now, moved slowly back from the table. Jonas looked straight at Harrison. "And maybe except guts."

Just as Harrison stood up, John shouted, "Fred!"

Harrison didn't take his eyes off Jonas as he replied through clenched teeth, "I think Jonas is talking about the willingness to die."

There was a long, tense moment. John looked over at Jonas. He didn't have to say anything. Jonas knew that he was asking him to back off.

Jonas finished his drink. With a thin smile he stood up. "Good night, gentlemen."

Malachy, Jake, and the rest of O'Toole's outfit were breaking camp, getting ready for the day's work. Jake nudged a sleeping soldier with his foot. Other soldiers, stiff from the cold ground, pulled on their boots. They went about their duties thoughtfully. They all knew that today they would surely see the elephant.

Malachy was finishing his usual meal of salt pork and hardtack. He picked up the coffee from the campfire and poured himself a cup. Noticing a rookie sitting off by himself, he went over and poured him some hot coffee.

The rookie looked up at him gratefully. "Were you scared, Malachy? Your first time, I mean?"

"Yep."

"How'd you get over it?"

"They gave me a medal. By mistake. After that, I was more scared of running than I was of dying."

O'Toole passed by Malachy. "Forty rounds for every man, Corporal. We'll be knee deep in rebs when we get outta these haunted woods." O'Toole had lost good friends in these woods, at the battle of Chancellorsville.

The Yankee column formed in the wagon-rutted road. The day before, the Engineers had covered the low wet spots along the way with planks. O'Toole's company stood in front of the long line. A mounted officer raised his arm. "Companeeee . . . march!" With the Stars and Stripes unfurled, they marched into the heart of the ghoulish woods.

As the column plodded along, here and there a veteran would pause and, crouching on the ground or using the back of another man, he would write his name on a small piece of paper. Then he pinned the scrap of paper to his chest. If a man was killed, he wanted the grave to be marked properly. They all hoped that later they would be gathered up by their families and buried back home. The idea of lying forever in this unholy ground was terrible to them.

They marched by a small clearing in the woods where an old farmer was turning over the poor sandy soil with a mule and plow. Here and there, scattered around the clearing, were skulls and bones from the soldiers who had fallen here last year. One half-buried skull still wore a moldering Yankee cap. The farmer was plowing the bones under, enriching the soil for the corn he would plant.

Only two hundred yards away, a reb cavalry officer unfurled the Confederate flag and held it high. Behind him the main body of Lee's army slowed slightly, taking their rifles off their shoulders. They were tense as they sensed the approach of the enemy.

Mark Geyser, John's oldest brother, double-checked his rifle as he marched, making sure it was loaded. A grizzled veteran of Lee's legendary Army of Northern Virginia, he was a skilled soldier now and a corporal in his company. He tried to keep his mind off the gloomy woods. Like his brother Matt, he now wore a full beard, but his had turned a little gray in the last two years. Things had not gone well for them since Matt had been sent to Vicksburg. He was glad Matt wasn't here in the Wilderness. This was a bad place for a fight.

A mounted reb officer pulled up next to him. "Mark Geyser!"

Mark looked up. Major Welles sat stiffly and solemn on his horse, his black preacher's coat worn over his gray uniform. Mark said nothing.

"God go with you today!" Welles said, and he rode on. Mark looked after him, and then shook his head.

Sergeant O'Toole stared down the road and saw a lone rider emerge from the tangled wilderness. It was Jonas. His horse reared up as he halted at the head of the Yankee column. "Rebs, coming down hard!"

Way down the road, coming around a bend, O'Toole saw them, peeling off to both sides of the road, disappearing into the underbrush. Mark and his company of rebs were moving swiftly and quietly into the dark woods.

Jonas rode off toward the rear as O'Toole deployed his men into the woods to form a skirmish line, while the rest of the Yank column dug in. The artillery set up in the road, completely unable to move into the brush.

When they were only a few yards from the road, Malachy and Jake could no longer see it. They groped blindly through the dense woods, hacking at the heavy growth and plunging ahead. All around them they saw spurts of flames from the reb rifles, but they couldn't see the enemy at all. They fired back at the flashes, hoping at least to hit something. The acrid smoke from the guns began to fill the woods, hovering in the low branches. The occasional rattle of skirmishers exchanging shots grew into a continuous roar of gunfire as the two blind armies flailed at each other.

* * *

Jonas galloped into the clearing at Regimental Headquarters, dismounting at General Meade's tent. He said
something hurriedly to Meade and together they walked
to a knoll in the clearing.

There sat General U. S. Grant on a stump, whittling.
As they approached, Jonas was struck by the fact that
Grant was dressed formally. It seemed odd because
Jonas had never seen Grant wear anything but a rumpled old private's uniform with his general's stars
tacked to his shoulder. Today Grant wore a frock coat
over his best uniform and a sash around his waist.
Wearing white cotton gloves, he idly whittled a branch
with his pocket knife, seemingly unaware of how incon-
gruous he looked.

Chomping a smoldering cigar, he looked up at the
approaching men, his beard flecked with ashes and
brown with tobacco stains. "Morning, Jonas. What's
the word?"

"General Griffin reports he's encountered strength, a
force as big as his own. What's more, the rebs are being
reinforced."

"You were there, Jonas. What's your opinion?"
Grant asked him.

"I think Griffin ran into Ewell's entire corps."

Grant turned to Meade. "Do you still think Lee's
fighting a rearguard action?"

Meade shook his head. "No, General. He's chosen to
fight here. I say let's throw the whole Army of the Potomac at him."

"I concur," Grant said simply. "Cancel the movement south."

Now that the strategic decision had been made, General Meade began making plans. "I'll order Hancock to double back on Plank Road. Jonas, tell Griffin I'm sending Sedgwick to bolster his right. And I better move Warren . . ." Meade turned to Grant. "Excuse me, General."

Grant nodded their dismissal. As Jonas and Meade walked away, planning the next moves, Grant picked up another stick. The soldiers marching by cheered him. They could see their general on the knoll, dressed in the clothes of victory, calmly whittling, and for the first time they felt like winners. No one could see how his knife cut savagely into the stick, nor could they detect the tension in his hands as the white gloves began to split at the seams.

O'Toole and Malachy tried to gather their company together, but it was impossible. They could see only a handful of their men. They called out to them, but no one could hear them above the deafening concussion of rifle fire. With the knot of men they had, Malachy and O'Toole crawled forward, keeping low and firing continually. They could hear the musket balls making a whirring sound as they whistled above their heads. Here and there around them men were felled by unseen enemies. All the trees were gradually being chopped down by the vicious rifle fire.

It was a nightmare of confusion. Each man could only see the soldier on either side of him, so no battle maneuvers were possible. Each soldier, blue and gray, had no choice but to seek out the invisible enemy.

Tiny slivers of bark and wood showered down on Malachy and his men from the splintering trees above. Then it began to happen. Small fires broke out in many places, caused by the firing and the exploding shells. Patches of tinder and underbrush burned all around the men. The dense smoke obscured the sun, causing a strange light, which fooled some into thinking the sun was going down.

As Jake and Malachy crawled through the underbrush, they came upon a wounded man who had already been caught by the spreading fire. Except for one arm, his entire body was charred beyond recognition. He had hoped in his last moments that, when he was found, they would know who it was that had died there. Unable to crawl, he had held one arm away from the flames. In his hand was a letter to his wife.

Other wounded men who could not crawl screamed for help. The tiny fires spread across the ground, the flames licking at their boots and their clothing. The smoke from the gunpowder and the burning woods mixed with the horrible stench of burned flesh, and the screams of dying men.

O'Toole and Malachy and their men came to the edge of a small clearing. As they crouched in the cover of the woods, loading their rifles, O'Toole peered across the clearing at the woods beyond.

He motioned to the men and spoke softly, "Fire one round." They fired a ragged volley across the clearing, then hit the ground and waited for an answer.

On the other side of the clearing, Mark and his company were advancing to the edge of the clearing. When O'Toole's squad fired their volley, they dove for cover, leveling their rifles at the Yanks.

"Hold your fire," Mark whispered. They waited silently.

O'Toole turned to Jake. "See anything over there?"
Jake shook his head. "Can't see nothing."

"All right, men. Move it." O'Toole led his squad into the clearing.

When they were ten yards out, Mark's company opened up. A minié ball hit O'Toole in the forehead, throwing him straight back. He was dead before he landed. Two more Yanks dropped lifeless to the ground.

Malachy, who was standing next to O'Toole, took a quick look at his dead sergeant and realized suddenly that he was now in charge. He raised his arm. "Back!"

The Yanks sprinted back to cover before the rebs could reload.

Jake crawled over on his belly. "Where's Sarge?"

Malachy was busy loading his rifle, trying not to think about it. "He caught one." Jake shook his head. He knew that O'Toole and Malachy had been close.

"They got us outnumbered, Malachy," the rookie shouted desperately. "We'd best skedaddle."

"Shut up, Harry. We stay put."

A shell exploded in the clearing, and the dry grass burst into flames. "That was one of ours, God dammit!" Jake yelled.

It occurred to Malachy that if their own shells were falling here, they must be very far forward. They probably were the foremost point of the whole Union line. He knew without being told that they had to hold this clearing.

With a loud whoosh another shell slammed into the clearing, hitting the base of an old dead tree. With a groan it slowly toppled in front of them. Immediately

Malachy waved the others forward, leading them to the fallen tree. Now they had good defensive cover to hold the rebs back.

The shelling had started fires on Mark's flank and he was rapidly losing his cover. He knew he had to take this clearing. Fanning his men out, he led them out of the woods in a sweep across the clearing.

Jake and Malachy peered out from the fallen tree. Smoke drifted across the open space, clinging to the ground. Out of the smoke came Mark's men, advancing slowly. Malachy smiled to himself. Now he would have his revenge for O'Toole. He would let them get very close, and then they would cut them down.

Malachy leaned over to his men and whispered, "Hold your . . ." At that moment the rookie fired, hitting nothing. Mark's men faded back into the smoke. The Yanks blindly fired a ragged volley into the smoke, but the moment was gone.

Malachy looked over at the rookie, who covered his face in shame. Malachy turned away, unable to say anything. He knew in his heart that as a rookie he himself had done worse.

The sun was almost down, and in the smoky darkness neither side could see anything. It was a standoff. The men on both sides just dropped where they were and slept.

Cries of "Water!" pierced the increasing darkness, punctuated by the gunshots of nervous soldiers, firing at anything that made a sound, sometimes even at their own stretcher bearers. Those who weren't blessed by sleep crouched in the gloomy night and listened to the screams of wounded men, trapped and alone, unable to move. These were the night sounds of hell.

* * *

At the far end of Regimental Headquarters John had pitched a lean-to tent. He stood outside, staring off into the Wilderness. The dead trees stood out black against the red glow that hovered over the burning woods. The roar of battle had died down, but he could hear sporadic rifle fire throughout the battlefield.

He paced nervously in front of the tent. I can't see a damn thing, he thought. How can I draw a battle I can't see? But it was more than that, for he couldn't shake the bad feeling he had about this awful place.

Jonas rode into the light of John's lantern and slid wearily off his saddle. He had been scouting for Grant since sunup, and he was worn out. He turned a keg on end and sat down.

"You eat yet?" John asked.

Jonas shook his head. John pointed at the salt pork and hardtack on the makeshift table just inside the tent. Jonas glanced at it, and then took out his flask. "This'll do me."

There was a long silence while he drank. John stared off into the gloomy woods. Jonas finally spoke. "Thousands of men in that hellfire. Lost men, huddled in pockets. Brigades facing every which way. Men afraid to move in the dark, 'cause the enemy's maybe just a few steps away."

He took another pull on his whiskey flask. "Smoke, hangin' low, stingin' your eyeballs. The smell of burning bodies . . ." He shook his head.

They looked at each other for a moment. John reached for his canteen and picked up his hat. Jonas finished the flask off and picked up his Spencer. As they mounted up, John spoke without looking at him. "Do you know where O'Toole's squad left the road?"

"I'll find it," Jonas said simply, as the two rode back into the darkness.

CHAPTER NINETEEN

The Wilderness

"Show blood!"

There was a barricade in the road at the edge of the Yankee lines. John and Jonas stopped and watched as a ragged procession of walking wounded passed through. Each man was challenged by a Yank lieutenant.

"Show blood!" he said to a soldier hobbling through the barricade. The wounded man opened his torn pant leg and showed the lieutenant his mangled calf. He was passed through.

"Show blood!" the lieutenant commanded of the next man in the road. In the light of the lantern the officer saw that the man's shirt was soaked from a wound in his chest. He passed the wounded man through. Only the maimed could retreat this battle. John and Jonas passed the line of wounded as they rode through the barricade toward the front lines.

A few hundred yards down the road, two Negro Yankee soldiers came toward them, driving a pair of

mules. Sam, a tall, powerfully built man, walked in
front. His partner, George, trudged behind. They had
been hauling ammunition for the battle under fire all
day, and they still weren't finished. Being Negro soldiers, they weren't allowed to carry guns, but they both
knew that it wouldn't be long. They had seen thousands
and thousands of dead white men in the last year of
hauling for the Yankee army. They knew that the Yankee army would soon figure out that a black man could
stop a bullet as well as a white man. And when they
figured that out, Sam and George would be handed rifles.

Jonas rode his horse in front of them and the black
men stopped. "I'm Captain Steele. I need those mules."

Sam's expression did not change. He would take orders, but he jumped for no man. "We got orders to
fetch mo' ammo."

George was more curious. "Wha' fo' you need 'em,
Cap'n?"

"To carry out wounded."

Sam's expression softened. "We heard 'em wounded,
down the road." He looked up at Jonas. "These mules
mighty ornery, Cap'n. They won't be no use less'n we
comes wid 'em."

"It's dangerous work," Jonas said.

Sam looked over at George, and they smiled slightly.
They had been shot at all day as they worked along the
front lines. Sam turned back to Jonas. "Mules don't pay
no mind to danger. They're too stupid."

Jonas grinned at Sam—he had two more good men.
They turned their mules and fell in behind John and
Jonas.

Further down the road they began to hear the pleading cries of wounded men. Suddenly Jonas halted.

"This is the place." Dismounting, they led their horses into the tangled brush followed by Sam and George and their mules.

They pulled their frightened and skittish animals deeper into the woods, weaving their way through the tangle toward the glow of a brushfire. With sparks drifting through the acrid smoke and the red-yellow glow of the flames, they seemed to have stumbled into the underworld.

Suddenly Jonas froze, pointing into the brush. Silhouetted against the glow were three reb soldiers, stalking single file among the trees. Jonas was content to let them pass by, but he kept his Spencer at his shoulder.

A wind-blown spark landed on one of the mules and he whinnied in pain. The silhouetted rebs turned at once, raising their guns. Jonas fired and pumped three times and the reb soldiers dropped. Not one of them had gotten off a shot.

The small band forged on, coming eventually to the ruins of a cabin, crumbling into the ground. The remaining half of a wall had been used by the Yankees as a barricade, but had been overrun by a rebel company. The dead and wounded of both sides were strewn around the floor of the cabin. It obviously had been a vicious hand-to-hand struggle.

Fire was creeping all around the yard, feeding on a foot-deep bed of dry pine needles. They saw a wounded Yankee soldier, his legs smashed and useless, trying to drag himself away from the flames, but the fire had spread faster than he could crawl. He cried out to them as they moved toward him, skirting the fire. But the flames licked at the leather cartridge case on his belt, and before they could reach him the cartridge case exploded, blowing out half his rib cage.

A wounded reb, his back propped against the cabin, saw them and cried out. "Help! Here!" A Yankee, lying on his side, the flames licking at his boots, called out, "Over here!"

George stayed with the four terrified animals as Jonas, John, and Sam darted around picking up wounded men. The wounded were flung over the mules, their smoldering boots and shirts stripped off. Jonas carried a reb on his shoulder, leaving his other hand free to carry his Spencer. Big Sam hauled two at a time, one wounded man under each arm. John carried out the last man from the cabin in his arms.

"The rest are dead." Jonas said. He turned to Sam. "There's a field hospital near the crossroads."

"We know the place," Sam said.

Jonas shook Sam's hand. "Thank you, men." John and George slapped each other on the back, and then George and Sam led the two mules off. Sam glanced back once, worried for the two white men.

John and Jonas blindfolded the horses to shield them from the smoke and fire and continued on. Ahead of them they heard the cries of wounded men. Suddenly there was a terrible scream, cut off by a dull thud. Then they heard the singing.

> "Glory, glory hallelujah,
>   Glory, glory hallelujah . . ."

Jonas stopped. "It's him," he murmured. I've been waiting for you, he thought. I knew you would be here, in this damned place. Jonas turned to John. "We'll split up. I'll try to catch up." He moved off at a trot before John could say anything.

John moved off toward the rebel lines, seeing the red glow of a fire at the edge of the clearing. A shell exploded ahead of him, the sparks showering down on him. His horse reared back in terror, but John held him by the neck, calming him as best he could.

Another shell landed near him and exploded with a deafening concussion. John's horse tore free and fled wildly into the woods.

Without a horse, he was of no use to the wounded. Looking around, he realized he'd lost his direction. He kept walking toward the clearing, stumbling over a charred body. He looked down in horror as he recognized the body of Sergeant O'Toole. A voice emerged from the smoky darkness. "You move, you're dead."

John froze. A bayonet appeared out of the night, followed by a blackened face. John couldn't make out what color the uniform had been, but now it was black with soot.

"John?" Malachy lowered his gun. "John! Well, I'll be danged. You finally joined up, did ya?" John lowered his arms. He slid exhausted behind the safety of the fallen tree, glad to be still alive.

Jonas tethered his horse and, pumping a shell into the Spencer, stalked silently forward. Out of the darkness he saw a huge white horse gleaming in the red glare of the flames. Its eyes were wild, rolling with terror. The saddle belonged to a reb officer. The scabbard for the saber was empty.

Then Jonas saw the corpse, impaled against the tree. It was a Yankee private, held to the tree in a grotesque standing position by his own bayonet. His cap had been placed at a jaunty angle. Jonas took the Yank's cap off. His eyes glazed over with fury as the black hatred inside him took over. The Yankee's head had been split in two, the same as before. I'm going to kill that butcher, Jonas thought. It'll be one hate-filled bastard against the other.

> "Mine eyes have seen the glory
> of the coming of the Lord . . ."

Jonas slipped into the underbrush. There was a long silence, and then a cry of terror from a wounded soldier. Jonas moved. Running through the woods toward a burnt-out hollow, he got a glimpse of Major Welles raising his sword over a wounded Yank soldier. He heard a cry, then the sickening crunch of the sword.

Jonas burst through the brush into the clearing. Welles was gone, leaving a decapitated soldier in the middle of a stagnant pool. A shadowy figure moved in the woods behind him.

At the edge of the burnt grass Jonas saw a reb soldier lying with his bloody cheek to the ground, one eye watching Jonas. With enormous effort, he motioned.

Jonas knelt at the dying man's side. "Some mad bastard . . . murderin' the wounded. Get him!" Suddenly the reb's eyes widened and Jonas knew Welles was behind him.

As he wheeled, he spun to the side, raising the Spencer. In the glare of the hellish red light, his eyes bulging, Welles towered above him. "You!"

Welles brought his flashing sword down on Jonas. The blade glanced off the Spencer and sliced into Jonas' arm, throwing him sideways.

Welles thrust at him, slashing across Jonas's ribs and plunging the blade into the charred ground. Jonas reached out with his good arm and grabbed the Spencer. Welles pulled the sword out of the ground and turned to finish Jonas off. With the rifle butt cradled in his useless left arm, Jonas leveled the Spencer at Welles.

Welles drew himself up to his full height, oblivious to the red sparks falling around him. "You can't kill me. I am the sword of God." Raising his sword, he came at Jonas.

Jonas fired, the bullet smacking into Welles's chest. He was jolted, but he still came on. Jonas fired again, this time hitting Welles full in the heart. He staggered and paused, but still he came on. Jonas emptied his Spencer into Welles's guts.

He pulled the trigger again, but the rifle just clicked. Welles raised his sword over Jonas for the final, lethal blow. Jonas looked up at the insane demon, knowing that he was about to die.

Suddenly a black arm slipped around Welles's neck. Another huge hand grasped the sword like a vise. Welles hissed and clawed viciously against the black man as Sam lifted the major bodily into the air, crushing the life out of him. Sam hurled him into the fire at the edge of the burnt-out hollow. The flames swirled around him. His long beard caught fire and illuminated his screaming face in a garish light.

Sam lifted Jonas over his shoulder, and without saying a word the powerful black man walked out of the inferno.

At dawn Mark's reb company ate their meager breakfast of hardtack. In the still dim light, filtered through the layers of smoke, they found that they had slept next to dead comrades who had fallen in the Yankee volley. They ate the wormy hardtack in sullen silence, their companions staring blankly at the sky.

After stationing pickets around his position, Mark finished the letter he was writing to his sweetheart, Sarah, the girl he had first kissed at Emma's wedding. He had matured as a man during the war, and he had come to realize that he loved this girl. He'd stopped and seen her this winter on leave and asked her to marry him. He was surprised when she said yes. She had grown up loving him too.

He wrote to tell her a premonition he had of his own death in this awful place. In his mind's eye he saw her, moving slowly through the flower garden back home, her blue calico dress blowing gently in the wind, her face beautiful and glowing with light.

> Oh, Sarah! If the dead can come back to this earth and float unseen around those they loved, I shall always be near you, in the gladdest days and in the gloomiest nights, witness to your happiest scenes and saddest nights, always, always.

He finished writing the letter and shoved it into his shirt pocket. He was ready now. He could hear scattered rifle fire throughout the broken woods as the battle began again.

The two small groups of men faced each other in the dark and the smoke across the large clearing. They had fired nervously at each other all night, feeling out each other's position. Mark knew he had to take this clearing if the reb line was to advance. Taking advantage of the thick cover of smoke, they could make it halfway across the clearing before the Yankees would see them. Mark knew that he had more men than they did, and he gambled that he had enough to run them over. The rebs steeled themselves for the charge.

Malachy, Jake, and their men took their positions behind the fallen tree. John stayed apart from them at one end, without a gun. They knew he would not fire on the rebels even to save his own life, and Malachy had placed him out of the line of fire.

With a rebel yell Mark led his men across the clearing. He held his felt hat high on his sword, so that his men could see him in the gathering smoke. They had gotten halfway across when the Yankees opened fire. The first volley took a ghastly toll.

Mark ran forward. Choking on the smoke, he turned to call his men on and found himself almost alone. A few men stumbled behind him, already hit, looking like sleepwalkers in ragged clothes.

At that moment John saw him. He screamed to Malachy to hold his fire, but they couldn't hear him in the firing. All the different loyalties and harsh words meant nothing in this moment. John knocked Malachy's gun down to keep him from firing and leaped over the fallen tree. Malachy, thinking John had gone crazy in the violence, held up his hand to stop the firing.

Frantically John ran toward Mark, stumbling to his hands and knees. He got up, calling Mark's name. Mark, seeing a man coming at him, leveled his gun to fire. Malachy saw the reb aiming at John and raised his rifle. Only a few yards apart, Mark saw John. His face lit up suddenly with surprise and joy.

A single shot exploded across the clearing, the musket ball crashing into Mark's chest. He fell into John's arms.

John cried to him as they embraced, "Mark! I'm sorry, Mark!"

Mark reached out to touch John's face. "John." He fought to breathe through his shattered lungs. "It's all right, John. There's a letter in my pocket. See that . . ." He choked on the blood filling his throat. "John, you tell them. Tell them to go home." His body slid down John's arm to the burnt ground.

John lifted his face and cried out. "Oh, God!" With each breath he screamed it. "Oh, God! Where are you?" He broke down and cried. "Where are you?"

The clearing was quiet now; the battle had moved on. John gently lifted the letter from Mark's shirt. It was open to the last page.

> And if there be a soft breeze upon your chest, it shall be my breath. As the cool air fans your throbbing temple, it shall be my spirit passing by. Sarah, do not mourn me dead, think I am gone and waiting, for we shall meet again.

John held his brother tightly in his arms and would not be consoled.

BOOK IV

CHAPTER TWENTY

Virginia—May 1864

The two Yankee cavalrymen hid among a stand of trees, watching the wagon coming toward them on the country road. The captain pulled his rifle from its saddle holster. The other soldier, wearing a long slicker over his civilian clothes and a wide-brimmed scout's hat, held his pistol drawn but out of sight in his slicker. Their faces were tense. Lost and in enemy territory, they were running out of time.

It was hot and dry, and the wagon kicked up a cloud of dust as it came abreast of the two men. With a shout the Yankees spurred their horses out of the woods and across the ditch onto the road, halting the wagon.

The captain leveled his rifle at the driver. "You know these parts, mister?"

John Geyser looked at them without expression. "Some."

"We're lookin' for Carpenter's Ford."

"The river's over the next hill. The ford's five miles upstream."

The two Yankees glanced at the coffin in the back of the wagon. It was draped with a Confederate flag. "Who's that?" the scout demanded.

John looked back at the coffin. "My brother," he said quietly. "We're goin' home."

The captain holstered his rifle and, nodding to the scout, they turned and galloped up the road. In the distance John could see a great cloud of smoke hanging over the horizon in the direction the men were headed. His eyes vacant, he whipped up the horses and rode on.

Matt was just finishing the chores when he heard the wagon coming over Geyser Hill and down toward the house. Walking with a rolling limp, favoring a stiff right leg, he was carrying two pails of water to the barn. He put down the pails and squinted into the sun. When he recognized his brother John, he knew what the wagon was hauling.

John pulled up by the barn next to Matt and jumped down from the seat. Not saying a word, the two men shook hands, both feeling a tangle of emotions. Matt reached over the side of the wagon bed and put his hand on the coffin. "We got your letter 'bout Mark a coupla days ago. I'm glad it was you that brought him."

John nodded. "It's good to see you, Matt." He motioned to Matt's leg. "Where'd you get the limp?"

"Caught one at Vicksburg, right after I saw you that time."

"That's a year back. It should be healed."

"She healed, all right," Matt said grimly. "An inch shorter'n the other. The war's over for me."

They walked to the porch as they talked. Just as they got near the house, Emma came out the door holding Jesse's hand. She stopped, smiling bitterly as she watched John approach. She waited until John was within earshot. "Pa! We have a visitor!"

"Who is it, Emma?"

"The traitor."

Ben came out the door behind her, his wooden leg knocking on the planks. The strain of the news of Mark and working the farm alone these years had taken its toll. John looked at his father with sadness. He seemed older than his years.

Ben's face hardened. The long moment of silent confrontation was broken by little Jesse. "Hi," Jesse said, eyeing John curiously.

"Hi, Jesse." John looked up again at his father. "How are you, Pa?"

"You turned your back on this house, on this land. You don't belong here."

"I won't stay long."

"Why did you hafta come at all!" Emma demanded.

"I brought Mark home."

Ben's eyes moved slowly from John to the wagon. His body sagged visibly, crushed by the awareness that his son was lying in a box across the yard. Emma jumped up and, steadying him, led him to a chair. Ben sat there, his eyes never leaving the wagon.

"I'll go see Ma," John murmured.

As he came up the steps and crossed the porch, his father spoke. "John." John paused. "Don't tell your ma about Mark. Not just yet. She's already worried sick."

John nodded slowly and stepped into the house for the first time in three and a half years.

Matt and Emma helped Ben as he walked out across the dusty yard to the wagon.

* * *

John sat on the bed beside Maggie, who was propped up by pillows. The curtains were drawn, allowing only a soft light to filter in through the windows. "Has the doc been here?" he asked her gently. She seemed shrunken since he'd seen her last, and more frail.

"I don't need him, now that you're here." Her eyes were shining. She couldn't stop looking at him. "Did you see your father?"

John nodded sadly.

"He's still bitter," she said. John looked away. "He had a hard time after you left. Folks got under his skin, askin' how come he raised a Yankee. You know how they talk. He's a proud man, John. It hurt him bad."

She reached out and John took her hand. There had always been so much love between them. "We haven't heard from Mark in weeks. His sweetheart, Sarah, came over the other day askin' for him. She's worried sick."

John had the letter that Mark wrote Sarah in his pocket.

"Mark will show up, one of these days," Maggie said hopefully.

John felt the knot tighten in the pit of his stomach. "Sure, Ma," he said.

Maggie sighed. "Will it last much longer?"

"It can't. Too many's been lost."

"I live for the day it's done. And Luke'll come back from that prison. And Mark'll come stridin' up the road. And we'll all be together again."

"That's how it'll be. You rest now."

Maggie watched John's face as he pulled the quilt up over her shoulders. "I heard the wagon in the yard," she said.

"I lost my horse at the Wilderness," John offered by

way of explanation. There was a long awful moment of silence.

"They told you not to tell me, didn't they?"

John couldn't look at her. His tears began to fall on her hand.

"What's in the wagon, son?"

John let out a long quivering breath. "They killed him."

She squeezed his hand to keep from crying out.

They sat like that for a long time. Finally John got up and leaned forward to kiss her.

They stood in the graveyard on top of Geyser Hill, overlooking the orchards and fields and woods beyond. John had often leaned against his grandmother's grave stone and drawn the scene spread out below. Now he stood beneath the tall swaying pine trees, waiting for his turn to dig his brother's grave.

Maggie stood by him, her arms folded in front of her, watching Ben working in the grave. He dug steadily and deliberately, his shirt off in the summer sun. His arms and neck were deeply tanned, but where his work shirt had covered his body, his skin was white. Maggie watched the muscles in his back as they moved beneath the skin. She knew he was tiring. With only a silent glance from his mother, John picked up his shovel and jumped into the hole. Putting his hand on his father's back, he said, "I'll finish it, Pa."

Ben stopped working and, with Matt's help, climbed out of the hole. He rested against his mother's tombstone. Maggie watched him, startled at how old and broken he suddenly seemed. She looked at the stone he leaned on—ANN GEYSER - WIFE OF JACK GEYSER - BORN 1780 - DIED 1856 - MAY SHE REST IN PEACE.

"I understand now why that quilt meant so much to Mother Geyser. She had her share of grief too. That quilt was her way of writing it all down, so she could remember. I saved Mark's gray tunic for my quilt. I want to remember everything about him."

She paused a moment. "I've been thinking about my sister. She lost one of her boys early on—young James. Now we've both given one up. That's enough."

Her face was drawn and exhausted. She'd cried all the tears she had inside. Emma, standing next to Maggie, put her arm around her mother's shoulder.

Storm clouds were gathering in the sky; lightning flashed silently in the distance. "I saw the lightning," Matt said. "But I can't hear the thunder."

When John had finished, they lowered the casket into the hole. A preacher from town said the last words. "Unto Almighty God we commend the soul of our brother Mark, and we commit his body to the ground. Earth to earth, ashes to ashes, dust to dust. In sure and certain hope of the Resurrection unto eternal life, through Our Lord Jesus Christ. Amen."

John tossed feverishly in his bed, his face sweaty and flushed. He mumbled incoherently in his sleep, as again he relived Mark's death, felt him fall into his arms, suddenly heavy and broken. Suddenly an ominous pounding intruded on his dreams and he woke to the sound of a rifle butt banging on the front door of the house.

John jumped out of bed and pulled aside the curtains, staring down at the yard below. It was almost dawn, and in the pink streaks of the day's first light he could see that the whole driveway was filled with reb cavalry. He pulled his pants on and ran downstairs as the pounding continued.

"Confederate cavalry! Open up!"

Ben, in a worn robe and carrying his shotgun, answered the door. Matt stood behind him, still putting on his shirt.

"My name is Lieutenant Hardy. This *is* Geyser Hill?"

"It is. I'm Ben Geyser. My son, Matthew."

"Who else in the house?"

"My wife, my daughter, my grandson."

"Who's that?" Hardy asked. John had just come up behind his father. Ben hesitated to answer.

"That's my brother," Matt said finally.

Hardy nodded. A veteran sergeant came up the porch steps. "Prepare to defend that wall, Sergeant. And find a safe place for the horses!"

"Sir!" The sergeant hustled back to his men.

Hardy turned back to Ben. "There's two regiments of Yank cavalry on the road to Louisa Court House. Our main force is movin' up to meet 'em. We figger a battle's gon' start most anytime now."

"That road's over a mile away," Ben said.

"It could spread this far 'fore it's over. My orders are to protect our right flank. That means holdin' this hill."

"I understand, Lieutenant. What can we do to help?"

"Get your family outta here."

Ben glanced at Matt, and Matt shook his head. "This is our land, Lieutenant," Ben said. "We aim to defend it."

"I reckon that's your privilege." He turned and barked an order. "Evans!"

A trooper, hurrying by, stopped in his tracks. "Sir?"

"Bring me three rifles, twenty rounds for each." The trooper dashed off. "At least get the women out, Mr. Geyser."

"The women stay!" Emma barked back, standing unseen behind the door. She had a robe on over her nightgown, her pistol in the pocket. The lieutenant looked at Emma. Her face was fiercely determined.

"I don't have time to argue, miss. Hide 'em in the cellar!" he ordered Ben, and turned to walk away. The trooper came up the porch stairs with three rifles and the ammunition. Hardy handed a rifle to Ben. "This'll do more good than the shotgun." He turned to Matt. "You done any soldiering?"

"Three years in the Army of Northern Virginia." Hardy handed Matt a rifle as one veteran would to another.

He held the third rifle out to John. John stood there, agonizing over the decision he finally had to make.

"You want this weapon?" Hardy snapped.

"I'm a correspondent . . . pledged not to bear arms against either . . ."

"Got no time for talk, mister! You want this rifle or don't you?"

"No," John finally said.

Hardy tossed the rifle back to the trooper and walked off the porch. Ben and Emma stared at John in disgust. Matt was stunned. "John! You won't fight! Not even now!" He was incredulous. "You won't defend your own *family!*"

"Get out of my sight!" Ben shouted at him. "Or God forgive me, I'll shoot you!"

John slowly turned and started into the house. "Take to the cellar, yellowbelly," Emma taunted.

All along the stone wall the line of reb cavalry crouched and waited nervously. Ben gripped his rifle, trying to get the feel of it. They could hear the constant roar of battle from Louisa Court House Road. Lieutenant Hardy trained his binoculars on the woods at the foot of the downhill slope, but could see nothing moving.

Matt had put on his patched-up reb uniform. He leaned against the solid stone wall and looked down the length of it as it encircled their fields and the yard around the house. He was proud of this wall. He and his brothers had spent years working on it, extending the work done by their father and his father before that. It had marked the boundaries of their home, made to last the Geysers for a hundred years. Now it was their shield from the enemy.

The cool dark cellar also had stone walls and was stocked with food. There were several boxes of carrots and parsnips stored in damp sand, apples individually wrapped in paper and packed in barrels, and jars of vegetables and cured meats lining the shelves. Maggie sat in a rocking chair, a heavy wool shawl over her shoulders. Near her, Jesse was asleep in his crib.

Emma stood at the foot of the stairs, listening. Her eyes had taken on a haunted look, for the cellar reminded her of the terrible closed-in feeling she had known in the cave. It even smelled the same, like a moldering grave. She shivered. With a glance toward her mother, as if to say I'm sorry, she darted up the stairs.

The wooden shutters had been closed over all the windows in the front of the house. John crouched in the corner of his darkened room. He felt as though he were being ripped apart by the torment of conflicting loyalties, as though he were losing his grip on sanity.

* * *

Lieutenant Hardy, crouched to the ground, moved down the line behind the stone wall. He stopped next to his sergeant and asked for a report. "Ain't seen nuthin', Lieutenant. But I feel 'em. I feel 'em down there in those woods."

Hardy looked down the slope at the tree line by the creek. "What are they waitin' for?"

Four Yankee cavalrymen, leading their horses, moved along the sunken wagon road behind the house. The Yank corporal knelt at the embankment and signaled them to stop. Two of the troopers joined him, handing the reins of their horses to a third Yank.

They peered at the farmhouse. "When the shootin' starts, we'll head for that back door," the corporal whispered. The two troopers pumped shells into their Spencers, now the standard-issue rifle for the cavalry.

"We gotta get in fast and set up. Soon as the rebs hear our shots behind 'em, they'll have to pull men out of the line. By that time our boys will have got up the slope and took the stone wall. Got it? When we're done, George, you set fire to the place on the way out. I don't want the rebs using it again. If anyone tries to stop you, kill 'em. Now check . . ."

He broke off. They could hear the deep Yankee yell as their infantry charged out of the woods up to the stone wall. The three Yanks sprinted to the back door.

John ran down the stairs and threw open the bolt to the front door. Yank minié balls crashed through the door, splintering the wood, flying past him through the house. He paid no attention to them. He walked out on the porch, looking toward the stone wall. The rebs along the stone wall fired steadily at the swarm of Yankees charging up the slope from the woods along the creek. John stood directly in the Yank line of fire, bullets smashing up the porch around him. His indifference was suicidal—he just didn't care.

Emma burst onto the porch, pulling the revolver from the pocket of her robe. John grabbed her around the waist as she reached the steps.

"Go back inside!" he growled.

"I'm takin' your place on the firin' line, coward!"

John wrestled the gun away from her and pushed her toward the door.

"Inside!" he commanded, but she just stood there in the doorway defiantly.

"Help!" Maggie screamed. Immediately John pushed Emma inside and darted through the door to the kitchen.

Maggie stood at the head of the cellar stairs, struggling in the grasp of the Yank corporal. She had heard the men above her when they entered the house and had come up from the cellar. The corporal now had his hand over her mouth, silencing her, but he was having trouble subduing her. She fought him with incredible strength.

As John rushed into the kitchen the corporal shouted to his men. "Brain her, will ya!" One of the Yank troopers raised his Spencer.

John snapped. His first shot hit the trooper in the temple, nearly tearing his head off at that close range. The second trooper whirled, swinging his rifle toward John. John's second shot entered his right eye, killing him instantly.

The Yank corporal pushed Maggie aside and reached for his revolver. Maggie grabbed his hand, holding it to the holster for the second it took John to pull off his third shot. John meant it to be another head shot, not trusting the knock-down power of the handgun, but he missed and caught the corporal in the throat. John watched him drop, clutching his neck, drowning in his own blood. When John was sure the Yankee wasn't going to get up, he turned to his sister.

"Emma!" She did not respond, but merely stood there in shock, horrified at the carnage she had witnessed, the kitchen floor slippery with blood. John grabbed her by the arm and shoved the gun into her hand. "Take care of Ma!"

He picked up the two Spencers and lunged out the front door.

Gunsmoke filled the air, hovering over the stone wall. The reb defenders had driven back the first wave of Yankees but had paid a terrible price. A dozen gray-clad men lay sprawled where they had fallen behind the wall. Since the wall protected everything but their heads, their wounds were mostly fatal. Ben and Matt quickly reloaded their rifles, preparing for the next attack.

"They're back!" Hardy yelled, putting down his binoculars and grabbing his gun.

Out of the smoke came a wave of Yank infantry, bayonets fixed, charging blindly up the hill, stepping over their comrades who had fallen in the first charge.

John dropped behind the wall between Matt and Ben. Matt fired and turned to load. "John!"

John threw him one of the Spencers. "How do you work this damn thing?" Matt asked with a slight smile.

For an answer John raised himself up and began to pump and fire. Ben looked at John in astonishment as Yankees fell before his gun. Then Matt joined him, and he and John stood shoulder to shoulder, without the protection of the wall, firing the savage Spencers.

The Stars and Stripes fell with its standard-bearer and the Yank charge wavered. All of John's pent-up anger and madness emerged now as primal, instinctive violence. The long agony was over. Things were suddenly clear.

John fired with blazing accuracy until the hammer clicked down on an empty chamber. He threw the Spencer at the Yankees and picked up a fallen reb's musket. Without thinking of the danger, he leaped over the wall.

Spontaneously the reb standard-bearer jumped over the wall after him, followed by the whole reb line.

"Over the wall!" Hardy screamed. "Charge!"

A Yankee bullet found the standard-bearer ten feet from the wall and he toppled forward. Matt climbed over the wall and picked up the flag, letting out a shrill rebel yell.

The screaming rebels hurtled down the slope toward the wavering Yankee line and the Yanks broke and ran. As they retreated down the slope, a backup line knelt and fired to provide cover. The Yanks were pros and gave ground reluctantly and then only at a great price.

Matt, bearing the flag, moving as fast as his bad leg would allow, caught up with John. Separated by their ideals yet bound by blood, they led the charge, running together strong and proud.

Looming out of the blue smoke, the Yank backup line fired their volley. Like a moment frozen in time, predestined and acted out, the two men ran straight into the rain of bullets.

Suddenly John ran alone. Matt, jolted many times, pitched forward. Hardy picked up the flag as the reb charge swept past Matt, driving the Yankees from the field of battle.

John looked back and saw that Matt was down. He ran back as fast as he could, kneeling at his brother's side just as Ben hobbled up. Matt was hunched over on his knees, his body torn apart. Bullets had ripped through him, coming out his back and his side.

Ben knelt by his son, not knowing how to touch him or how to hold him. He tried to look at Matt's wounds, but Matt shook his head slightly. He didn't want his Pa to look.

"Pa," Matt whispered softly. "We drove 'em off, Pa. We kicked 'em off our land."

"Matt . . ." John whispered hoarsely.

Matt reached a bloody hand out to John and John held it. "We did it, John—all of us, together."

Matt looked up at both of them. "I'm so glad to be home."

His body slumped gently against John. Ben began to weep. John looked up at his father. He had never seen him cry before.

"You were always the best one, Matt," John said simply. "You were the flower." But he did not cry. He had no tears left.

Maggie stood on the porch looking out at Matt lying in the field, her hand over her mouth. John picked his brother up in his arms and walked slowly through the field toward their mother.

CHAPTER TWENTY-ONE

Elmira, New York—Fall 1864

The prison camp squatted in a low swamp of marshes and rotting trees and was surrounded by a twelve-foot-high board fence. The outside of the fence was framed by a sentry walk on which armed guards patrolled the entire perimeter.

There were no trees in the camp—they had long ago been hacked down by the prisoners for firewood in their constant effort to keep warm. The ground was hard, packed down by the bare feet of thousands of men with nothing to do but walk in circles.

A little stream ran through the camp, but its water barely moved in the festering mire from the latrines placed along it. A putrid smell hovered over the whole camp, and flies and mosquitoes moved in clouds above the stream.

The long wooden barracks were laid in rows, monotonous and barren. And among them thousands of prisoners wandered aimlessly. Every hundred yards along the wall there was a raised guard box. In each one a sharpshooter stared intently at the prisoners, his rifle positioned to fire.

Luke Geyser stood near the fence along the back of the camp. His shoulders were hunched over, his curly blond hair was long and matted. His sparse blond beard and gaunt, weather-beaten face made him look older than his twenty-one years. The once gray uniform was now only a filthy rag, cut off at the knees and elbows where even the layers of patches had worn through. In front of him was a hand lettered sign—ANY MAN THAT TOUCHES THIS FENCE WILL BE SHOT DEAD.

Luke stared out through the wide cracks in the fence boards. He could see the river that rushed by the camp, and the fall leaves on the trees, burnt orange and flaming red, gently falling into the water. He saw the water sparkling in the late afternoon sun. His hollow, sunken eyes stared at the river, reflecting nothing, only watching.

He stood for a long time without moving, as he did every day. And he thought about how easy it would be to end the misery of this place. He had only to reach out his hand and touch the fence. He had seen others do it, when they knew that they weren't going to be able to stand it anymore. They just touched the fence and waited for the bullet that would take them away.

"Keep moving, folks! Just fifteen cents to see the captured rebs! Get your tickets here!"

Running along the outside of the prison fence was a dirt road. On the far side of the road was an observation tower, built by a local entrepreneur. Crude stairs led almost straight up to a platform thirty feet high, which was jammed with spectators. Below there was a long row of townspeople and tourists, waiting to climb the tower and watch the reb prisoners in the camp. A sign was posted to the base of the tower: SEE ELMIRA PRISON! ADMISSION 15¢. REFRESHMENTS SERVED!

The barker called out his spiel. "Keep moving, folks! Just fifteen cents to see the captured rebs! Get your tickets here!"

He competed with a vendor who moved through the crowd, a tray jutting out from his stomach. "Ginger cakes! Spruce beer! Lemonade!"

The sightseers climbed the stairs to the platform, eating and drinking, elbowing each other for a place at the rail overlooking the prison. One plump little girl, chomping on a ginger cake, pointed at Luke in his tattered uniform, and at the other rebel prisoners being mustered for their daily count.

"Look, Daddy. They're *funny!*"

A Yankee sergeant walked past the line of prisoners. Weakened by scurvy, dysentery, and starvation, they shivered in the chill fall air. Many were half naked, wearing only underwear or ragged pieces of their uniform. Lice ridden, their scratches infected, they were ghosts of the soldiers they once were.

"Anybody sick, report to the dispensary. Now!"

No one moved. They knew that men rarely returned from the dispensary, that the Yankee doctor openly boasted that he'd killed more rebs than any soldier at the front.

The sergeant smiled. "Glad to see you're all healthy! Dismissed!"

At the dismissal, a few men sank to the ground. Others drifted off, while a few helped their weak buddies back to the barracks.

The huge barracks room was mostly dark, with only an occasional window to let in light and air. There were double bunks along both walls, with dirty, lice-infested straw in each one.

Luke walked slowly into the barracks, leaning heavily on a cane, his slim shoulders bent over. Sick and weak, he made his way to his bunk, his swollen joints aching as he sat down.

Another prisoner hurried by, a wild-looking man with large darting eyes. His head twitched and jerked nervously. "Luke, how's the cane? Are you done yet?" He said it with a monotone quality, as if he had been asking the same question for a long time.

Luke picked up his cane and studied it. It was carved from a hardwood branch he had found when he first arrived at the camp. A little more than three feet long, it had a curving handle like the butt of a pistol, carefully carved to fit his hand. The cane was an intricately carved replica of the branch of a flowering fruit tree, like those he remembered from the orchard back home. Each blossom, all up and down the branch, was delicately shaped. In the spaces between the blossoms, Luke had carved the bare history of his life in the army.

He had carved his full name, his company and regiment, and, in bold letters, The Army of Northern Virginia. After that he had carved the date of his enlistment, June 21, 1861. The only thing he had yet to carve into his cane was the date he left the army. He knew that as long as he had the cane to carve, he would not surrender. He would still be a Confederate soldier.

"I was just thinking," Luke said quietly. "Today is

November first. It's been two years and four months, exactly."

He looked around the barracks. The men were lounging in their bunks. The more recent arrivals played endless games of cards, or wrote letters, not knowing yet that the letters were opened and read by prison guards and usually not delivered. This deception caused some of the worst suffering of all, for when the men got no replies, they felt that surely they had been forgotten. Most of the men in Luke's area were prison veterans, who merely lay on their bunks and stared up at the ceiling.

"I can feel myself fading away," Luke whispered. "I can feel it."

The frantic little man suddenly looked around the dim barracks. "Luke, you seen my wife? Damn that woman, she keeps runnin' off on me!"

Coming out of his own thoughts, Luke watched the other prisoner dart away, mumbling to himself. He could tell that the man would not last long now. He had seen many of the soldiers that had been imprisoned with him die off, one by one, usually the same way. When they gave up and went crazy, they didn't last long.

He turned the cane over and over, studying it carefully. Its workmanship was beautiful and he was proud of it. It was the sum total of two years and four months of his life. It had kept him sane. Now he hoped that it would be sent home to his folks when he was dead, to remember him by.

Luke took out his pocket knife and carefully carved the day's date on his cane: November 1, 1864. Now he was done.

* * *

The wind picked up and blew across the Geyser farmland and through the orchards, rustling the yellow leaves on the gnarled apple trees. John turned from his work and faced the crisp, clean wind. He could smell the smoke from the leaves they were burning at the edge of the orchard. He turned and loaded another bushel of apples onto the harvest wagon.

John and Ben were gathering in the apple crop, as Geysers had done every fall for as long as he or his father could remember. Helping with the farm work, John had become tanned and strong again, filling out his old shirts with hard muscle. The six months that John had been home had been a time of healing, both in his mind and his heart.

Since the Wilderness, he had stopped drawing. There were no more violently scrawled scenes of mangled corpses with hellish faces devouring the dead. Even the nightmares, his feverish visitations of dread, came less often now. He had made his choice. The only thing that mattered anymore was piecing his shattered family back together.

So he was not really surprised when, as he turned to load another bushel of apples, he saw the line rider coming up the road toward the house. Jonas still wore the uniform of a scout, with the broad hat and high boots. His blue pants with the strip of yellow along the pant legs were the only indication of what army he served. Then John saw his empty left sleeve, neatly pinned to his shoulder.

Jonas dismounted and walked up to John. With warm easy, smiles, they shook hands much as brothers would.

"I was wondering where the hell you were. How long you been hidin' out down here?"

John grinned. "I'm not hiding. With Matt dead, Pa needed me."

"You could have paid for a hired hand." Jonas was feeling John out.

"I suppose," John said with a shrug.

Ben came limping out of the orchard carrying a bushel of apples. He was changed in every way by the loss of his sons, Matt and Mark, and by the worry over Luke in prison. He seemed withered and defeated, preoccupied by his own sadness. He no longer carried himself with the same sureness and pride. He blamed himself for the loss of his sons.

"I'm Jonas Steele. Mary's husband."

Ben's reaction was guarded. Jonas was a Yankee, and the last time Yankees had come on his land he had killed as many as he could. But he knew that John trusted Jonas, and that was good enough. Ben held out his hand and they shook.

"I've heard much about you, Jonas. Mary was a fine woman. I'm sorry."

Jonas nodded. The three men walked up to the house together as they talked. "You got my letter?" John asked.

"I came as soon as I heard. How did they get word to you?"

"Luke's friends must have bribed a guard. Their letter said Luke was taken to the dispensary."

"He'll get no doctoring there," Ben said bitterly.

Jonas nodded in agreement.

"Jonas!" Maggie called out as they came up to the porch. "So good to meet you at last."

"Thank you, ma'am."

"Evelyn wrote and said the army had given you an important new job and made you a colonel."

"No, ma'am, major."

Maggie smiled at him, liking him right off. "Good for you!" She turned to John, her smile fading. "Emma's upstairs packing. It's in her head she can get Luke out somehow. John, she can't make that trip alone, and it wouldn't do any good if she did." She paused a moment, confused. "Would it?"

"It might," Jonas said simply. They looked at him in surprise. "I have something in mind. We need to do some plannin'."

Emma was bustling around her bedroom, throwing things into a pair of saddlebags. John looked in, entered, and gestured for Jonas to follow. Emma glanced at them. She and Jonas stared at each other. They were both scarred, wearing their hate and anger like badges.

"Don't try to interfere! I'm going! And it'll take more'n you and this Yankee to stop me!"

John tried to reason with her. "Emma, they never release a prisoner without an army order."

"I'll find a way!"

"We have a way," John said.

Emma paused in her frantic act of packing and stared at them. Jonas cleared his throat. "I have this new job in Washington. The title's too long to remember."

"He's chief investigator for the Joint Committee on the Conduct of the War," John said.

"What does that get us?" Emma demanded.

"Maybe it'll get us an order to release Luke," countered Jonas. "I think I can work it."

"When? Next year?"

"After I get to Washington, two, three days," Jonas said.

"Time enough for Luke to die. Days are important. Hours are important." She turned to John. "You expect me to put Luke's life in the hands of this bluebelly colonel?"

"Bluebelly major," Jonas said with a slight smile.

"I'm not gonna stay here and do nothing!"

"Nor am I," John said. "Emma, we go to Elmira while Jonas goes to Washington. Our job is to keep Luke alive till Jonas gets the order. We'll take food, medicine, blankets—we'll make a list."

Emma looked from one man to another, pondering their plan. "Are you willing to leave at dawn?"

John smiled. "Yep."

"That's it then," Jonas said, moving to the door.

Jonas and John paused in the hallway just down from Emma's room. Emma stood in her bedroom, her hands on her hips, listening.

"Snippy little thing, ain't she?" Jonas said, just loud enough to be heard. Emma slammed the door. "Pretty though," he continued with a grin, not loud enough to be heard.

Just inside the main gate of Elmira Prison stood a low guardhouse made of rough-cut, unpainted boards. Attached to the side of the building was a drab, bare anteroom. John sat in the anteroom, slumped on the bench that ran along one wall. Emma leaned against him, her head on his shoulder. This was their second day of waiting. The box they had brought for Luke, tied with string, sat on the bench next to John. They didn't know yet if Luke was still alive, and they were prepared for the worst.

In the middle of the room was a desk, presided over by a studious young corporal with tight, thin lips and thick wire-rimmed glasses. He seemed totally occupied by the paperwork on his desk, frowning occasionally at the two reb civilians slouching on his bench.

Captain Potts, the commander of the prison, came out of his office and placed some papers on the corporal's desk. John and Emma were instantly alert. John sized up the captain and nodded to Emma. She jumped up and intercepted him.

Potts was a chunky, self-important bureaucrat whose main objective was to keep everything running smoothly. His concern, in addition to his own career advancement—which he longed for mightily—rested entirely with the welfare of the prison, not the prisoners.

As Potts turned from the desk, Emma stepped into his way with an eager smile. "Captain Potts, I jes' know you're gonna spare me a few moments of your time."

"Not now, not now! I'm busy . . ." Potts noticed Emma's pretty face, and he looked her over. She was wearing a long dark wool coat with large deep pockets. Even with the frumpy winter coat on, he could see she was a very handsome woman. What he did not see was the pistol she carried in her coat pocket, leveled at his fat stomach.

"Please, Captain. I been waitin' all day, and all day yesterday."

"Who is this little lady, Corporal?"

"Emma Geyser, sir. Sister of a prisoner, Luke Geyser."

He took her arm in a fatherly way. "What can I do for you, Emma?"

"I was hoping and praying you would let Luke have

the stuff we brought him," she said sweetly. And if you don't, she thought, you fat-ass Yankee, I'm going to blow a hole in you and let the hot air out.

Potts pawed through the box, taking out blankets, a sweater, medicines, tins, and small boxes of food.

"Who're you?" Potts snapped at John, thinking Emma had brought her husband.

"The prisoner's brother, sir."

Potts seemed satisfied with the box. "I don't see any contraband, Corporal."

"No, sir," the corporal said, disappointed.

"Then why'd you keep the little lady waiting?"

"I was suspicious, sir. She's a reb from Virginia, and she tried to vamp me. I thought . . ."

"You can put this gear back in the box, Emma." He gave her a leering pat and walked back toward his office.

"See that the prisoner gets his package," he growled at the corporal.

"Yes, sir!"

The corporal slumped down at his desk. "Let me know when it's ready." With one hand on his forehead, he returned to shuffling papers.

Emma quickly repacked the box, leaving the sweater till last. She glanced back over her shoulder. "Just keep on messin' with those papers, you fish-eyed little toad," she said under her breath. She slipped her gun into the sweater and stuffed it into the box.

The corporal, while pretending to work, watched her out of the corner of his eye. He saw the gun and leaped over his desk and pounced on her, grabbing for the sweater. Emma, easily as strong as the corporal, struggled with him.

"Captain!" he cried out.

John, at the other end of the bench, looked up startled, and ran to help Emma. Potts came out of his office just as John was about to smash the corporal.

Suddenly the pistol fell out of the sweater and hit the floor with a loud clunk. All four of them froze, staring at the gun.

Potts pulled his revolver out of his holster and leveled it at John and Emma. "Corporal, fetch the prisoner. What's his name?"

"Luke Geyser," he said, panting.

"I want him here! Now!"

The corporal dashed out. Potts, now flushed with rage, never took his eyes off Emma and John. "You're both under arrest!"

Outside the guardhouse, a large black coach drawn by two horses skidded off the dirt road and stopped at the swinging wooden gate. The sentry at the entrance of the prison camp examined the papers that Jonas handed down from the driver's seat and then waved him through. Jonas drew up in front of the guardhouse and jumped down. Throwing off his dark winter coat and his wide-brimmed hat, he strode into the prison anteroom.

"Answer me!" Potts screamed at them. "Or you two reb spys will rot in this place with your brother! Who else was in on this escape plot?"

When Jonas entered he saw Potts standing over John and Emma with his pistol pointed at Emma's head. They all turned to look at Jonas, resplendent in his new major's uniform, looking tall, polished, and very formal. With the sleeve of his left arm affixed carefully to his new shoulder straps with a golden pin, his medals blazing against his breast, he looked as solid as if cut from granite.

Startled by the obvious complication, Jonas adjusted his plan slightly. Ignoring John and Emma totally, he strode confidently up to Captain Potts and handed him a document. "Good day to you, Captain. I'm Major Steele, Washington, D.C., Chief Investigator, Joint Committee. You have a reb prisoner here, my most important witness in a highly sensitive case. Here's the order for his release into my custody."

Potts barely glanced at the document. "Glad to oblige, Major. My corporal will be back in a moment."

Jonas glanced casually at Emma and John. "Who are these people? Why are you holding a gun on them?"

"They're rebs. Under arrest. The woman tried to smuggle a revolver into the prison!"

"She did?" Jonas walked over and glared down at Emma. "She must be a very headstrong woman." Emma's eyes narrowed. "Fortunately for us, she's stupid." She started to leap at Jonas, but John held her arm.

The side door opened and the corporal staggered backward into the anteroom, carrying Luke in his arms. Panting with exhaustion, his legs shaking under him, the corporal lurched toward the bench. Emma and John rushed to Luke's side.

Potts glared at the bespectacled corporal. "Just why are you carrying that filthy reb!"

"Only way I could bring him, sir. You said 'now'!"

Emma held Luke's face, her own reflecting both delight and despair. He was incredibly frail and gaunt, and they could see that he was sick and near death. His only sign of strength was in the way he clung to his carved cane.

Emma fought back her tears. "Luke! Luke, it's me, Emma!"

"Luke?" Jonas asked Potts. "This isn't Luke Geyser, by any chance?"

"That's who it is—the man she was smuggling the gun to."

Jonas seized Potts' hand, shaking it warmly. "Excellent work, Captain! Now I can prove conspiracy! You've made my case!"

Jonas, seeing that the corporal was about to deposit Luke on the bench, stopped him. "Corporal! Put that man in my coach!" The exhausted little corporal looked at Jonas with pleading eyes, then staggered toward the door.

"But, Major . . . !" Potts exclaimed.

"Look at the release order. He's the man I came for." Jonas turned back to the corporal, who was sinking to his knees. "You heard me—put him in the coach!" The corporal lunged out the door in a crouching position before anyone could change their minds again.

"I'm taking them, too," Jonas said, pointing at Emma and John.

"But, Major . . ." Potts objected.

"Potts! That order's signed by two generals and a senator!"

"It doesn't mention these two! How can I release them, I just arrested them!"

Jonas put his arm around Potts's shoulders, and said in a low and icy voice. "Captain. Do you want this cesspool of a prison investigated?"

"No . . . no!"

"Good. Into the coach, rebs!" Pulling his revolver from its holster, Jonas jabbed Emma in the ribs with it, marching them out to the coach. Emma winced and gritted her teeth.

Potts stood in the empty room and listened to the coach drive away. Then he sat down very slowly on the bench where Emma had been sitting. He sat there for a long time and tried to figure out just what had happened.

As they raced down the dirt road, inside the coach Luke opened his eyes weakly. Lying in Emma's arms, he could see through the windows of the coach. He saw the stand of trees pass by that he had watched for two years. I'm not dead, he thought. I'm free.

"Are you hungry?" John asked, digging into the boxes of food they'd brought for him.

When he spoke, his voice was so weak they had to bend down to hear him. "I'm so hungry, I could eat a rider off his horse and snap at the stirrups."

CHAPTER TWENTY-TWO

Appomattox Court House, Virginia—April 9, 1865

It was Palm Sunday. Alongside a dirt road on the out-skirts of the sleepy little village, John and Jonas sat on their horses and waited for General U.S. Grant. Several Yankee officers sat with them in grim silence. They had come because they had heard that the end was near, that the nightmare was finally over. They had come this far and they wanted to be there at the fin-ish.

Finally Grant came riding up from the Union lines and stopped in front of the men. They exchanged a sa-lute. He wore a rumpled blue private's tunic with his lieutenant general's stars carelessly tacked to the shoul-ders, his trousers and boots were mud-spattered, and the chewed stump of an unlit cigar hung from his mouth. He looked more like a lost mule-skinner than the commander of all Union armies.

"Is General Lee up there?" Grant asked.

One of the officers replied that he was. Grant looked

up the road toward Appomattox and nodded. "Very well, let's go up."

Grant and the Army of the Potomac had doggedly pursued Lee for more than a year, hitting him again and again, relentlessly grinding him down. Finally they had brought him to bay. Grant had maneuvered his army to a position in front of Lee's starving, exhausted men, and now they had nowhere to go. General Lee simply did not have enough men to break out, and of the soldiers he had left, about half had lost their weapons. Yet they stayed with the army, willing to fight until the end.

Scattered around the small village green of Appomattox Court House was a general store, a tavern, a courthouse, and a few houses. A large gray horse stood on the lawn of one house, owned by a man named McLean. McLean had once lived near a little stream called Bull Run, but when the war broke out and his farm had been overrun by battle, he had moved his family away from the war to this quiet little village. Now, four years later, the war had found him again. Only this time fate had decided that this was where it would end.

When Jonas and John pulled up to the McLean house with Grant and his officers, General Lee was standing just inside the doorway, his hands clasped behind him. Tall and handsome, with a closely cropped gray beard and gray eyes, he was dressed immaculately in his finest tailored uniform, complete with sash and embroidered belt. His sword was encased in a scabbard of leather and gold, and his boots had golden spurs.

As they mounted the porch, Grant shook Lee's hand, and then the odd pair stepped into the parlor of the house and sat down at separate tables. These two men,

two warriors, two completely different versions of the
American ideal, sat face to face, one victorious, the
other defeated, both proud.

Jonas stood at the end of the porch with the other
officers. John sat down in the shade of a tree and took
his sketchbook out of his worn satchel. Here he would
make his last sketch of the war. He would see it
through to the end.

When it was over, and Lee had signed the surrender,
he stepped out onto the porch. The Yankee officers
tipped their hats in respect to their long-fought enemy,
and Lee tipped his hat in reply. Lee's horse Traveler
was brought around, and the general stepped up to him.
A tuft of the horse's hair was caught under a strap. Lee
gently freed it, patted the horse's neck, and mounted
up.

Grant and his officers stepped out on the porch. Lee
paused in front of the steps. The two men looked at
each other for a moment, as if seeking in the other
man's eyes the hidden purpose to all the suffering that
had happened. There was a stillness all around them.

Finally Grant saluted him, and Lee, returning the sa-
lute, turned and rode away.

The Confederate flag, torn and splashed with blood,
snapped in the breeze. The reb army was stretched
along a ridge in a battle line, waiting for General Lee to
come back. They did not know if they would be fighting today or going home. Most of them were prepared
to die. They refused to believe that the long road they
had traveled would end here—in defeat.

From the high ground they saw Lee riding up the
slope toward them. The sun gleamed on his golden

sword and spurs, and for a moment his soldiers felt a thrill of hope. They would fight today after all. The men stood as he rode among them.

Lee looked out over his army of ragged men. They stood there, starving, gaunt, many without shoes or guns, their hopeful, sun-burned faces turned toward him. Faced with telling his men that they were beaten, for a moment his legendary courage wavered. He realized that the awful responsibility for these men and for the thousands who had already died for him was manifest in those before him. He had used them up.

They surged around him as he rode through. At first they tried to cheer him, but they broke into tears instead, for they could see the truth in his face. The press of men forced Traveler to a halt. Unable to speak, Lee looked at them with sad eyes brimming with tears.

One lean veteran spoke to him. "General, are we surrendered?"

Lee took off his hat. "Yes, my men. You are surrendered." Lee saw the dazed faces. Fighting back his own tears, he spoke gently to them. "Men, we have fought the war together. I have done for you all that it was in my power to do. All of you will be paroled and transported to your homes." He paused, his head bowed. "The odds against us were too great."

"We'll fight 'em yet, Marster Lee. Just say the word."

Lee shook his head. "I will not lead you to further fruitless slaughter. Good-bye, my men. Good-bye."

Lee rode through them. The awful truth that had hovered over them now pierced their hearts. These leather-tough veterans, who had endured everything asked of them for four terrible years, cried like children. They surged toward Lee, knowing that they would never see him again. They reached out to touch his horse, to touch his boots.

Finally Traveler was clear of the men and they stood in silence, watching General Lee as he rode away.

One young Yankee soldier, looking over at the ragged, starving men in gray huddled in front of him, ran from his ranks and up the slope to walk among them. He talked with them and shook their hands. They joked about how it appeared as if they would now live to see Easter. These men are just like me, he kept saying to himself. It seemed as though they had been fighting on the same side all this time together. He felt a bond to these men, like no other bond he would ever know.

An hour after Lee's surrender, Grant rode through the Virginia countryside back to his headquarters. In the distance he could hear the booming of artillery. He turned to the officer next to him. "That artillery. Is it our men celebrating?"

"Yes, sir. A messenger was sent through the army spreading the news." Grant frowned as he rode on.

"General, something has occurred to me." Grant turned to him. The officer worded his question as carefully as he could. "In view of your momentous accomplishment today, sir, I thought perhaps you would like to send the news to Washington."

Grant reined his horse. "I *knew* there was something I forgot!"

Sitting on a rock at the side of the road, the officer at his shoulder, Grant wrote a terse telegram. He handed it to the officer. "Telegraph that to Secretary Stanton immediately and add a copy of the surrender terms."

"Yes, sir."

"And tell our artillerymen to stop that racket! These men are no longer our enemies."

CHAPTER TWENTY-THREE

Outside Appomattox

Jonas lay sprawled across his blanket on the grass floor of the tent, still fully dressed except for his boots. He had almost collapsed in exhaustion and had fallen into an immediate deep sleep, as though the years of struggle and loss could be redeemed in one night of rest. With long, stertorous moans, he began to dream his fearful, familiar dream.

Curled up against the other side of the tent, his back to Jonas, John slept deeply for the first time in years, peaceful in the knowledge that the long agony was over. A bayonet was stuck in the ground between them, and in the bayonet ring a candle burned low. The wick sputtered in the pool of wax, causing the diminishing light to flicker on the walls of the tent.

Suddenly Jonas opened his eyes, staring blankly at the dancing shadows. He was still asleep. His breathing was labored, tortured by the forces struggling within him. In his vision he again saw the stormy sea and a long narrow harpoon boat moving swiftly through the water, though its oars were unmanned.

Jonas stood on the shore, peering into the mist and fog. Once again he glimpsed a tall man dressed in black, standing at the stern of the boat, steering the course to shore. Cold winds tossed the vessel, dark waves lashing out at the somber figure.

The boat skimmed over the water and crashed on the shore with a sharp crack, a sound like a pistol shot. Jonas ran into the stormy sea to the shattered boat and lifted the body of the man in black from the waves.

Staggering through the breaking waves, he laid the body onto the white sand. Jonas moaned in his sleep when he saw the face of the man. It was Mr. Lincoln. A pool of blood stained the white sand under his head. His eyes were covered by silver coins.

Jonas cried out in grief and shock, waking John with a start. At that moment the candle went out, plunging them into darkness. Jonas hurled himself out of the tent, gasping, struggling to fill his lungs with the cool night air. John quickly followed as Jonas wiped the sweat from his face, steadying himself.

"Are you all right?" John asked, putting his hand on Jonas's shoulder. Jonas nodded, lost in thought. "It was one of your dreams, wasn't it? A vision."

"It's a curse," Jonas mumbled.

"What did you see?" John asked, and the whole terrible dream flooded back on Jonas.

Suddenly Jonas rushed back to the tent. He grabbed his boots and his saddle, checking to be sure his Spencer was holstered.

"I'll tell you on the road! We have to ride! It's Lincoln! He has to be warned!"

John was moving to the horses before Jonas finished.

Washington, D.C.—April 14, 1865

President Lincoln's Cabinet sat around the long table, waiting for the President to arrive. Today they
would begin to plan for the postwar reconstruction of
the defeated South. A formal and crusty group, they
spoke in low, ominous voices of how dearly the South
would pay in both labor and money for the terrible cost
of the war. They knew that only Lincoln and his plans
for charity stood between their vengeance and the helpless South.

When Lincoln arrived, he was followed by U. S.
Grant. The Cabinet applauded spontaneously as Lincoln and Grant shook hands. Grant was his usual dour
self, but Lincoln seemed in a happy, expectant mood.

The Secretary of the Interior, John Usher, spoke up.
"I was hoping for news that General Johnston had sur-
rendered his army. Have we heard anything from North
Carolina?"

Secretary of the Navy Gideon Welles shook his head.
"Such news would come through the telegraph at the
War Department. Perhaps Mr. Stanton will have word
for us—if and when he arrives."

"I've been expecting word hourly from Sherman,"
Grant said. "I am, I confess, somewhat anxious that I
haven't heard from him."

Lincoln was the only one smiling. "Calm your fears,
gentlemen. Last night I received a good omen. I had a
dream. One that I've had before, several times. The
dream is always the same, and invariably it precedes
some great and important event of the war. I expect,
therefore, to get news of Johnston's surrender very
soon."

Around the table the members of his Cabinet glanced at each other nervously, their eyebrows raised. They found it difficult to countenance Lincoln's belief in dreams and omens.

"What is the nature of the dream, Mr. President?" Secretary Welles asked politely.

"It relates to your element, Mr. Welles . . . the water. I am in some singular, indescribable vessel, and I am moving in it with great rapidity toward a dark and indefinite shore. That's all there is to tell of it, except that I had this same dream before our victories at Antietam, Stone River, Gettysburg, and Vicksburg."

Lincoln had their interest now. They leaned forward to hear more. Only Grant seemed unimpressed. "Stone River was no victory, Mr. President. In fact, a few such victories would have ruined us."

"Perhaps we differ on that point, General, but I repeat: the dream has always preceded some great event. Last night's dream must mean that Johnston has surrendered, for I know of no other great event likely, at present, to occur."

Just after ten o'clock that night, Jonas and John galloped at full speed down Pennsylvania Avenue. The clattering of their horses' hooves on the cobblestones echoed along the nearly deserted streets.

Their horses reared up when they reined at the White House gate. Jonas shouted at the gatekeeper, "We have an urgent message for the President!"

The man looked up at their desperate faces, grimy from the road and flecked with the lather from their nearly spent horses. "He's not on the premises, sir."

"Where!" Jonas shouted. The gatekeeper hesitated. "Tell me, man!"

"Reckon it's no secret. The President and Mrs. Lincoln are at Ford's Theatre."

John and Jonas turned and galloped back up the avenue. They passed squads of soldiers running in the same direction. As they turned the corner at Tenth Street, they ran into a crowd of people, gathering at the corner and looking down the street. The people seemed dazed—some wandered around aimlessly, some weeped openly, but most just stared in disbelief. There was a deep murmuring sound spreading through the crowd, an intense, angry roar, a rage. They were becoming a mob.

Leaping from his horse, Jonas grabbed the first person he saw, a black man, tears running down his face. He seemed in a trance.

"What's happened!" Jonas shouted to him over the roar of the crowd.

The black man looked at Jonas with vacant eyes. "They done shot him," he murmured, dreamlike. "They done shot Marster Lincoln." The black man stumbled on.

Leaving his horse with John, Jonas raced down the street. In front of the Ford Theatre a knot of people were slowly making their way across the street, through the crowd, carrying the wounded President.

Jonas plunged into the crowd. As he fought his way through the hysterical people, most of them from the audience of the theater, he prayed that it would not be as he had seen it in his dreams. Then he saw the shaggy head of the unconscious President, matted with blood. For a moment he was frozen with horror.

The four soldiers carrying Mr. Lincoln, jostled by the pressing crowd, were thrown off balance. Jonas reached out to help steady the President as they forged a path through the mob.

A doctor, walking at the President's head, stopped them as they were almost across the street and with his fingers removed a blood clot that had formed at the bullet hole.

"How bad, doctor?" Jonas asked him.

The doctor spoke without looking up. "His wound is mortal."

A man waved them into Peterson's boardinghouse, across the street from the theater. As they carried him in, Jonas heard Mary Lincoln screaming hysterically as she crossed the street. "Where is he? Where have they taken my husband?"

At her side was Major Rathbone, who had fought with John Wilkes Booth after he had shot the President. Booth had slashed the major in the arm, and both he and Mary Lincoln were covered with his blood. In the chaos no one recognized Mrs. Lincoln, and she was carried along by the surge of the maddened crowd. She dug her evening slippers into the mud of the street as she dragged the major with her to the boardinghouse.

They carried the President down a narrow hallway and into a small bedroom. As they laid him down, Jonas helped lower President Lincoln's head to a pillow, as white as the sand in his dream. And then he sat down to wait.

Jonas hadn't noticed it was dawn until one of the doctors turned out the gaslight, and morning light creeped into the small room. President Lincoln was lying diagonally across the bed, being far too tall to fit between the bedboards. His right eye, where the bullet had lodged, was swollen and discolored. His breathing was labored and heavy, with alarmingly long intervals between breaths.

President Lincoln drew a troubled breath, gasping a little as he exhaled. They waited for his next breath, but it did not come. The doctor listened a long time to his heart and then straightened up. "The President is dead."

Jonas stood up slowly. John, who had been waiting in the hall, came in and stood by his side.

Mary Lincoln threw herself on the President, sobbing. "Oh, my God! And have I given my husband to die!"

Secretary of War Stanton, standing in front of them by the bed, took his last look at the President. "Now he belongs to the ages."

The pillow under the President's head was soaked with blood. The doctor took two silver coins from his pocket and placed them gently over Mr. Lincoln's eyes.

CHAPTER TWENTY-FOUR

Washington, D.C.—Spring 1865

It was twilight in the Union camp. Up and down the hillsides the campfires blinked in the gathering darkness. Outside their tent, the remnants of O'Toole's company were sprawled in a circle around the fire. Malachy, Jake, the rookie from the Wilderness fight, and five other men had been joined by Jonas and John. This was their last night in the army, the last night of familiar camp life. Earlier that day they had been mustered out and paid. A bottle of whiskey was passed around the circle.

"Jonas, pass me down that bottle of tanglefoot," Malachy said. He took a long, slow swallow and shook his head. "I still have to laugh when I think about brother Jake there when we finally cornered Bobby Lee. We were coming in on their flank and their big guns opened up on us. It was so loud our ears went deaf. So Jake pulls some of the cotton off the stalks and stuffs it in his ears."

Jake laughed in remembering. "Then one of them reb

shells hits a chicken coop and out they came, all squawking and fluttering. Malachy grabbed a couple of them and hung them on his belt for lunch. Some general came riding by, waving his damn sword. But half the boys in the company started catchin' chickens and the rebs about got away."

Even Jonas joined in the laughter. Malachy pointed at John. "What about ole John boy, back at the Wilderness. That took a lotta guts. If I hadn't recognized you, I'd a shot you dead on the spot." He took another swig of liquor and handed it to John. "Yes, sir. You'd be in hell right now, pumping thunder at three cents a clap."

When the bottle was empty, Jonas took out his silver flask. After a deep drink, he passed it around. As they drank, the euphoria passed, and they began to feel sadness. All the memories came rushing back.

"I've been thinking about those we've lost," Jake said. "Young James, dying in that hospital tent, before Bull Run. Before the war ever got started."

"An' good ole Sergeant O'Toole," Malachy said, taking a slow sip, thinking of the Wilderness.

John nodded. "And my brother, Mark, who died with O'Toole there in that hell." He paused, letting the whiskey warm him. "And Matt, at Geyser Hill."

Jonas stared into the fire. "And Mary . . ."

John went into the tent and came back out with a bag of candles. He lit one and stuck it into the muzzle of a rifle. It was a still, windless night and the flame barely flickered. Malachy and Jake watched the candle for a few minutes and then each lit one, sticking them into their guns. Jonas lifted up his Spencer, the one Abraham Lincoln had given him, and silenced it with a candle.

Other soldiers all up and down the line of tents began to put candles in their guns, raising them above their heads. A few began to walk around the parade ground, their rifles silenced by the quiet flames. Gradually the entire camp began to gather for the last time. There were no officers to impress, no politicians, no witnesses at all.

The men marched in silence, weaving in and out. These were tough, grizzled soldiers, paying their last respects to the men they had fought with and against. They had all fought together, through dark rainy woods, across sunny fields, in swamps, over stone walls, through orchards white with blossoms. Now, at last, it was done.

The candlelight twinkled in the night, illuminating their faces. Then the men began to cheer, a sound that moved and swelled like a roar from the earth. They cheered themselves, their survival. They were alive. They would go home now and raise families and grow old in peace. Malachy and Jake and Jonas and John cheered until they were hoarse. And the candles burned for them.

Jonas galloped up Geyser Hill, urging his horse ahead. Below him he could see the peaceful countryside, lush and beautiful in the early summer sun. He was the last to arrive at the family reunion and they had gathered in the yard to wait for him.

Where on one terrible day Yank and reb bodies had fallen, there now stood long harvest tables set end to end. Sheets staked on poles rippled and billowed in the breeze, shading the yard where the feast was laid out. Below the canopy of cloth the tables were piled high with ham, turkey, cider, whiskey, breads, fruits, and vegetables of all kinds.

The dogs barked and the chickens scattered as Jonas rode up to the yard. He leaped off his horse and was immediately surrounded by family. Ben took his hand and said heartily, "Welcome home." Maggie reached out and hugged him. Luke raced by, strong again, pursued by his old girlfriend, Mandy.

A country fiddler played lively mountain music as everyone chattered and drank. Jacob Hale, gray and portly now, reached for a tidbit, but Evelyn slapped his hand away.

John began rounding everyone up. Under his direction, Malachy and Jake were setting benches in a row. "Come with me, folks. You have to pose before you can eat."

Emma came out of the house carrying a big cake, with Jesse at her side, hanging on to her skirt. "Emma, you and Jesse sit right here," Jonas said, holding out his hand to guide her. She felt her cheeks burning as she sat down. Jonas wrapped his arm around Jesse and lifted him up to his shoulder.

Luke and Mandy came by, arm in arm. "We need you, Luke—you too, Mandy. Stand next to Malachy."

"What's goin' on?" Luke asked.

"John's going to make a picture."

"Of who?"

"Of all of us," Jonas grinned.

"That'll take hours!"

John rushed by, lugging a huge camera over his shoulder. "A few seconds is all I need now."

He fixed the handsome wooden box, with its ornate brass fixtures and wide lens, on a rickety wooden tripod. "Positively the latest thing in photographic cameras, all the way from New York. Just like the one Brady uses."

Sticking his head under the black velvet cloth, he focused the lens. The children were held still, and the women reached up and checked their hair. Then John emerged, looking over the group with an artist's eye.

In the back row stood Jonas, Jake, Malachy, Mandy, and Luke. On the benches sat Emma, Maggie, Ben, an empty space for John himself, Jacob, and Evelyn. On the grass sat Jessie and Annie Hale.

"Jonas, move in a little, right behind Emma." Jonas hesitated, and then moved behind her.

John made the final adjustment and set the timer. "Hold the pose till I run into the picture! Ready?"

He flicked the timer, which began to buzz, and dashed to his seat. In that moment they were all still.

Click. The photograph captured all the excited, proud faces, smiling into the future.

Just before the photograph was taken, Jonas put Jesse on Emma's lap and moved behind her, resting his hand on her shoulder. Both of these veterans had been wounded, and the scars of hate were deep. But now, as he smiled, the furrows in Jonas's face seemed less chiseled. He had a family to come home to.

Emma's face showed a slight smile of pleasure, too, and of hope. Her eyes were shining.

At the moment the camera clicked, John's face was turned slightly. He had wanted to look at his family, to see that the circle was finally joined. There was peace on his face.

The healing had begun.

A SELECTED LIST OF FINE NOVELS FROM CORGI

☐	11962 8	**Chinese Alice**	*Pat Barr* £1.75
☐	11185 6	**Typhoon**	*John Gordon Davies* £1.25
☐	11241 0	**Hold My Hand I'm Dying**	*John Gordon Davies* £1.50
☐	10437 X	**The Years of the Hungry Tiger**	*John Gordon Davies* £2.50
☐	10268 7	**Taller Than Trees**	*John Gordon Davies* 50p
☐	99019 1	**Zemindar**	*Valerie FitzGerald* £2.50
☐	12043 X	**Prima Donna**	*Nancy Freedman* £1.50
☐	11981 4	**Chasing Rainbows**	*Esther Sager* £1.50
☐	11575 4	**A Necessary Woman**	*Helen Van Slyke* £1.95
☐	11321 2	**Sisters and Strangers**	*Helen Van Slyke* £1.75
☐	11745 5	**No Love Lost**	*Helen Van Slyke* £1.50
☐	11068 X	**Forever Amber (Vol. 1)**	*Kathleen Windsor* £1.25
☐	11069 8	**Forever Amber (Vol. 2)**	*Kathleen Windsor* £1.25